The City When It Rains

The City When It Rains

Thomas H. Cook

OVERLOOK DUCKWORTH
New York • London

This edition published in the United States and the United
Kingdom in 2015 by Overlook Duckworth, Peter Mayer Publishers, Inc.

NEW YORK:
The Overlook Press
Peter Mayer Publishers, Inc.
141 Wooster Street
New York, NY 10012
www.overlookpress.com
For bulk and special sales, please contact sales@overlookny.com,
or write us at the above address.

LONDON:
Gerald Duckworth Publishers Ltd.
30 Calvin Street
London E1 6NW
www.ducknet.co.uk
info@duckworth-publishers.co.uk

Cataloging-in-Publication Data is available from the Library of Congress

Printed in the United States of America
ISBN: 978-1-4683-1062-7 US
ISBN: 978-0-7156-5020-2 UK
2   4   6   8   10   9   7   5   3   1

For Justine, of course.

Chapter 1

CORMAN'S EYES DRIFTED SLOWLY OVER THE ENOR-mous vault of Saint Patrick's Cathedral. Even at night, the stained glass windows shone brightly with small glittering wings of electric blue, red and green. Up ahead, an old man was trying to pray, but a single fly kept distracting him, swooping at his ear. He swatted at it from time to time without lifting his head. It was an odd scene, and for an instant, Corman felt the impulse to reach for his camera and record it, then realized it would be the kind of photograph that only pretended to deal with the greater ironies by focusing on the little ones. A fake, he thought, and yet?

"Why'd we come here?" Lucy asked.

Corman drew his eyes from the old man and settled them on her. "The people who built Saint Patrick's weren't allowed to drink," he told her. "Did you know that? The Archbishop made that rule."

Lucy looked suspicious. "How do you know?"

"Mr. Lazar told me," Corman said. The two of them had been walking silently through the deepening snow, and as they neared the cathedral, Lazar had stopped suddenly, nodded toward its gray facade, then gone into a detailed discussion of how the blue granite had been shipped from Maine, the marble from New York and Massachusetts. From the building itself, he'd moved to the travail of the men who'd built it, how they'd dug the immense foundation out of solid bedrock. As Lazar spoke, Corman had been able to see them working through twenty years of summer heat and winter cold, growing old in their long thirst, while a succession of robed Archbishops and red-capped Cardinals had patrolled the site, glancing suspiciously at their lunch pails. He remembered a picture he'd come across which showed a crowd of workmen as they sat on one of the high steel girders of the skeletal cathedral, one of them with his hand lifted high in the air, boldly toasting heaven with a small square flask. It had been one of the photographs he'd planned to use in his picture history of the old city, a book without words, not even a title, a book that would let the eyes do everything.

Lucy looked at him wonderingly. "You okay, Papa?"

Corman nodded, half-regretting all the hours he'd spent thumbing through the *Herald*, *Leslie's Illustrated*, the old *Police Gazette* and scores of other lost recorders, while Lazar had smiled at him indulgently from the corner of the North Hall Reading Room.

He pulled his camera bag onto his shoulder, stood up, glanced at Lucy. "I'm ready to go," he said.

He took her hand, drew her from the pew, then down the aisle past racks of weaving candles, the church gift shop and poor box, finally through its enormous carved doors.

"Where are we going now?" Lucy asked once they were outside.

"Home, I guess," Corman said.

They threaded briskly through the still heavy Fifth Avenue traffic, then ambled more slowly down 50th Street until they reached Broadway. The crowds had grown thicker by then, congealing around them as they would have done in the old city too, in great swirling throngs that swept across the unpaved avenues, encircled the music halls, gathered in dense laughing clusters beneath the gaslights of the sporting clubs. It was their vast anonymity which moved Corman each time he looked at pictures of them, the way time made their once different faces seem featureless as bits of plankton.

He took Lucy's hand, closing his fingers tightly around it, as if to seal her frail identity within its sack of skin.

"You don't have to hold on," she said as she pulled at his hand. "Let go."

Reflexively, he released her, and the two of them headed south until they reached 45th Street. The great neon crater of Times Square shone before them. A huge Minolta sign flickered brightly from the top of one of the buildings, and Corman thought of his own cameras. Not the ones he used in his work, but the dusty, unsalvageable relics he kept stacked up in his closet, boxy old museum pieces that reminded him of the shutterbugs who'd gone before him, recorded the world, then departed, leaving only their cameras behind, the still surviving eyes of the beholder.

"Can I get gum?" Lucy asked.

"I guess," Corman said.

The theaters had let out, and crowds of well-dressed people were heading toward the restaurants and drinking holes of the theater district. Limousines stretched east and west from Broadway to Eighth Avenue, shining elegantly in the blinking lights of the theater marquees. The people who got out of them looked happy, energetic, untroubled, as if nothing remained for them but to live on stylishly, strive to perfect the tango.

Lucy grasped the arm of his jacket, tugged him forward. "Let's go faster," she said excitedly, taking on the pace of the street, moving through it effortlessly, as if her body had been streamlined to its flow.

Corman adjusted his pace immediately to keep up with her. The crowds parted to let them pass. He smelled powders and perfumes he could recall from the days when he'd still lived with Lexie.

Lucy glanced up at him, smiled brightly. "We can get it there," she said, pointing up ahead.

At the shop, Corman lingered on the sidewalk while Lucy went inside and roamed the counters looking for just the right gum. Not far away, workers were cleaning out one of the last of the area's slum hotels. Large metal containers had been placed at the curb and workmen were filling them with old mattresses. A wave of yellowish light washed over them from inside the hotel. They seemed to push through it heavily, as if it were made of millions of small fibers.

Corman took out his camera and began to ease slowly toward them in the way Lazar had taught him, bearing down upon a picture like a matador, getting close, holding steady.

Through the lens he could see the workmen as they dragged the mattresses by their edges, then hoisted them into the bins. In his hand, the camera felt warm, pliant, alive, as if it were a keen-sighted animal he'd trained to be his eyes. He calculated the light, adjusted for it, began shooting.

For a time, he concentrated on the workmen, their enormous black work gloves, sweaty shirts, trousers white with plaster dust. Then, moving steadily closer, he began to focus on the mattresses instead. He could see how stained they were with food, drink, the body's various fluids, and it struck him that each mattress presented a scaled-down portrait of its owner's individual biological history, the times he'd made love, bled, thrown up, sweated something out. It absorbed the physical elements of his destiny better than any photograph ever could, and as he continued to inch forward, shooting one picture after another, Corman could feel the camera's old inadequacy once again, its distance from the source, the way it seemed to keep him just one small step away.

"We can go now," Lucy said as she rushed up to him. "Before it starts to rain."

Corman remained in place for a moment, then tilted forward slightly, focused on a single reddish stain. It was impossible to know what had caused it, blood, nail polish, raspberry jam, any of a thousand separate things. And yet something about the stain drew him toward it, the way it spread out across the fabric, flowery, petaled, and to Corman's eye at least, curiously beautiful in the odd way that only things in themselves could sometimes be.

They stepped under the large awning of the Broadway just as the first wave of heavy rain broke over the city.

"We barely made it," Lucy said.

Corman nodded, glanced at the building's creaky revolving door, and imagined the thousands of men and women who'd glided through it, leaving trails of cologne and aftershave that still floated somewhere in the stratosphere.

The owner of the building was converting it to cooperative apartments, and he'd placed a stack of brochures for prospective buyers on the small table in the lobby. Corman picked one up as he headed toward the elevator, and read it idly while he waited.

The writer had done a good job, and as he read, Corman saw elegant people going in and out of the building, heard cabs honking impatiently outside, felt the syncopated rhythm of this part of the old city, its once jazzy life. And yet, in the end, the writing had come out faintly sad and sentimental, nostalgic in a way that turned nostalgia itself into a form of letting go, of hoisting the white flag.

He dropped the brochure into the small metal garbage can between the elevator doors and looked at Lucy. "What'd you do today?"

"Nothing," Lucy said, rolling her eyes slightly.

"What's the matter?"

"You always ask that."

"It's something I want to know."

"But it's always the same," Lucy told him. She shifted about impatiently, popped her gum. "We read about Columbus, that's all."

"The man who discovered America."

Lucy looked at him scoldingly. "Not really. The Indians were already around."

"Yes, they were," Corman said. "Even in Manhattan."

The elevator arrived. They rode up slowly, then walked down the long, somewhat smelly corridor toward their apartment.

"Mr. Ingersoll's cooking sausage again," Corman said. He twitched his nose. "Jesus."

A small white envelope had been taped to the door of the apartment. Corman quickly snapped it off, sank it into his coat pocket.

"What's that?" Lucy asked.

"Just a note," Corman said. "From the landlord."

Lucy looked at him worriedly. "Are we behind again?"

"Just a little," Corman told her as he opened the door.

Once inside, Lucy went directly to her room while Corman sat down at the small dining table and read the note with the little edge of panic that always pressed against his flesh when money was tight. He waited a few minutes for it to subside, then began assembling the rolls of film he'd taken during the day: a fire in the Village, but nothing spectacular, an auto accident on the Upper West Side, a broken water main in the Garment District. He'd taken seven rolls of film but there was nothing worth developing.

He unstrapped the police radio from his belt, set it down on the table and turned it on. For a few seconds it was quiet. Then a patrolman mentioned a woman who'd jumped out a window on West 47th Street almost an hour before. He ended with something about a baby or a doll or something. Static covered the last of it.

He sat back and waited for something else to break, but the radio remained silent except for the usual traffic mishaps, petty thefts, domestic squabbles, nothing Pike or any of the other photographic editors would be interested in, no heroic measures or last minute rescues.

He stood up and paced the room restlessly. He could feel his own edginess building slowly, insistently, like a pressure beneath his skin. He knew part of it was money, the rest just his nature. Finally it overtook him and drove him to Lucy's room. He tapped lightly at the door.

"Come in."

Corman opened the door, peeked inside. "I have to go out for a shoot," he told her.

Lucy looked up excitedly. "Can I come?"

"No."

Her face fell slightly. "I never get to go on the night shoots."

"You have school."

"But I want to see things, too."

Corman shook his head. "No."

Chapter 2

THE RAIN WAS FALLING HEAVILY BY THE TIME CORMAN got to 47th Street. The photographer from the Crime Scene Unit was perched on a small portable ladder, his body bent forward, the camera pointed toward the woman. His name was Shepherd. Corman had seen him many times before, knew the old brown hat, pea-green raincoat, thick white socks, all now completely soaked in rain.

"Just finishing up," Shepherd said dully as Corman stepped up to him. He aimed the camera steadily, seemed to freeze.

Watching him, Corman admired the care he took, the way he never let things distract him. He supposed the photographers of the old city had worked the same way, as if they'd had no lives outside, nothing to break their concentration, but only the darkness beneath the short black hood, the single tunnel of silver light. And yet, he thought, there was a dark flip side to such intense concentration, since focus shut out everything it didn't center on.

A bright flash swept the street as Shepherd shot the picture. Corman flinched, turned to the left and made his way toward the two men who slouched idly under a green cloth awning a few yards away.

The awning was badly tattered. Its torn flaps snapped softly in the breeze. It would make a marketable picture, had what Pike called "symbol potential." In this case, urban decay. As Corman moved toward it, he could see that it only fitfully protected the two men from the hard, pelting rain.

"Lousy weather," Santana said as Corman joined him under the awning.

Santana was a shooter for a lower Manhattan weekly who sometimes turned up at fire and crime scenes when things were slow in Soho or Tribeca. He was always friendly, almost jaunty, insensibly happy in the way birds seemed happy, along with other lower forms.

"It always rains on a street shoot," Santana added. His skin was smooth and brown. He looked around thirty, but Corman had noticed that he liked to act the old pro, even when talking to men who'd been on hundreds of street shoots when the air had been bright, hot, dry, no rain in sight.

"Christ, look at that," Santana said. He pointed to a cascading sheet of water that plunged from the top of a tenement to the street below. "Like fucking Niagara."

"Yeah," the other man said. His name was Fogarty, a shooter for a Brooklyn biweekly.

"You're late on this one, Corman," Santana said after a moment. "The whole world's come and gone. What's the matter, you don't keep glued to the police frequency anymore?"

Corman's fingers reflexively moved to the radio handset which hung in a black holster from his belt. "I was taking a walk with my daughter."

Santana waved his hand. "Well the ME's already been here. And Shepherd's the only guy left from CSU." He shook his head. "He's taken a full roll already. God knows why."

"He's got a morbid streak, that's why," Fogarty said with a grim smile.

Santana looked at him doubtfully, the little black moustache twitching to the right.

"No lie," Fogarty said firmly. "He hangs around like a fucking fly, sniffing, sniffing, rubbing his skinny little fingers together." He did his standard imitation of a fly frantically raking its front legs. "Like that, you know?"

A single car swept by, throwing arcs of water from behind. Fogarty's eyes followed it, squinting slightly to see who was behind the wheel.

"Shepherd's a pro," Santana said. "The way I hear it, first he shoots the hole, then the splinters on the floor."

Fogarty faked a shiver.

Santana laughed. "You got a moral streak, Fogarty, a belief in humanity. I admire it."

"Bullshit."

Corman's eyes shifted back to Shepherd. He'd stepped off the ladder and was now breaking it down, getting ready to tuck it under his arm, return it to the CSU wagon. As he bent forward, small bursts of water leaped from the back of his coat, as if to strike at him was the whole secret purpose of the rain.

"A couple shooters rushed over right after the jump," Santana told Corman. "One from the *News*. One from the *Post*. Some video cams, too. But nobody looked that excited."

Corman looked at the woman, then the mound of blue blanket her naked arm seemed to be reaching for. "What happened?" he asked.

Fogarty's head drooped forward as he scratched his face. A line of moisture spread out from the brim of his hat. "Same old shit," he said to Corman. "You been following the cop house long enough to know that."

Corman's eyes returned to Shepherd. He was loading everything into the back of the CSU wagon. Two men lounged in its front seat, both of them smoking cigarettes. They had cracked the window slightly on the driver's side and a steady cloud of white smoke curled out of it.

"You got the field now," Santana said to Corman, "but you'd better make it fast. The EMS boys'll scoop it up pretty soon."

Corman looked at Fogarty. "Did you get an ID?"

Fogarty shook his head. "It's not my beat, Hell's Kitchen."

Santana laughed. "He just came over because the wife's riding the pink pony, right, Artie?"

Fogarty glanced at Santana, winked. The two men laughed together, old comrades in the wars of love.

"Listen, Corman," Santana said after the laughter had trailed off. "I hear Lazar died."

"Not exactly."

"Went to Florida, something like that?"

"He had a stroke," Corman told him. "He's in a home up on 106th Street."

"You two were real close, right?"

"Yeah."

"Your rabbi. Taught you everything."

Corman nodded quickly. "I'm going to take a few shots," he said as he stepped out from under the awning, into the rain again.

The woman's body was sprawled across the smooth wet street. She wore a long white dress, but as the rotating lights of the EMS ambulance rhythmically pulsed over it, they turned it faintly orange. She lay face down, her body bent slightly at the waist. One of her arms pressed against her side. The other stretched out over her head, nearly perpendicular to her tangled hair, the fingers thrust out rigidly, so that they nearly touched a torn strand of the blue blanket. Her head was lifted, as if balanced on the tip of the chin, her face raised, despite the fact that her nose was crushed nearly flat. A trickle of blood ran from her ear, then moved in a gently curving line along her throat. In a standard black-and-white, it would look like a piece of soft black cord.

For a few seconds, Corman merely circled the body, looking for the best shot. Finally, he stopped just to the left of the woman's face and bent down to bring the top of her body into the frame. As he snapped the picture, the bright light of his flash swept over her like the tail of a comet, throwing her shadow across the slick gray pavement.

"You're wasting your time, Corman," Santana said dryly as he passed by, heading for his car. "Even the locals'll pass on this."

"Maybe."

Santana nodded toward the blue blanket. "That's the only angle. And you ask me, it's not much."

Corman glanced up at him. "Do they have any witnesses?"

Santana nodded in the opposite direction. "The Incorruptible Detective Lang dug one up," he said facetiously. "He's still at him."

Corman turned slowly to see the witness, a tall man in a New York Mets sweatshirt, as he talked to Lang just inside the doorway of a neighboring building.

Santana tapped Corman's shoulder. "Listen, could you spare me a sawbuck for a couple days?"

Corman stared him dead in the eye. "No."

For an instant Santana looked offended, then his face relaxed into a light chuckle. "Well, at least you didn't give me some bullshit song and dance." He laughed again, waved his hand. "Catch you later," he said as he walked away.

Corman turned his attention to the bottom edge of the blue blanket. He knew that his second picture had caught the tip of it in the frame. It would be a distraction in the final print, drawing the viewer's eyes away from the woman, its real subject. It would confuse the composition, throw the frame off balance. He squatted close to the ground, edging the camera up just enough to take it out. The narrow wedge of blue sank beneath the bottom line of the frame like a small boat.

From that angle, he took several more pictures, drawing the camera down slightly, then to the right, up the woman's arm. A line of needle marks ran from the upper arm to the elbow, where they gathered in a cluster of pitted purple dots. Several tan scars, raised and pointed, crisscrossed the same area like tiny mountain ranges. He moved the camera on down along the nearly smooth lower arm until he reached her fingers. Her nails had once been painted bright green, but most of the polish had chipped away. He shot one of her hands, centering the frame around a single jaggedly outstretched finger.

It was pointing toward the blue blanket and the small doll that lay wrapped inside it. For a few seconds, Corman concentrated on the doll's face, the glittering plastic eyes that stared up at the overhanging building, the dirty white stain gathered in its mouth.

Inside the blanket, the doll was naked, with rounded arms and large, bulging stomach. The head was scrunched down into the fleshy folds of its neck so that from a certain angle, it looked like a miniature sumo wrestler.

But that wasn't the angle Corman liked. He circled the body slowly, as he had the woman's, staring at it through the lens, trying to find an appropriate frame. Every picture has a heart, Lazar had once told him, it's the shooter's job to find it.

Corman finally decided to shoot the doll from the left side, with most of the body covered by the blanket, then straight down, with the face just enough off-center to pick up the glistening pavement.

After he'd taken several shots, he straightened himself, let his eyes drift back and forth from the woman to the doll, as if following a length of rope which stretched from one to the other.

"Some fucking night," Lang said as he stepped up beside him. "Raining like hell, and I get a jumper."

Corman nodded.

"You get all the pictures you need?"

"I guess."

"Good," Lang said. He headed toward the tenement.

"If you're going in, I'd like to take a look," Corman said.

Lang studied him for a moment. "Okay," he said finally.

Corman walked a few paces behind him, watching Lang's back. He thought about snapping a quick picture, concentrating on the dripping hat, the fall of his shoulders, the way the tenement walls drew in around him so that he looked like a man walking into a dark concrete trap. But it was a picture he'd seen a thousand times. No matter what the angle, it always came out on the side of hopelessness. Give up the fight was its advice.

A narrow alley led along the southern wall of the building. Lang trudged down it listlessly, his feet scraping through the usual debris, cans, bottles, bits of paper, until he got to a rectangular flap of unpainted plywood that leaned against the side of the building. Then he jerked it down and let it crash into the alley.

The hole behind it was barely large enough to crawl through. Lang took a flashlight from his raincoat, stooped down with a low groan, and crawled on his hands and knees through the opening.

Corman came in behind him, feeling the ground carefully for nails, broken glass, old hypodermic needles. Inside, it was dark, the windows completely covered over, and as he rose to his feet, Corman could see nothing but the single yellow beam from Lang's flashlight as it glided smoothly along the floor of the building. The walls were wet, peeling, the ceiling pulled down, its plumbing stripped away. The floor was bare, swept clean, except for the far left corner, where the light grew more faded and diffused, and settled finally on a small pile of empty cans.

Corman walked over to the cans and stared down at them. "Similac," he said. He looked at Lang. "Baby formula." He fingered the strap of his camera bag as he thought of the stain on the doll's mouth. "She was feeding it."

"Yeah," Lang said without interest, peering about. "There must be a set of stairs around here." He walked to the middle of the room, his feet scraping through the broken pieces of plaster and sheetrock which covered it. Then he stopped, pointed the flashlight toward the far rear corner. Metal stairs led upward to the second floor. "There we are," he said idly as he headed for them.

Corman followed him up the stairs until they reached the top floor of the building.

"The witness said the jumper had been living here for quite a while," Lang said as he made his way to the window. "He said she threw the doll out first. Like trash, he said. Then she jumped herself." He glanced quickly out the window, then turned back toward the dark room and headed for the stairs.

Corman stepped up to the window and peered out. Two ambulance attendants were moving toward the body. One of them had a zippered plastic body bag slung over his shoulder like a slick black pelt.

Corman lifted the camera to his eye and moved it slowly over the scene below, concentrating on the two bodies, his lens cruising smoothly from the plump plastic one wrapped in a blue blanket to the emaciated legs of the woman in the white dress. In the faintly silver street light, her skin took on a slick, scaly sheen. It was the high gloss of starvation, and he'd seen it only in pictures before. He stepped away from the window, quickly grasped a shattered edge of jutting brick, and held on for a moment while he put it together in his mind. Then he snapped the lens cap back on his camera and headed for the stairs, finally catching up with Lang in the alleyway.

"She was starving," he told him.

Lang kept up his pace. "It happens."

"But she bought all that Similac."

"So?"

"For a doll."

Lang continued on until he reached his car. Then he opened the door, slid in, glanced back at Corman through the half-open window. "Keep an eye to your back," he warned. "It's always more dangerous than you think."

Chapter 3

ON THE WAY BACK TO HIS APARTMENT, CORMAN STOP-
ped off at Smith's Bar on Eighth Avenue. The usual customers had
already assumed their usual places, and from his own seat at the end
of the bar he could follow the action as closely as he liked. For a time,
he'd thought of doing some sort of photographic study of the burned-
out cases who hung around late at night, retired cops, street hustlers,
drifters, vagrants, barflies, the usual spillover from the slum hotels. They
had hard, weathered faces, but in pictures that only made them look
like characters from central casting, actors in some docudrama about
the wretched of the earth. Through the generations, they'd been gone
over by the best of them. The illustrators of the old city had done them
in woodcuts, charcoal, and after the illustrators, legions of shooters
had poured into the slums, shantytowns and ghettos. He'd gone over
hundreds of their pictures for his book, everything from the groggeries
of the Five Points to the murderous alleyways of the Old Brewery.
He'd seen children buried waist-high in garbage heaps, piles of women
sleeping in open wagons, swollen bodies left for days in unlit corridors
and abandoned airshafts.

"What'll you have, Corman?" Mike asked as he wiped the bar
and put down the little paper mat. "The usual?"

"Yeah."

Mike smiled, poured the shot of J&B. "How you been?"

"Okay."

"Long night?"

"A jumper," Corman said. He downed the shot, glanced to the
left. A nearly bald, middle-aged man was whispering vehemently to
himself, his hand pressed against his face.

21

"Been like that all night," Mike said, "Somebody must have opened up one of those fruit bins upstate, let 'em loose."

Corman took out a cigarette and lit it. "They used to put them on a boat," he said idly. "Then they just sent them drifting down the river. You know, the ship of fools."

Mike chuckled. "Put them on a boat, huh? Where was this, Poughkeepsie?"

Suddenly, the bald man peeped out from behind his own hand. "Animal cages have been recommended," he blurted loudly in a high, staccato voice. Then he fled back behind his tightly closed fingers and began giggling wildly.

Mike shook his head, picked up a glass and began polishing it. "You remember that redhead in here couple nights ago?"

Corman didn't.

"Flaming red hair," Mike added. "Big hooters."

Corman saw her now, the long red hair dangling from her shoulders, the way she plucked at her lower lip while Mike did his best number on her, the one about his days as a big band singer.

Mike winked. "One of Mike's Girls now," he said. "Number one sixty-two." He laughed. "I told her so. After, I mean. While we were both having a smoke. About the count. She thought it was funny." He shrugged. "Least it didn't bother her."

Corman glanced at the empty glass. "One more."

Mike was still pouring it when the bald man shot his face out from behind his hand again.

"Elephant-size capacity," he said loudly, then swiftly retreated behind his hand.

"He means cages, I guess," Mike said. "The ones they recommended." He filled Corman's glass, chuckled to himself. "Yeah, she laughed when I told her, the redhead. A real good sport, you know?" He shook his head. "If it weren't for the ladies, what would life be, huh?" He was probably in his early fifties, but well kept, with slick black hair and an aging matinee idol face. His eyes were light blue, and Corman could easily imagine them as two small cold lights in the afterglow of passion, distant, calculating, already looking for the next hit.

"She was a real dish, I'll say that for her," Mike said. "Definitely worth the strokes."

Corman's mind shifted to the jumper, her wet, glistening skin. "Did you ever see a woman around here?" he asked. "Skinny, carrying a doll in a blanket?"

Mike took up another glass and began polishing it while the younger bartender worked the other half of the bar. "Don't sound like one of Mike's Girls," he said.

"The jumper only lived a few blocks from here," Corman said. "I thought you might have seen her pass the window."

Mike shook his head. "Just sounds like another escapee from Looneyville, you ask me."

"Maybe," Corman said. He thought of the empty cans of Similac, the white stains around the doll's mouth, and regretted he hadn't gotten closer to them, concentrated on the way the rain had frothed them out from the rubbery pink lips.

Back at the apartment, Corman pulled out the sleeper sofa and prepared to bed down, as he always did, in the middle of the living room. It was an old sofa, dark green and rather soiled. It was the first thing he and Lexie had bought after getting married, and each time he pulled it out, something of those vanished days swept over him in a soft invisible tide.

Someone knocked at the door just as he was about to undress. He walked to the door and opened it.

Mrs. Donaldson stood in the doorway, erect as her aging bones could keep her. She was a large woman with an almost perfectly round head. Her white hair shone like an aura around her pink face. It gave her a strangely unreal look, as if she were someone's fairy godmother and could change things with a wand.

"I was wondering if you were home yet," she said. There was a faintly accusatory edge in her voice, which made Corman uncomfortable. It was in her eyes too, and it made him see himself as he thought she saw him, aloof, roguish, a man who could ditch his children whenever the mood struck him.

"I came home earlier," he told her. "But then I had to go out again. I had a shoot."

"Lucy was here alone," Mrs. Donaldson said.

"She has to be, sometimes."

Mrs. Donaldson eyed him pointedly. "There've been a few break-ins, you know," she said.

"There're always a few break-ins."

"On the third floor," Mrs. Donaldson added significantly. "Just under us. Mr. Baxter's apartment. They got everything. Even his humidifier. He has asthma. He needs his humidifier."

Corman said nothing. The edginess was creeping up his back like a line of tiny insects.

Mrs. Donaldson frowned slightly. "And what if Lucy was alone at a time like that? You know, they might . . . abuse her."

"I don't have a choice," Corman said. His voice sounded lame, weak, as if he should have arranged his life to have the very choices that were beyond him now. He hardened it a little. "I do the best I can."

Mrs. Donaldson looked slightly offended, as if she'd been rudely dealt with. "It's just with all the break-ins, I . . ."

"Would you like a cup of coffee?" Corman asked, trying to make amends.

"No, thank you," Mrs. Donaldson said. She smiled thinly. "Say hello to Lucy for me."

"I will," Corman said. "Good night." He forced the smile again as he closed the door. It felt like a wet string clinging to his lips.

For the next few hours Corman tossed about, then decided to get up and do some of his work. It was useless for him to try to make his body sleep when his mind wasn't in the mood.

He walked to the small closet near the bathroom he'd converted to a darkroom five years before. It was a tiny space, barely large enough for his trays and chemicals, but it was adequate nonetheless, and its feeling of highly concentrated space gave a physical sense of intensity that went well with the scores of pictures he'd strung on lines or thumb-tacked to the sheet of cork he'd nailed to the left wall of the room.

Once the door was tightly closed, he took out the rolls of film he'd shot during the day, then went through the routine of developing the long strips of negatives onto contact paper. Meticulously, he mixed the chemicals, pouring the various liquids into their separate trays. Then he looked at each individual shot, trying to decide which to keep, which to throw away. He'd hoped to sell a few of them to one of the city-wide dailies. Failing that, he'd have to concentrate on the weeklies scattered around the outer boroughs. The rest of the pictures had no value as news shots. They were for himself, photographs of street life he vaguely thought of as evidence he was slowly accumulating for some great trial that was yet to come. They were always black-and-white, always centered around people. He stayed away from things that had lost their human scale: towering buildings, bridges, monuments. He thought of them as accidents of science or engineering, impermanent, tentative creations. It was part of what he'd truly learned from Lazar, never to shoot higher than a human face. And so he shot people in alleys, subways, taxis; people eating, rushing away; people together or apart, connected or adrift; people who rescued children from cars, rivers, fires, or threw them out of windows, as the witness had told Lang, "like trash."

From the contact sheets, he selected a few pictures worth printing, dipped them in the bath and watched as the images rose from the blank white of the paper in that odd, ghostly way that still struck him as miraculous.

When the first print was complete, he lifted it from the liquid, strung it on the line, then stared at it silently. It was one of the pictures he'd taken of the doll, a close-up of the face, its hooded eyes lifted upward, the long black eyelashes beaten back against the half-closed lids by the falling rain. There was no doubt about it, as a photograph it had tremendous symbol potential. The painted eyes glistened brightly in the street light. Huge droplets gathered in their corners like swollen tears. Tragic ironies spilled over both sides of the wet, rubber face and gathered in pools along the pitted street. It was a picture he'd seen a thousand times, a doll lying among the ruins of a still smoldering house or circling slowly in the flood waters that had engulfed the town. He knew Pike would drool over it, perhaps pay as much as fifty dollars.

Chapter 4

LUCY WAS ALREADY COMPLETELY DRESSED AND STARING down at him when Corman's eyes opened the next morning. He'd finally nodded off in the chair by the window, his head slumped forward, hands curled together in his lap.

"Your mouth was open," Lucy said. "It looked funny."

Corman stood up, stretched, rolled his shoulders. "Did you eat yet?"

"Corn flakes," Lucy said. "The milk had that taste. You know, sour. So I had water."

"With corn flakes?"

"Yes."

Corman groaned.

"It doesn't matter," Lucy told him. She glanced at the photograph which still remained in Corman's hand. "What's that?"

"Just a picture I printed last night," Corman said.

"A doll," she said, almost to herself. Two small creases spread across her forehead as she continued to stare at the picture. It was as if she were studying it from separate angles, tasting, smelling, feeling it, all her senses sending out their wires. "It makes you feel funny," Lucy said as she handed it back to him.

Corman nodded, got up and headed toward the bathroom. "I'll be ready in a minute."

They were on the street a short time later. Lucy walked beside him, her bookbag strapped to her back like a camper. She tucked her hand beneath his arm, as if he were escorting her. It was a gesture she'd developed not long after Lexie's departure, and Corman saw it as a way she'd devised to give him the feel of having a woman in his life, someone on his arm, rather than clinging, however sweetly, to his hand.

"Maybe we'll go to the movies this weekend," he said. "What do you want to see?"

The idea didn't seem to excite her.

"I'd rather go ice skating," she said.

"I don't skate."

"You never do anything like that."

She was still complaining about it, mumbling darkly under her breath, as they continued toward the tall wrought-iron gate of the school.

"I'll try to be home by six or so," Corman told her. "Mrs. Donaldson will be with you until then."

"Are you going out with Joanna tonight?"

"Yeah."

"What are you doing today?"

"I'm supposed to see Julian."

"About your pictures?"

"Yeah."

Lucy smiled quietly. "Maybe he'll like them."

"Maybe."

They walked on in silence for a time, huddling closely beneath the black umbrella.

"You want to go for another walk tonight?" Lucy asked after a moment.

"If you want to."

"Maybe," Lucy said hesitantly. "But not back to that church."

"Okay," Corman said.

At the school, he bent forward, kissed her lightly. "See you tonight," he said.

She darted away almost instantly, her body merging with the stream of students that moved through the gate and up the wide cement stairs. They were talking loudly, scuffling about, and as he watched them, Corman remembered how his brother Victor had talked about his days in the Mississippi Delta, working in the Freedom Schools that had dotted the state in those days, small wooden shacks manned by northern kids who'd come down to teach the southerners how to treat one another. He'd come back with lots of stories. Some were edged in threats and violence, but even Victor's darkest tales had always ended on a hopeful note. Kids were all potential, according to him, they were the future of mankind.

But as Corman watched the kids of PS 51, he didn't think they looked like the future at all, only the most recent expression of the past. It was in their accents, clothing, what they went through, talked about. The past was a fat man sitting on their chests. A little shake wouldn't budge him. Potential didn't raise a sweat. Hope was no more than a buzzing in his ear. Victor could have talked all night, but to Corman it all came down to just one notion: if you wanted to change the world, you really had to *change* it.

"You waiting for somebody?"

Corman looked away from the gate and confronted a fresh-faced young policeman on foot patrol, the type the old cops called "Portables" and ridiculed. His eyes were utterly youthful and unshadowed. There were sights he hadn't seen, but they were on the way. "I just dropped off my daughter," Corman told him.

The Portable looked relieved. He shifted slightly, jiggling the required nine pounds of equipment which hung from his belt: the two-way radio handset, handcuffs, flashlight, nightstick, citation booklet, regulation .38 special, holster, ammunition belt and accompanying cartridges.

"The thing is," he said, "we've had some suspicious characters hanging around the schools. We're supposed to keep a close eye out for guys like that."

Corman nodded.

The Portable smiled brightly, and Corman thought that the first cops of the old city must have looked like him, young men who'd nervously patrolled the streets at night for $1.87 a tour. A fireman's leather helmet with the frontpiece removed was all they'd taken with them to meet the droves of thugs who nightly swarmed from behind Rosanna Peers' vegetable stand at the northern edge of Foley Square.

"You work around here?" the Portable asked.

"All over," Corman said. "I'm a photographer."

"For the papers, something like that?"

"Sometimes," Corman told him. Instantly he thought of all the pictures that were for no one but himself and wondered if the shooters of the old city had also stored them up by the hundreds, until they bulged from every room, poured from every drawer, swept out in curling waves from beneath their beds and chairs, endlessly extending the history of their eyes.

Julian took his hand and shook it affectionately. "Good to see you, David. Come on in."

Corman stepped into the office and reflexively positioned himself for a shot that could take in the whole room.

Julian sat down behind his desk and smiled cheerily. "So, how you doing?"

"Okay."

"Have a seat."

Corman sat down, glanced out at the rain-swept city behind the window, the clouded spires and flat gray walls. Julian's body seemed pressed against it, holding it back.

"How's Lucy?" Julian asked.

"Fine, Julian," Corman said a little impatiently. "I guess you looked at the pictures."

Julian's face shifted slightly, turned just a shade grayer. "Yes, I did."

Corman waited while Julian searched for the right words, then gave up without finding them.

"It's not that they're not good," Julian said. "Technically, I mean." He waited for Corman to react and continued when he didn't. "It's more the subject. What you shoot." He shrugged. "These things have to go through several editors. It's not up to me."

Corman nodded.

"Several people," Julian continued. "Several people have to comment, and a couple of them thought the pictures were more or less the sort of thing Weegee used to shoot, crime scenes, the underworld, that sort of thing." He glanced away, then back. "Diane Arbus was also mentioned. The grotesque, a fascination with that." He put his hands up quickly, as if parrying a blow. "Not that they don't have their place, pictures like that. They do. Absolutely. But not for us ... this house ... not right now." He leaned forward. "Photography books are very expensive to produce. And the market ... well."

Corman smiled quietly, tried to let him off the hook. "Yes," he said then started to get up.

Julian stopped him. "One thing, though," he said quickly.

Corman eased himself back into the seat.

"One of the editors came up with an idea that might interest you," Julian said. "Take one case, follow it all the way through to the end."

"Case?"

"Like a murderer, something like that."

Corman stared at him expressionlessly.

"Do a study of this person," Julian explained. "A photographic study." He laughed. "From the cradle to the electric chair, you might say."

"A murderer?"

"Or a victim," Julian said. "It wouldn't matter. A full record, though. Carefully edited. Only the later pictures would be yours."

"Later pictures?"

"Well, you wouldn't have been there for the early years," Julian told him. "I mean, you would also be working on the edit. You'd be more than a photographer. You'd help compose the whole thing."

"Pick somebody and do his whole life?" Corman asked.

"Yes," Julian said. "And the more infamous the better. Some well-known killer, someone in the news. Or at least some twist, something to hang the tale on. You know what I mean, an angle that would give the pictures some resonance."

Corman thought a moment, shook his head. "I don't know, Julian, I don't see ..."

"Slow decline, that would be the hook," Julian said. "Incremental fall. Movement, you know, downward. As they say, toward the abyss."

He sat back in his chair. "You'd be perfect for something like that," he said. "All the people who looked at your pictures, they agreed on that. No one is questioning your eye."

Corman got to his feet. "I'll think about it."

Julian looked at him pointedly. "For a really good proposal, we'd be ready to give you an advance."

Corman could feel the landlord's crumpled note like a small bomb ticking in his jacket pocket. "I'll think about it," he said again.

"Good," Julian said happily. "I thought it might interest you." He smiled. "It'd be good to work with you again. Like the old days, when we were at Columbia together."

Corman nodded.

"Remember that?" Julian said. "You, me, Lexie? The Wild Bunch."

The "old days" came back to him in a series of pictures, Lexie alone in front of St. Paul's Chapel, then he and Lexie posed comically beside the high black gate, then all of them together in the snow, Lexie lifted high on his and Julian's shoulders while some anonymous passerby shot the picture from a few feet away.

"I often think of those days," Julian said wistfully as he got to his feet. Then he snapped out of it. "Anyway, think about it. The proposal, I mean."

"Slow decline," Corman said musingly.

"Toward the abyss."

Corman stood up. "I'll think about it," he said, then turned and headed for the elevator. By the time he got there, he had completely dismissed it from his mind.

Chapter 5

THE CITY ROOM OF THE *NEWS* WAS ON THE FOURTH floor. Hugo Pike was the paper's picture editor, and he played the part exactly, everything from the half-lens reading glasses perched on top of his head, to the smoke-filled betting parlor where he gulped his egg salad sandwich.

"What you got for me, bub?" he asked, as Corman walked into his office.

Corman draped his camera bag over the metal peg beside the door, took out an eight-by-eleven manila envelope and sat down in a chair opposite Pike's desk. "I took some pictures of that woman who jumped out of a window in Hell's Kitchen last night," he said, as he drew out his contact sheets and offered them to Pike.

Pike waved them away. "We had our own people over there, but there was nothing we wanted to use."

"There may be an angle," Corman said.

"Yeah, I know," Pike said dully. "She took her Barbie doll with her."

Corman pulled out the picture he'd taken of the doll, playing it like a trump card. "She was feeding it," he said.

Pike was not impressed. "So, she was a nut case, so what?"

"She was starving herself to buy the baby formula."

Pike shook his head. "I don't think that's enough," he said. He returned everything to the envelope and then handed it back to Corman. "Better luck next time."

Corman remained in his chair, the envelope dangling from his hand.

Pike looked at him closely. "What's the matter, you coming up short this month?"

"Maybe a little."

"You need to work the nights more," Pike advised him. "We don't even have a staff shooter after two in the morning."

"I can't do that," Corman said. "I have a daughter."

"So what does that mean, you don't have a life?"

"It means I have two lives," Corman told him.

Pike shrugged. "What can I say, Corman? All the great shooters were loners. In your racket, other people just smudge the lens."

Corman nodded, said nothing.

Pike studied him carefully. "Ever think about a steady job?" he asked tentatively.

"Doing what?"

"Well, this is not for publication, you understand," Pike said. "But Harry Groton's got a serious condition."

Corman looked at Pike questioningly.

"Cancer," Pike added reluctantly. "It could be chemotherapy for a long time. We would need a quick replacement if that happened."

"When will you know?"

"He's supposed to tell us how he is by Monday," Pike said. "It could be a six-month thing, or, if he goes down . . ."

"Permanent," Corman said.

Pike nodded. "Interested?"

"I'd be shooting the same stuff Groton does?"

"Light stuff, you know that," Pike told him. "Society shit, but it's day work, all of it, just the kind you say you need. And it's steady."

Corman continued to think about it.

"Used to, Groton hung around your neighborhood," Pike added. "If you see him, you could have a word. Just don't let on you know anything."

Corman nodded.

"What are you, Corman? Thirty-nine? Forty?"

"Thirty-five."

"In the ballpark," Pike said. "Anyway, you're not getting any younger. Maybe you're getting tired of sleeping next to a police radio."

"I'm not sure."

"How about being poor, then?" Pike asked. "Are you getting tired of that?"

Corman drew in a long, slow breath. "Maybe something else will break."

Pike laughed. "Like what? Lotto?" He shook his head. "All the freelance shooters end up the same, Corman, looking for something steady. In the end, they all want to come in from the rain."

Corman said nothing.

"They all figure it out, believe me," Pike added. "That they can't keep it up, that life has a downward pull."

Downward pull, Corman thought as he returned the envelope to his bag, incremental fall, toward the abyss. The whole world was beginning to sound like Julian Carr.

There was an old Automat not far from the newspaper. Corman found himself going through its revolving glass doors a few minutes after his meeting with Pike. It was his favorite place on the east side of the city. He liked the furious speed with which the attendant scooped up exactly twenty nickels when he gave her a dollar bill. No matter how empty the place was, she jerked up the coins with the same flashing speed, her whole attention narrowed to the green bill, then the tray of faded gray coins. It was a focus Corman could understand. Since going freelance, he'd come to realize that watching money was a way of seeing. Suddenly the price of a magazine loomed larger than the cover story. Lately he'd even begun to compare the prices of various brands of laundry detergent and tuna. Edgar didn't have such worries. He was kept by a big law firm, and because of that there were times when Corman envied him, not because he was rich, but because his security gave him an aura of dignity, competence, even mastery. Hustling for a dollar made you look like a kid, froze you in an adolescent pose. If you didn't own property, had no broker, figured your taxes on the short form, your voice never changed and your shoes squeaked when you walked.

Corman dropped the coins in the slot, pressed the lever and watched as the coffee cascaded into the plain white mug. When it was full, he walked to a table by the window and sat down.

Outside, the rain had started again. The street looked dark and slick. Traffic moved slowly back and forth, while people darted through it, their umbrellas flapping in the wind off the river.

He turned from the window, took a quick sip of coffee, then riffled through his camera bag again and took out a stack of pictures, searching for one he could sell. Slowly, meticulously, he went through them one by one, staring closely, combing his mind for some way to place each one. He was still doing it when Eddie LaPlace came through the door a few minutes later.

"Yo, Corman," Eddie called from across the room.

Corman waved to him.

Eddie bounced energetically up to the table, pulled out a chair and sat down. "Been up to the City Room?"

"Yeah."

"Sell anything?"

"No."

Eddie shook his head. "Hey, it's a tough life, am I right?"

"For the last few weeks, anyway," Corman admitted.

Eddie looked at the pictures Corman had spread haphazardly over the table.

"Some of this stuff looks pretty good," he said.

"Only to you, Eddie."

Eddie looked surprised. "Oh, yeah? Really?" He picked up a long shot of the old man on the balcony. "Holy shit," he said with a chuckle. "Where'd this go down?"

"Brooklyn," Corman said. "He'd just shot his wife."

"No shit," Eddie said. The photograph slipped from his fingers, fell back down on the table. "You don't sell pictures with dicks in them, my man. Pussy hair, that may get by, and tits and ass, they're just fine for everything but the dailies. But dicks? Forget it." He smiled. "You know why?"

Corman shook his head.

"Because editors are usually men," Eddie said, "and they feel embarrassed for the guy. For a fox, no problem. They'll spread woolly pink cover to cover. But for a guy, they're embarrassed."

"You may be right," Corman said dryly.

"I'm absolutely right," Eddie said. "That's why I if I get a dick, I airbrush it right out. I cover it with leaves."

Corman said nothing. It was good advice, and Eddie was no moron when it came to human motives, either. He was probably right about everything. And yet?

Eddie snapped up another photograph. It showed the body of a teenage boy lying faceup on the sidewalk. He was clothed in blue jeans, running shoes and a dark peacoat. "What's the story with this one?" he asked.

"Cops figure it for a drug burn."

Eddie nodded thoughtfully. "Couldn't sell it?"

Corman shook his head. "It's a common sight, Eddie. Nobody needs a stringer for a shot like that."

Eddie continued to stare at the picture. "Looks like the East Side."

"That's right."

Eddie's eyes peeped over the edge of the photograph. "Forty-ninth Street, right?"

"Yeah."

"Well, there it is then," Eddie said with a sly smile. "The way you sell the picture."

"What are you talking about?"

"For Christ's sake, man, that's Katharine Hepburn's block. This hit went down practically right in front of the old broad's window."

"So what?"

"That's your angle, asshole," Eddie said triumphantly.

Corman stared at him silently.

"You play that up," Eddie said insistently. "You play the shit out of it." He leaned forward, planting his elbows on the table. "The editor looks at the picture, says nothing, unimpressed, you know?"

Corman nodded.

"He says no, right?" Eddie said. "You say, okay, fine, no hard feelings. You start to pick up the picture, then you say, 'Nice block, huh? Hepburn lives on it.' You tap the print. 'Right there,' you say. 'Jesus,' you say, 'imagine that. A drug hit right on Hepburn's block.' You slap your forehead. 'What a city?' you say. 'Drug burns even on Hepburn's block.' You shake your head at the thought of it. 'My God,' you say like it's just hit you, 'what if she'd been passing by,' you say. 'She coulda caught some lead.' It doesn't change the picture, but it gives the editor an angle on the story. The angle goes with the picture. You give him both, but you act like you don't know it." He leaned back again, his arms folding proudly over his chest. "You make the sale."

Corman stared at him, wonderingly. "You actually make sales like that, Eddie?"

"Do I?" Eddie cried. "Do I? Jesus Christ, man, I got a map of the city tacked to my wall." He spread his arms out wide. "Big fucking thing. Big as you can get. I got little numbered pins that tell me where every celebrity in this town lives." Again, he smiled proudly. "So what do you think?"

"It's good, Eddie," Corman said quietly, with a small, very slender smile. Anything seemed better.

Chapter 6

AFTER A DAY OF CHASING SMALL FIRES AND FENDER benders, Corman returned home just before sunset and found Trang staring at the bulletin board which the tenants had hung on the wall.

"Ah, Mr. Corman," Trang said as he turned toward him, "I was hoping to have word with you."

Corman stopped, stared at him expressionlessly, said nothing.

"You know you must make decision soon," Trang said gravely. He was the new owner of the building, a South Vietnamese immigrant who had, according to his disgruntled tenants, accumulated large sums of money by shipping drugs out of his country before the fall of Saigon. He wore perfectly tailored blue suits, but in a 1940s style, three-piece double-breasted, with wide lapels and pleated, slightly baggy trousers, the style, as some residents liked to claim, of a French imperialist. His teeth had been capped somewhat oddly, too, so that almost all of them were the same length, like piano keys.

"I mean concerning apartment," Trang explained.

"I made it a long time ago," Corman told him flatly.

"What was decision?"

"I don't want to buy it."

Trang looked mildly hurt. "But Mr. Corman, the insider price is very good," he said, his eyes sweet, sorrowful, as if he were a good friend trying to prevent Corman from making a disastrous mistake. "And it is very good apartment, as you know."

It was a dump with loud radiator pipes and rattling windows, but Corman didn't feel like going into it. "I just don't want it," he said.

Trang's face tightened. "Perhaps you have specific problem?"

"No."

"If you do, it could be repaired," Trang assured him. "It could all be part of purchasing agreement."

"I'm not interested," Corman repeated.

"But why?" Trang asked. "We could come to arrangement. I am willing to provide financing to insiders."

"I don't want to own an apartment," Corman said firmly.

"And that is final?"

"Yes."

Trang cleared his throat loudly. "Well then," he said darkly. "I have to bring up other matter."

"The rent."

"I am afraid so."

"I've been a little short recently."

"Short, yes," Trang said curtly.

"I'll get it to you as soon as I can."

Trang didn't look convinced. "The people here, they think I am rich man, that rent does not really matter to me." He shook his head. "But I have mortgage, you see. It is quite big one, too, as you know from prospectus. I have to pay it, just as you have to pay rent. Every month."

Corman nodded, his eyes staring evenly into Trang's face. It was not an evil face, just flat and faintly yellow with oval eyes and soft, almost purple lips. But there was something behind it, an edginess and brutality that added up to a capacity to do whatever the scheme of things demanded. He looked like the sort of person who was perfectly willing to accept the law of the jungle as the only one there was or ever would be. His body always looked tightly coiled, as if around a low-slung limb, poised to drop, entangle, squeeze.

"You very smart person," Trang said. "I am sure you understand about mortgage."

"I need a little more time."

Trang looked at Corman as if he'd asked to sleep with his wife, daily with his twin daughters. "You make it difficult for me, Mr. Corman," he said flatly. "I am not bad man. People, here, they think I am bad person."

Corman said nothing, and his silence seemed to set Trang on edge, stiffen his resolve. His eyes shriveled into two small green dots. "At this point," he said, "I believe that you are two months in arrears."

"That sounds right," Corman told him.

"Of course, this problem with rent could be figured into purchase price of apartment," Trang added, now shifting again, becoming more conciliatory. "As discount, you see."

Corman shook his head, his eyes still focused on Trang's face. There was a small birthmark just above his right eyebrow. It was dark pink, and roughly in the shape of a fish. For a moment Corman thought it might be a tattoo, the mark of some murderous Oriental gang of drug runners and assassins to which Trang had once belonged. He wondered if Trang had ever killed a man, slit a throat or bashed in a skull. It was entirely possible, if the rumors were true, and the odd thing was that in America he would never think of such a thing. He would use the law instead, wielding it like a dagger, hurling it at you like a pointed throwing star.

"The figure is eight hundred and forty-two dollars and seventy-two cents, I believe," Trang said.

"Yeah," Corman told him, "I got your letter."

"I wrote it with regret," Trang said. "It is not personal matter."

It was an interesting choice of words. For an instant Corman dealt with the hidden element within it. Nothing personal meant that they could do anything to you, but it wasn't exactly to you they were doing it. They were just doing it in response to some phantom sense of the way things were. That's what dictated their action, and you weren't supposed to get mad about it.

"I'm working on a few things," Corman said.

Trang's eyes widened hungrily. "Things?"

"An angle on some pictures."

"Angle?" Trang said uncomprehendingly. "Pictures?"

"I'm hoping to make some money."

"I hope you do," Trang told him. "Do you think it will be soon?"

"Yes."

"Good," Trang said, his words now quite precise, lawyerly, emphatically stated. "If not, it is necessary I have to ask you to leave."

"I understand."

"Eviction proceeding very slow. I would like better to avoid."

"So would I."

Trang stepped back, edging himself against the bulletin board. Angry tenants had posted a newspaper article which had been written about Trang and other developers who were transforming the theater district, turning old Broadway hotels and rooming houses into state-of-the-art co-ops and condominiums. It showed Trang heatedly wagging his finger at an old man in a sleeveless undershirt and suspenders, and although Trang had never noticed it, the photo credit in the right-hand corner of the picture was Corman's.

Trang flashed an uneasy smile. "Well, good night, then, Mr. Corman," he said. "I am glad we understand each other."

"Me, too."

The smile vanished, the eyes grew small again. "I am sure I will be hearing from you about rent."

Corman nodded quickly, turned and walked to the elevator.

Mrs. Donaldson was playing Chinese Checkers with Lucy when Corman came into the apartment.

"He's going out with Joanna tonight," Lucy told her matter-of-factly.

"Is that so now?" Mrs. Donaldson said, as she turned quickly and gave him a faintly disapproving glance, as if he'd once again failed to deliver on some vague promise of paternal responsibility.

"That's right," Corman said. "And I was wondering . . ."

"If I could stay at your house," Lucy blurted to Mrs. Donaldson.

"Yes," Corman said. "Until around midnight, something like that."

"So he can be with Joanna," Lucy said.

Corman dropped his camera bag on the small metal chair he kept by the door, unstrapped his police radio and walked into the living room.

"Did you finish your homework?" he asked as he sank down in one of its chairs.

"The child did it all," Mrs. Donaldson declared. She looked at Lucy and smiled sweetly. "Like the grand little girl she is."

Corman continued to stare at Lucy doubtfully. "Did you?" he repeated.

Lucy shot him a withering glance. "I said I did," she cried. "Jeez."

"I just wanted to be sure," Corman told her.

Lucy returned her attention to the checkerboard. "It's not due till Monday anyway," she muttered.

Corman stood up again, walked into the bathroom and slapped some cold water onto his face. In the mirror above the sink, he could see that he was losing a little hair, and that small puffy patches had begun to form beneath his eyes. He'd noticed them in Joanna, too, and Lexie before her. Far out in space, he imagined, you could turn around and see puffy patches on the earth itself, wrinkles forming, gray wisps, the whole vast process slowing down. At times, it even seemed the best solution. And yet?

Joanna ordered a margarita. When it came, Corman watched her move her finger around the salted edge of the glass just as she always did. He had known her for almost two years, and little things had become predictable—the way she lit a cigarette, always with the tip held slightly upward, or the way she rubbed her eyes, never with her fist, her palm, her little finger, but always with the side of her index finger. It was as if there was a code which dictated these movements precisely, locked all history in a helpless chain reaction.

"Have any luck today?" Joanna asked.

"In what?"

"Money."

Corman shook his head. "I pitched a few things," he said, "but nobody moved on them."

He added nothing else and instead let his eyes rove the restaurant, taking in its ocher walls, dotted with huge red sombreros and cowboy gear, bridles, stirrups, a pair of leather riding chaps, the tools of someone else's trade.

Joanna smiled sympathetically. "It's been a long dry spell," she said.

Corman glanced up from his own drink. "It's been raining for two days."

"I mean as far as money's concerned," Joanna explained.

"Trang's threatening eviction," Corman told her.

Joanna looked alarmed. "Really? Is it that bad?"

"Bad enough."

"Well, I'm good for ..."

"No, thanks."

"It happens to a lot of people," Joanna said gently. She remained silent for a moment, then added hesitantly, "There's an alternative."

"A steady job, I know. I'm looking into something."

"What?"

"With one of the dailies," Corman said. "Light stuff."

Joanna smiled. "That seems promising."

"It's society stuff," Corman added. He elbowed away a bowl of taco chips. "Trivial stuff. It doesn't mean anything."

"Yes, it does," Joanna told him flatly. "It means money. Survival. That's what it means."

Corman nodded resignedly and took a sip from the beer. "So, how's Larry?"

Joanna's face darkened slightly. "You really shouldn't ask me about him."

"Why not? He's your husband."

Joanna's eyes darted away. "Well, what can you say? Kids make strange bedfellows." Her finger circled the rim of the glass again, dislodging small granules of salt. "Does Lucy know about him?"

"Larry?"

"Yeah."

Corman shook his head. "No. Why should she?"

"Honesty."

"Bullshit," Corman said.

"Travis knows about you," Joanna said.

"Travis is in college."

"What are you afraid of, Corman?" Joanna asked him, her face turning very serious. "That your kid will hate you because you slept with a married woman?"

"It would complicate things a little," Corman said dismissively. "She's nine years old."

Joanna smiled weakly. "And you want to protect her?"

Corman ducked behind his drink, took a quick sip.

Joanna's finger made a third circle, as she eyed him carefully. "I'm not sure I love you, you know," she told him bluntly. "I never have been."

Corman smiled softly as he lowered the glass. "Same here," he said.

They made love late in the evening, slow, already somewhat tired, Friday night love. When it was over, Joanna walked to the window, her body wrapped in a sheet, and stared out at the city.

She'd come from the Midwest, and her body had a lean, prairie emptiness to it, a sense of something which lived openly and needed very little tending. The urban crouch Corman often noticed in other women was completely absent in Joanna. She walked the streets almost heedlessly, as her mother must have walked the limitless fields of Illinois.

"Larry's in Florida," she said, without turning toward him.

Corman said nothing. He lay on his back and watched her. He could see how the folds of the sheet nuzzled her softly, rested smoothly on her hips and clung with a kind of ghostly affection to her shoulders.

"He'll be back on Monday," she added.

Corman sat up, pressing his back against the back of the sofa bed. "What's the matter, Joanna?"

She didn't answer, and Corman slid back down beneath the covers, thought of the old city, wondered if love had been simpler there. If it had been, he was reasonably sure it was oppression that had done the trick, made everything look harmonious. "Want a drink?" he asked after a moment.

She shook her head, still watching out the window.

His eyes drifted away from her, and he could see the small red light of his closet darkroom. On the small shelf just inside the door, the woman still lay sprawled across the rain-swept street, her doll nestled in a soggy blue blanket. To the extent that history would remember her, it would be like that, just as it remembered all victims in their darkest moment. The old shooters had known exactly how to capture the dead in their muddy fields, the stricken in their frozen grief, the bony faces gathered behind the rusting wire. He wondered if, in a moment of irony, they'd ever been tempted to call out some brief instruction: *Okay, now, say cheese.*

"I'd better get home now," Joanna said as she suddenly turned from the window.

Corman nodded softly. "Okay."

She gathered her clothes and walked into the bathroom. When she came out again, she looked exactly as she had in the restaurant, hair neatly combed, not so much as a loose strand to betray the night.

"I'm sorry," she said as she came up to him. "I'm a little down."

"I'll walk you to the train," Corman said.

She decided on the bus instead, the 104, which lumbered up Eighth Avenue, then crossed over to Broadway at Lincoln Center.

"I'll call you in a couple of days," she told him.

They were standing near the northeast corner of 47th Street, shielded from the rain by one of the small porno theater marquees that stretched out over the sidewalk.

"Larry's due back on Monday," Joanna said.

"Yeah, I know."

She drew in a deep breath, her face oddly strained. "He found a lump," she said.

Corman looked at her. "Where?"

"Groin."

"Did he go to the doctor?"

"On Monday," Joanna said. "He's scared. I've never seen him scared."

"I'm sorry, Joanna."

She turned away from him, her eyes following the quickly moving traffic. "People grow on you, don't they?"

"Yes."

She faced him again, squarely, like someone laying it on the line. "We'd have to ..."

"Of course."

She smiled slightly. "I'll let you know."

The bus arrived, leaning heavily, its long black wipers gliding rhythmically across the windshield. An old woman sat at the front of it, fingering the top of her red-tipped cane.

"See you, Corman," Joanna said as the hydraulic doors wheezed open.

He kissed her quickly, affectionately, without desire. "If there's anything I can do," he told her.

She stepped onto the bus, glanced back at him as the doors closed. "Just answer the phone," she said.

Corman nodded as the bus pulled away, then stood for a moment, watching it move more deeply into the heavy night-bound traffic.

"How much to get in?" someone asked suddenly from behind him.

Corman turned, saw a stocky little man standing at the ticket window of the theater. The woman behind the glass looked up, her eyes sharp, animal-like, a wolf nudged from sleep.

The little man lurched slightly, dragging a huge elevated shoe beneath him. "How much?" he repeated.

Corman couldn't hear what the answer was, only saw the woman's lips twitch crisply behind the glass, then the little man shake his head disappointedly as he walked away.

Chapter 7

LUCY WAS SLEEPING VERY SOUNDLY ON MRS. DONALD-son's sofa, her hands tucked under the pillow. Corman could see her small white feet, and just above them, the rolled cuffs of her dark blue jeans. "I'll take her home now," he said.

"She could stay the night," Mrs. Donaldson told him, as if it would be safer that way, as if no little girl could ever be more secure within a man's rough care. "You wouldn't have to wake her."

"No, I'll take her home," Corman said determinedly as he walked past her, through the small square foyer and into the living room to where Lucy lay motionless on the sofa.

There were little shrines all over the place, plaster saints, nativity scenes. Christ hung from almost every wall, wracked with pain and disillusionment. The Virgin was all around, too, poised on the edge of a table or standing on either side of the mantel, her face more serene than any parent had the right to be, unfeelingly composed, too accepting of her child's dark fate.

"She didn't give you any trouble, I hope," Corman said as he knelt down to pick Lucy up. Her body was warm, terribly soft. She moaned gently as he lifted her, ran her tongue across her lips, then nestled her head into his shoulder.

"She's a sweetheart," Mrs. Donaldson said.

"Yes, she is."

At the door, Corman turned back toward Mrs. Donaldson. "I'll pay you tomorrow, if that's okay."

"Whenever."

"Anyway. Thanks."

"Good night, then," Mrs. Donaldson said as she closed the door.

Corman walked the few yards down the hall, fiddled awkwardly with his keys until he finally got the door open, then took Lucy directly to her bed. It was never made, and so there was nothing to turn back or tuck in. He simply laid her body across the mattress, tugged loose one of the covers that formed a tangled bundle at the foot of her bed, and drew it over her.

He watched her a moment, then walked back into the living room and stood by the window as the rain ran down the glass in silvery streams.

After a while, he glanced back at the sofa, thought of taking out the bed but decided not to. Instead, he pulled a chair up near the window, unstrapped his police radio and let it rest in his lap. It was a simple UNIDEN handset, and, next to a camera, it was the one indispensable tool of the city's freelance shooters. Corman kept it tuned to the frequency of the SOD.

Special Operations Division was a central clearinghouse for all the city's hour-by-hour distress. When a car slammed into the Brooklyn Bridge or a train caught fire in the Bronx or a man anywhere walked into a fast food restaurant and started shooting, it came first over SOD. It worked twenty-four hours a day, and there was hardly a second of that silence which the stringers called "dead air."

Now, as Corman turned it on, something was happening at Broadway and 174th Street.

Click: *In his hand? What?*

Click: *Uh, we don't know at this time. We just got an EDP in the hallway.*

Click: *Eighth floor, right?*

Click: *That's right.*

Click: *Okay, Ten-17.*

A soft whoosh came over the radio for an instant. Then another click and the voices continued, but different voices, another call, this one for a medical unit, a fire in a restaurant.

Corman lit a cigarette, edged himself onto the wide windowsill, and listened. Outside, the soft beat of the rain continued through the night.

48

Click: *We got a problem with the EDP.*
Click: *Advise.*
Click: *A Ten-27.*

Things had suddenly gotten more complicated at 174th and Broadway. The EDP had a gun.

Click: *You got a positive on that?*
Click: *Affirmative.*

He had been spotted with it.

Click: *Identification?*
Click: *Negative.*

They didn't know who he was.

Click: *Request location.*
Click: *Ten-11.*

Or exactly where he was.

Click: *Do you think he's still in the building?*
Click: *Affirmative. Request backup.*

It was getting dangerous. The radio responding unit wanted help.

Click: *Ten-17.*

It was coming.

For an instant, the frequency went silent, then another click, another call, a bus had overturned on the Major Deegan Expressway and several people were wandering half-dazed among the stalled cars and onlookers. Another EDP was running half-naked along the FDR Drive.

Corman walked into the small kitchen and made himself a cup of coffee. He could tell it was going to be a long night. It was almost two in the morning already, and he had not even begun to feel the first fleeting drowsiness.

He brought his cup back into the living room and sat down once again on the windowsill. The voices had returned, and the first had grown a bit more tense.

Click: *We have a definite negative at the exits.*

The EDP had not left the building.

Click: *How are you proceeding?*
Click: *Floor search. Up and down.*

Click: *Any response on the Ten-17?*
Click: *Negative.*

The backup had not arrived. The Jake was alone.

In his mind, it was easy for Corman to get a good clear picture of what was happening on 174th Street and Broadway. A foot patrolman had responded to an EDP call. The EDP, Emotionally Disturbed Person, was now wandering the halls of a large apartment building with a gun in his hand. The Jake was following him, moving cautiously up the dim stairwells or along the empty corridors, his hands already on his pistol. He was sweating under his arms, and he could feel a tightening in his muscles. He jumped a little, each time his radio clicked on.

Click: *Any response on the Ten-17?*
Click: *Negative.*
Click: *I can hear him. He's right above me. I can hear him yelling. It's really loud. It sounds like … like … he's stomping up and down, too.*
Click: *Did you say stomping?*
Click: *Yes.*
Click: *And yelling?*
Click: *Affirmative.*
Click: *Is he yelling at other people?*
Click: *I don't know.*
Click: *Can you make out what he's saying?*
Click: *Negative.*
Click: *Are civilians involved?*
Click: *I can just hear the guy. I don't hear anybody else.*
Click: *I read you.*
Click: *Please advise.*

For a moment, there was silence. The SOD central dispatcher was young, inexperienced. He wasn't sure what to tell the Jake. For an instant, he hesitated. Then he made his decision.

Click: *Proceed with caution.*

Corman leaned forward in his chair. The dispatcher had made a serious mistake. The Jake was alone. A Ten-17 was in place, on the way. He should wait. There were no civilians in danger. He should wait. The dispatcher had screwed up. If everything went well, he'd be chewed out in the morning. If anything happened to the Jake, he'd never pin on a badge again.

Click: *Proceed with caution.*

The Jake didn't respond. He was afraid. Corman could hear his fear, smell it. The Jake thought he was going to die in this little shitcan apartment house high above Broadway; he was going to open a grimy metal door, peek out and take a bullet in the face.

Click: *Repeat.*

Click: *Proceed with caution.*

Click: *Ten-4.*

He was going to do what he'd been told, follow the dispatcher's orders. He wasn't going to wait. He was going ahead, slowly, cautiously, the sweat now beading on his forehead, gathering in a little pool in his navel. But he was going ahead, and he was wrong.

In the meantime, restaurants were burning, cars colliding, and at the southern tip of Manhattan, yet another EDP was dancing around a smoldering ashcan while he hurled small stones at passing cars.

Corman took a sip of coffee and continued to listen as radio cars and emergency vehicles were sent hurtling along the empty, early morning streets, their sirens echoing through the towering glass corridors.

Click: *EDP in sight.*

It was the Jake on 174th Street. He'd spotted the EDP.

Click: *Request location.*

Click: *Ninth floor. Southeast, no, south ... southwest corner.*

Click: *Describe him.*

Click: *White male. About thirty years old. He's wearing jeans, I think, some kind of blue pants. He went around the corner, that's all I could see.*

Click: *Did you see a weapon?*

Click: *Negative. Any word on the backup?*

Click: *Ten-17. Proceed.*

Again, the radio went silent very briefly, before the usual round of calls began. Through the city, the usual night's work went on, but Corman found his attention now entirely focused on the ninth floor of a building that was over a hundred and thirty blocks away.

Click: *Okay, he's at the end of the corridor.*

Click: *Where are you?*

Click: *Southwest corner.*

Click: *Are there exits?*

Click: *Negative.*

The EDP had gotten himself into a corner. He was facing three blank walls and a corridor with a single patrolman at the end of it.

Click: *He's still screaming.*

Click: *He's alone?*

Click: *Affirmative. He's stomping, too. He keeps stomping.*

Click: *Ten-17 is in place.*

Click: *But where?*

Click: *We have confirmation on the Ten-17.*

Click: *Just a minute …*

There was a sudden silence, then the SOD dispatcher called again.

Click: *Unit 4. Ten-2.*

The dispatcher was trying to raise him.

Click: *Unit 4. Just a …*

Corman leaned forward. He could hear the screams of the EDP, the stomping.

The SOD dispatcher was getting worried.

Click: *Unit 4. Please respond. Ten-2. Ten-2.*

Silence.

Click: *Unit 4. Ten-2. Ten-2.*

There was no response. Corman could feel the air electrify around him, hear the frantic care in the dispatcher's voice when he finally acted.

Click: *All units. We have a possible Ten-30 at 2942 Broadway. Repeat, we have a Ten-30. Officer in danger. Respond immediately. Ninth floor. Southwest corner. 2942 Broadway. Request all available units to respond immediately.*

The silence continued for a few more seconds, then, suddenly, the patrolman's breathless voice broke through the steadily vibrating air.

Click: *Uh, we had a problem here. The EDP charged me. But it's okay now. It was a water pistol. Repeat. Water pistol. Subject is under control. Request medical unit and backup. Repeat. The subject is under control.*

Corman felt a small rush of air whistle through his teeth. Something had turned out well. A threat had been met, mastered, and the feeling which followed was unexpectedly sweet and exhilarating. He felt a barely controllable urge to wake Lucy up, tell her that somewhere nine floors above the sleeping city, the beast had been driven back. Joanna needed to know that such things were possible, despite the downward pull. Everyone needed to know it, Groton, the little man at the ticket window, everybody. He even thought of the Hell's Kitchen jumper, saw her long dark hair still wet with rain, wondered if such knowledge might have urged her from the ledge in time to amaze Julian's phantom audience with a happy ending.

Chapter 8

ON SATURDAY MORNING CORMAN SPENT SEVERAL HOURS arguing intermittently with Lucy over what movie they'd see that afternoon. Lucy sat cross-legged on the floor, carefully going over the entertainment section of the *Times*. She preferred movies that edged cautiously into the forbidden zone of sex and violence, but Corman suspected that this had less to do with the actual film than with her need to feel grown-up. It was the sort of attitude that could become a way of living, so that in the end you grew to adolescence hating childhood, then to adulthood hating adolescence, went all the way to death, hating life.

"How about this one?" Lucy asked suddenly. She pointed to a full page advertisement that showed a grim-looking cop nuzzling a forty-five automatic against his cheek.

"Not my thing," Corman said.

"How about a play then?" Lucy said. "You promised you'd take me to a play."

"When did I promise that?"

"About a year ago," Lucy told him. "You said you'd take me to the one about the fairy tales."

Corman thought about the money, the promise, the collision course between the two. "Okay," he said finally.

Lucy's face brightened. "Really?"

Corman pulled himself to his feet. "A promise is a promise."

The theater was on Broadway, and as Corman stood in line to buy the tickets, he stared at its wildly teeming lights. Despite the gaudiness, it struck him as beautiful. He admired the energy that swept out from it, the self-assertion, the refusal to lie down and take it. It had always been like that, first as an Indian warpath, then as a street of burning effigies, secret conclaves, plots, riots, scandals. As part of his scheme to bilk the city, Aaron Burr had sunk his only water-well alongside it. Not a drop of water had ever come from the well itself, but later someone had used it to hide the body of a murdered girl.

Lucy knew nothing of all this, and as the line inched toward the ticket booth, Corman wondered if there were any real way to teach it to her. He could take her on a tour, of course, point out this and that, but he wasn't sure that anything could find its way into a mind that wasn't ready for it. That was the reason he'd finally given up teaching, because he could teach only skills, nothing beyond them; how to read and write, but not how to feel about what was written in a way that was immediate and searing, the way he'd dreamed a photograph might teach.

"This is supposed to be good," Lucy said enthusiastically as her eyes swept over the billboard at the front of the theater.

Corman nodded. "You're staying with your mother next Saturday night," he told her.

"I know."

"And all day Sunday."

She looked at him. "I always stay all day Sunday." Her eyes remained on him. "She's taking me to a play Sunday afternoon. Jeffrey's coming with us."

"He's a nice man," Corman said, forcing himself.

He bought the tickets a few minutes later, then escorted Lucy to their seats.

The lights dimmed slowly. The play began, an amalgam of fairy tales which started with the happy endings then went on to what happened after that, untimely deaths and unfaithful princes. Corman thought it interesting, but glum. After a time he found himself drifting back to Julian's suggestion, money, finally the stacks of photographs he'd gathered in boxes, stuffed in drawers, every picture he'd taken since the first time he'd gone out with Lazar.

That had been over five years before, but he could remember it very clearly. A woman had called a local precinct, claimed that she'd swallowed a bottle of sleeping pills, that she was dying, that they had to hurry, hurry, before it was too late. Even so, Corman and the old man had made it to the hotel before the police, then followed them as they kicked down the door to the woman's room and plunged inside.

Corman could still recall the precise details of what he'd seen that first time. The woman was stretched out facedown across the plain wooden floor. The phone was still in her hand, but her fingers had released it, so that it simply lay in the palm of her open fist like a dead bird. A few feet away, a two-year-old boy jumped up and down in a rickety playpen, gurgling happily while the cops stripped his mother to the waist and began pumping her back to life.

She'd finally come to, dazed, but still able to walk shakily to the ambulance downstairs. A big cop had taken the child, cradling it gently in his arms, as if posing for a publicity photograph for the police department. "This is what it's all about," the cop had said to Lazar on the way out, and Corman remembered thinking that for one of the few times in his life, he'd actually heard someone say something that struck him as absolutely true.

"This is what it's all about," he repeated now in his mind as he watched the action on the stage. A world-weary man was singing to a little boy, trying his best to teach him how to live. "Careful," he kept saying. "Careful."

Once home, Corman prepared dinner for the two of them, read to Lucy awhile, then washed the dishes, his mind thinking of Lazar again, a story the old man had told him several years before. It was a kind of fairy tale, like the ones in the play, he realized now, with its own oddly happy ending. In his mind he could see Lazar as he'd appeared that night, puffing at his cigar while his voice sounded over the featureless hum of the barroom crowd.

"I was in the coalfields, you know," Lazar had said. "When I was a boy. There was a strike, and I hired on, you might say, as a courier. At night, I'd run from one striking mine to another, telling the miners the latest news, keeping everybody up to date on what was happening." Here he'd paused, taken a draw on his cigar. "Well, I got caught one night, and some of the gun-thugs gave me a bad beating." Here he'd waved his hand, dismissing it. "But I survived, and before long I was here in the city, working for the *Tribune*." A quick, ironic smile. "Well, a few years after that, there was another strike down in the coalfields and the *Tribune* sent me down to take some pictures. I took a lot of pictures, and during the course of the whole thing, I found out that one of the couriers for the miners was really an informer." Here he drew the cigar downward, like the muzzle of a gun. "I didn't know what to do about it, so I finally decided to take it into my own hands." A pause, mostly for effect. "So, I tracked down that courier one night, and I gave him a good beating." The voice deepened slightly. "I learned something from all that, Corman. I learned a little part of what it's like to live a balanced life." The face grew very calm, the voice exquisitely soft. "Once to receive the blow, once to deliver it."

Corman put the last of the dishes away and walked determinedly to his darkroom, as if it were a research laboratory on the rules of life. He sniffed the clean, sweet smell of the chemicals, peered at the soft red light, felt the way the room's continually building heat gave him the sense of moving toward the core of something. Outside, the world seemed hopelessly diffused, but in the darkroom, it became concentrated, intensified, and the vast blur gave way to small rectangles of highly focused light. Sometimes, in brief visionary glimpses, the mosaic struggled toward a decipherable design. Coils and spirals disentangled, and when that happened, he felt as if he were edging not so much toward some great revelation, as just a small, faint suggestion of what life ought to be.

After a while he returned to the living room, snapped on the television, and collapsed onto the sofa in front of it. Lucy came out of her room a few minutes later and eased herself beneath his arm, her eyes focused on the flickering screen. An old black-and-white detective movie was playing, and in the film, a wiry little snitch had just handed a battered-looking private eye a picture. "See. See," he told him excitedly. "Now you know." As Corman watched the screen, he thought again of Lucy, Trang, his work, all the other imponderables, and it struck him that basically what everyone needed was a skinny little snitch just like the one on television, someone who could clear things up, get to the bottom of something, hand over a single exquisite photograph of what had really happened.

Chapter 9

IT WAS STILL VERY GRAY AT MIDMORNING, BUT THE RAIN had stopped and the streets had begun to dry slightly in the brisk fall air. Corman had been up all night by then, with nothing but a short nap around dawn. But the nap had been just long enough to rejuvenate him, so he was able to feed Lucy her breakfast of cereal, then watch leisurely as she did her usual Sunday morning chores, cleaned her room, straightened her closet, folded the laundry he'd washed earlier while she was still sleeping in her room.

"I guess we can go to Uncle Edgar's now," she said when she'd finished.

"We're not supposed to be there until the afternoon," Corman reminded her.

Lucy pivoted one of her hips out melodramatically. "Well, can we at least go to the park before that?"

"It's not a very nice day."

"It's not raining now," Lucy said. "We could try it. We could meet them there."

"Okay," Corman said, giving in. "Get your bike."

It was the usual time-consuming struggle getting the two bikes out of the basement storeroom and into the elevator. They were rickety affairs, with nearly treadless tires, rusty chains, handlebars that were slightly off-center. They looked old the way people looked old, used beyond their days. Corman had hoped to buy Lucy a new one by summer, but now that seemed unlikely, and as he finally managed to wheel his own bike into the elevator, the pinched quality of his life overtook him again. He thought of Pike, Groton, the kind of work that made your nights better because your days were worse.

Once on the street, they turned west, rode quickly to Tenth Avenue, then swung north toward the park, with Corman in the lead, Lucy close behind. The whole distance was a worry for him. Traffic sped by at high speed, half-clipping bikers as they passed, a far cry from the old city, when taxis had been electric, and all other cars had been limited to nine miles an hour and forced to warn pedestrians with a gong. And yet Corman had long ago realized that despite the danger, he didn't have the patience to walk, dragging the bike beside him, and he knew Lucy didn't either.

They reached 59th Street in less than fifteen minutes. From there it was only a short pull eastward to Columbus Circle. The air was still very heavy, and the fall chill had not lifted. A spectral haze clung to the upper reaches of the trees, floating through their dark leafless branches, giving the whole area an eerie, moorish look that Corman found vaguely unsettling. He stopped dead and stared out toward a particular line of trees. Only a few days before, a woman had been raped and murdered beneath them, and during the last minutes of her life, she had probably lain on her back and stared helplessly at the same bare branches that spread out before him now. As his eyes lingered on the trees, Corman suspected that every inch of earth contained similarly wrenching ironies, and that a thorough knowledge of them would inevitably create a different way of seeing.

"What are you looking at?"

Lucy had come up beside him and was busily zipping her dark blue parka more tightly against her throat.

"Nothing," he told her.

"It's colder than I thought," she said when she'd finished.

"Put up your hood."

She looked at him sourly. "I don't like hoods. You know that." Corman shrugged. "Okay, you ready?"

"I've been ready," Lucy said.

She pressed down on the pedal, shot forward instantly, then headed down the gently curved road that led into the park. Corman followed along after her, pedaling slowly, careful to keep his distance so that she wouldn't feel surveilled.

Within a few seconds she was almost out of sight. It was her favorite trick, and he began pedaling a bit more rapidly to stay closer to her. He could see her parka billowing out slightly as she raced ahead, but it was little more than a blur which darted in and out from behind the other riders. Once again, he speeded up until he was near enough to see her glance back at him with one of her teasing, "gotcha" smiles.

They made two complete rounds of the park, then glided into the large esplanade that surrounded a white band shell which the city had erected for some of its outdoor concerts. Green wooden benches lined the area, and Lucy quickly plopped down on one.

"I went fast," she said as she unzipped her parka.

"Yeah," Corman told her as he pulled up behind.

"It gets you hot," she said. "Can I take it off?"

"You'll forget and leave it on the bench," Corman said. "You've done that before."

"No, I won't," Lucy said. "Please?"

"Okay," Corman told her. "Just make sure you remember it when we leave."

"I'll put it in my basket," Lucy said. Then she quickly stripped it off and crammed it into the small wicker basket which hung from the handlebars.

"Can I get a hot dog?" she asked as she returned to the bench.

"Why don't we wait for Giselle?"

"She's probably already eaten."

"I doubt that."

"How about a pretzel, then?"

"All right," Corman said. He fished a dollar bill from his pocket and gave it to her.

"Be right back," Lucy said as she dashed toward the hot dog wagon at the other end of the esplanade.

Corman leaned back and stretched his long, slender legs out in front of him. Here and there other people lounged on the benches or walked quietly across the brick-covered ground. From time to time a lone bicyclist would glide nonchalantly by, sometimes nodding quickly, but usually offering only a brief, apprehensive glance.

Lucy came bounding toward him, a huge salted pretzel dangling like a bridle bit from her mouth.

"It's a good one," she said. She stretched her hand toward him. "Want the change?"

"You keep it."

She smiled brightly. "Thanks."

For the next few minutes they sat together silently while Lucy finished off the pretzel. Some sort of band was beginning to set up on the orchestra shell. They were all dressed in black shirts and trousers. From the look of their instruments, it was going to be a fully electrified performance. Tangles of thick black wire hung over the side of the platform or spread out in ever-widening coils along the stage itself.

"It's the Heebee-Jeebees," Lucy informed him. "It's heavy metal."

"I see."

"You wouldn't like it."

"I might."

Lucy shook her head determinedly. "No, you wouldn't."

"I like all kinds of music," Corman insisted.

"Not this," Lucy said. She got to her feet. "Let's go."

She was pedaled away in an instant. Corman trailed after her, following her out of the esplanade then around the park again. He thought she might wheel back around the band shell, but she continued on, past the wide wet expanse of the Sheep Meadow, then to the whirling carousel, and still onward around the park, circling it again and again, stopping only once, briefly, near the exit at 72nd Street, where a lone troubadour stood almost within the dark shadow of the Dakota, crooning one John Lennon song after another, as if in perpetual reverence for the things he had imagined.

Toward early afternoon, Corman called Edgar and told him to bring Giselle to the large playground near the southern end of the park. They arrived a few minutes later, Giselle bounding happily ahead while her father lumbered behind, his somewhat portly body wrapped in a Humphrey Bogart-style trenchcoat and floppy hat.

Edgar glanced doubtfully at the bench as he came toward it. "Is this thing dry?"

"As much as it's going to get," Corman said.

"Okay," Edgar said as he sat down. He pulled off his hat and slapped it against his knee, then abruptly stopped himself. "Christ, Dad used to do that."

Corman said nothing.

"It's weird," Edgar added. "The stuff we pick up."

Lucy and Giselle rushed up to the bench, hand in hand.

"Can we climb the rock?" Lucy asked.

Edgar looked hesitant. "That's pretty high." He cast an evaluating glance at Giselle. "You sure you won't fall?"

Lucy squeezed her cousin's hand. "I'll watch her."

"Let Giselle watch after herself," Corman said.

Edgar unnecessarily straightened the collar which circled Giselle's throat. "Just be careful," he said to her. "And watch for glass."

The two girls nodded obediently, then darted toward the immense gray stone which rested at the other side of the playground.

Edgar turned to Corman, smiled. "So, how you doing these days?"

"Okay."

"Still shooting the city?"

"Yeah."

"I cover the waterfront," Edgar said, his standard line for Corman's work. "Shot anything interesting lately?"

Corman thought of the woman, the blue blanket, nodded.

Edgar didn't go into it. "I'm handling that plane crash outside Las Vegas. It's a real tangle. Multimillion-dollar damages. Excluding punitive."

"How's Frances?"

"Sick," Edgar said wearily. "Like always." He shrugged. "The whole thing could be in her head."

"I doubt it."

"I'm not so sure," Edgar admitted. "But what can you do? Nobody can get to the root of it." He stroked his sleek, clean-shaven chin. "When you get to be our age, things start to break down."

"She's only thirty-seven," Corman reminded him.

"With some people, it starts early," Edgar said casually. He glanced toward the rock. Lucy and Giselle had nearly made it to the top. "If she gets hurt, Frances'll kill me," he said.

Corman's eyes drifted toward the traffic on Fifth Avenue, for an instant envisioning the carriage parades of the old city, opera singers in their barouches, couples in sleek white phaetons, the elegant black victoria of Madame Restell, the Avenue's luxuriant abortionist.

After a moment, Edgar touched his knee gently. "It really is good to see you, David. We should see each other more often."

Corman nodded. "Victor, too."

Edgar frowned, waved his hand sourly. "Forget Victor. He's in his own world."

"You always say that."

Edgar shrugged. "Anyway, as far as we're concerned, the two of us, we should get together more often."

Corman said nothing.

"But your work," Edgar added tentatively. "It keeps you busy."

"Yours, too."

"But you're out at night again," Edgar said. He looked at Corman pointedly. "Or am I wrong about that?"

"Sometimes I work at night."

"Sometimes? Or is it pretty much a permanent thing?"

"It varies."

"Two, three nights a week?"

Corman sat back slightly, stared evenly into his brother's eyes. "Why all the questions about how often I'm out at night?" he asked.

Edgar laughed edgily. "You've got a good eye," he said. "You always had a good eye."

"What's on your mind, Edgar?"

Edgar cleared his throat sharply, glanced away, then returned his eyes to Corman. "I got a call from Lexie. She's making noises. Like a couple of years ago."

"About Lucy?"

"Yes."

"What is it this time?"

"She wants to talk to you about a few things. She's a little concerned about how things are working out."

"Things are fine."

"She doesn't see it that way."

"What's that supposed to mean?"

"I don't know where she gets her information," Edgar said. "But she knows you've gone back to working nights."

"How could she know that? It couldn't be Lucy. She knows to keep quiet."

"No, I don't think it came from Lucy."

"Frances," Corman blurted. "It must be Frances."

"It could be," Edgar admitted reluctantly. "She doesn't mean to let things slip, but sometimes she gets on the phone with Lexie and, you know how it is, the ladies exchange information."

"So she's told Lexie I'm working nights again?"

Edgar nodded. "You're not supposed to be working nights, David. You know that. It's part of the custody arrangement."

"I don't have a choice right now."

"Well, that's also a problem."

Corman looked at him quizzically.

"I'm talking about your ability to support Lucy," Edgar added.

"I can support her."

"But to do it, you work this night shift thing," Edgar said. "That's a problem when it comes to custody."

Corman turned away. He could feel his blood heating and worked to cool it off. "What can I do?" he asked finally.

"My advice is for you to talk to her," Edgar said. "You know Lexie. She's not a bitch. She's concerned about Lucy, that's all. It's not a spiteful thing. No bitterness. With you two, the whole thing was mutual. Even in the decree. Mutual. Mutual. Mutual. Every other word."

Corman's eyes shot over to Edgar. "It's about money. It always is."

Edgar stared at Corman sternly. "David, if I thought it was just the money, I'd tell Lexie to do her worst, and we'd see her in court."

"But money's what it comes down to," Corman said. He looked at Edgar knowingly. "Look, Edgar, you and I both know that whenever anybody says it's not just the money, it's just the money."

Edgar shook his head. "Not always. In this case, it's part of it, but it's not the whole thing."

"What else?"

"Well, for one thing, where you live."

"What about it?"

"Not just the apartment," Edgar said. "Although that could be an issue too."

"How?"

"It's pretty cramped, you got to admit."

"Cramped?" Corman blurted. "Cramped? Jesus Christ, Edgar, in this city in the nineteenth century people were piled into . . ."

"Nineteenth century?" Edgar cried. "Nineteenth century? Who gives a fuck about the nineteenth century? We're talking about the here and now, David."

"But you have to . . ."

"Face the facts," Edgar said sharply, finishing the sentence. "That's what you have to do." Suddenly his face softened, his voice grew less tense. "Look, David, you're my brother. I know how you feel about things. You have a—what would you call it—a romantic streak. Not everybody does."

"Romantic streak?" Corman said. "Edgar, what are you talking about?"

"Photography, that sort of thing. Working the nights. It's not the usual thing."

"So I have to do the usual thing to keep my daughter?"

"No, but you have to make a living at it."

"See what I mean?" Corman said icily. "Money."

"Money," Edgar repeated. "All right, money. I mean your apartment, where it is, the neighborhood around there, the school Lucy goes to." He lifted his hands, palms up. "All of that's a problem for Lexie. She has concerns about it." He waited for Corman to respond, then added cautiously, "Legitimate concerns."

Corman gave him a withering look. "Christ, you sound like her lawyer."

"Not at all," Edgar said. "But I'd be a fool to ignore the nature of her complaint. I know how a judge can see it."

"See what?"

"The way you live. Things you've done. Leaving your teaching job. At least Lucy could have stayed at that little private school if you hadn't quit."

"And been a society doll, like the other girls there?"

"A what?"

"A debutante at some stupid ball."

"David, I hate to break it to you, but not everybody sees that as a fate worse than death," Edgar said. "They see that Lucy had a few chances which she doesn't have anymore because you quit your teaching job and ran off to be a photographer."

"But that's the point, isn't it?" Corman said insistently. "I didn't run off. Lexie did."

"And maybe that was a little self-indulgent on her part," Edgar said. "I'm not denying that. But quitting your teaching job, that could be seen as self-indulgent, too."

"The bottom line is that Lexie gave me custody," Corman said flatly.

"Yes, she did."

"Well, doesn't that mean anything?"

"It means something, but not everything," Edgar said. "Lexie thought Lucy would be better off with you. Mainly because of the school. She hadn't married Jeffrey yet. She didn't have any money. You couldn't have paid any alimony even if she'd asked for it. And without it she couldn't possibly have supported Lucy. You could. At least at that time. The way she saw it, giving you custody was the best thing she could do for Lucy. That's the way the court could see it, too."

Corman's eyes drifted down toward his hands. They seemed good to him, strong, capable of expressing complex and indecipherable forms of love; rich, abiding, infinitely subtle forms that held no status in the law.

"I told her I'd speak to you," Edgar added softly. He touched Corman's shoulder. "I suggest you talk to her, David. That's my professional opinion." He waited a moment, then added, "Also personal, my personal opinion."

Corman shook his head despairingly. "She's going to do it. Try to get Lucy."

"It's too early to tell exactly what she's going to do."

Corman remained unconvinced. "Do you think she's started anything?"

"You mean, legal action?"

"Yeah."

"No, I don't think so," Edgar said. "If she were determined to start something, she'd go directly to an attorney. She wouldn't call me, and she certainly wouldn't be interested in talking to you."

"Then what do you think this is all about?"

"I think she wants to persuade you," Edgar said bluntly.

Corman stared at him unbelievingly. "Persuade me? You mean to give up Lucy? You mean, just do it, voluntarily?"

"That's my guess," Edgar said.

Corman shook his head silently.

"What can I say, David?" Edgar added quietly. "We're not talking about who gets a puppy. We're talking about a child here. People change their minds."

Corman remained silent.

"I thought Saturday might be a good time for you two to get together," Edgar said. "I understand Lexie's supposed to pick Lucy up on Saturday, and before that you two could go out for a drink, talk things over." His voice took on a hint of gentle warning. "I wouldn't let things drift if I were you, David."

Corman's eyes shifted over to the rock. Lucy was sitting at the rim of it, her legs dangling over the rounded ledge, her arms flying about as she talked to Giselle. Inside, he could feel a hollowness growing in him, a great engulfing emptiness expanding outward like the ripples of a cosmic blast.

Toward evening, they went to Edgar's apartment for dinner. Frances greeted them at the door, bussing Corman brusquely on the cheek, then drawing Lucy protectively into her arms, as if trying to comfort her for the way she had to live.

"Want a drink?" Edgar asked as he stepped into the large living room.

"Scotch," Corman said.

Lucy and Giselle bounded up the stairs to Giselle's room while Frances bustled about, serving first one hors d'oeuvre, then another, her long, stringy arms buttoned to a silver tray. She seemed curiously drained both by petty service and by being served, and as he watched her, Corman wondered if perhaps the solution to the old war between the sexes might be the reemergence of the woman-warrior, women who resisted protection as fiercely as they did abuse—sent out that message loud and clear: No more!

"Canapé?" Frances asked as she bent toward him, the silver tray flashing in the lenses of her wide designer glasses.

Corman shook his head. "No, thanks."

They had dinner almost an hour later, everyone situated around the large rectangular table Frances had bought from an East Side antique gallery. It was made of rosewood, and the purity of the grain, its smooth, effortless flow, gave a strange comfort to the entire room. For a moment, Corman imagined himself living among such lovely things, digging for a separate treasure than the one he found in his darkroom or on his walks with Lucy. It was as if elegant, expensive things were what life offered in place of that distant, ineffable richness which began to seem unattainable as time wore on and disappointments accumulated. And so after a while, you joined in a conspiracy with things that gave you comfort, style, prestige, a sense of being more than you really were, having more than you really had. It was perfectly natural, and the trick was simply to forget that there was anything else at all.

"Lucy could spend the night with us, you know," Frances said quietly after dinner, as the three of them sat in the living room again while the children ran about upstairs.

"Thanks, Frances," Corman said, "but I'd rather take her home."

Frances smiled thinly. "You like to keep your eye on her, don't you?" she asked, as if there were something perverse in his attachment.

"Not exactly."

"Doesn't she sort of get in the way sometimes?" Frances continued cautiously.

"Of what?"

"Your other . . . activities."

"Like what?"

"Frances," Edgar warned. "It's not your business."

She gave him a scolding look, then turned back to Corman. "Well, you're a single man, now, David, you must have . . . needs."

"Yes, I do."

"But, surely, with Lucy . . ."

"She comes first," Corman said flatly. "She'll always come first."

Frances stared at him doubtfully. "But a man your age, without Lexie . . . it must be difficult to . . ."

"Not really," Corman said. He shrugged. "Duty is a feeling like any other feeling," he said softly. "As a matter of fact, it's a passionate feeling."

Frances stiffened somewhat and said nothing.

"Maybe the most passionate there is," Corman added. He smiled, then stood up. "I'd better get us home now."

Once back in the apartment, Lucy went to bed almost immediately, and a few minutes later Corman walked quietly into her room. She was sleeping as she often did, on her back, arms and legs spread, the posture of a child who had little fear. Somehow she had reached a strange concreteness, a sense of herself that came across equally in moments of rebellion and acquiescence. He realized that he had no idea where this solidity had come from, only that it was now in place, and suddenly, at the thought of her going to Lexie, riding her bike through the opulent Westchester suburbs, heading down the predictable track that would lead to the right school, marriage, life, he felt a trembling along the fissure that ran from his mind to his heart, and in that instant he decided he would fight for her, and began immediately to formulate a plan.

Chapter 10

"YOU SURE ARE QUIET," LUCY SAID AS THEY MADE THEIR way toward school the next morning.

"I have a lot on my mind," Corman told her.

"About the rent?"

"That's part of it."

Lucy's eyes drifted over to the opposite side of the street. "That restaurant's changing its name again," she said.

Corman nodded quickly. "Uhm."

"It's like it changes every two weeks or something," Lucy added, almost irritably, as if such changes signaled a grave lack of resolution.

"Yeah," Corman said dully.

Lucy tugged at his arm. "You're really out of it," she said. Corman glanced down at her and hoped she wasn't right.

After dropping Lucy off at school, Corman walked quickly to the subway and took the Seventh Avenue Express downtown. On the way, he went over the murderers or victims Julian might be interested in, silently repeating the words he'd used: slow decline, incremental fall. That was what he needed, a book of pictures, something Lexie could hold in her hand, show to her friends, a Product, for Christ's sake, that could convince her he was still worthy to keep Lucy in his care.

Once above ground, Corman hoisted his bag more securely onto his shoulder and headed south, moving quickly until he reached police headquarters.

One Police Plaza was a massive brick cube which sat like a huge red block between Chinatown and the East River. Its straight parallel lines of small square windows made it look exactly like what it represented, the inflexible authority of the law. The old police headquarters had been very different, a beautiful beaux arts building, domed, graceful, as aristocratic in appearance as some of the old chiefs had been aristocratic by birth. The developers of the new city had already turned it into a luxury condominium.

The police darkroom and photographic laboratory was in the basement of the building. Its dark green double doors faced a well-lighted corridor which was usually filled with the familiar smells of photographic work.

Charlie Barnes was sitting at his desk when Corman came into the room. Long black strips of negatives were lined up in front of him, each neatly numbered with a red grease pencil. Harvey Grossbart stood over him, peering at the negatives. "That one," he said.

Barnes marked it, then glanced over to Corman. "You look like hell."

Corman shrugged, said nothing.

"Lang would like something like that," Grossbart said as he pointed to a particularly gruesome picture.

Barnes shook his head in disgust. "He stinks to high heaven, Lang does. I'd bet my life savings he's on the pad, a big one too, a horse couldn't swallow it."

Grossbart shook his head. "Not in Homicide. There's no money in Homicide."

"Just what you can snatch from the room of the recently deceased, right?" Barnes asked with a smile.

Grossbart looked at him tensely. "You wired, Charlie? You got an IAD wire up your ass?"

Barnes laughed.

Grossbart leaned toward him slightly. "Because if you do, I'll tell you every fucking thing I know."

Barnes laughed again, this time a little nervously. Then he took a single photograph from the stack on his desk. "Here's a good one from that hotel killing."

Grossbart took the picture and lifted it slightly for better light.

"You showed up for that one, didn't you, Corman?" Barnes asked.

"Yes," Corman said. He stepped over and looked at the photograph.

It showed a woman lying facedown on a bed, naked from the waist up, the lower part of her body wrapped in a dark brown towel. A large red bra hung from one of the bedposts. Over the other one, a man's hat, an old gray homburg, was tipped, almost jauntily. The woman stretched across the full length of the bed, her brown feet near the headboard, her hair pouring over the end of the bed like a wash of brackish gray water. She was somewhat overweight. Rounded folds of skin hung from her sides, tan and doughy.

From the photograph, it was easy to tell what had happened to her. Her husband had pressed her face into the mattress, probably to muffle her screams. Then, for some reason Corman could not imagine, he'd swept her hair over the top of her head before nosing the barrel of the pistol into the fleshy hollow at the base of her skull.

She hadn't died immediately, and because of that, almost the entire end of the bed was soaked in blood. It seemed to drip from the bottom edge of the picture, moist and glistening, the kind of shot Lazar called a "blood slide."

"Were you still there when the husband came out?" Barnes asked.

Corman nodded. The man had gone berserk after shooting his wife, waving his pistol out the hotel window while he raved about what a bitch she was. The woman had lain unconscious, bleeding to death, for almost a half-hour while the SWAT team got into position. By then, the hotel had become the center of neighborhood attention, and Corman had stood by, watching quietly as the frenzy grew steadily around him.

"Came out naked as a jaybird, I hear," Barnes added.

"Yeah, he did," Corman said. With his hands high above his head, he remembered, his smooth, hairless belly almost completely white in the bright afternoon sun. From the second floor landing, the crowd around the hotel had been able to see his small shrunken penis quite clearly as it peeped out from its nest of gray pubic hair, and they had cheered and hooted loudly while the man stood trembling uncontrollably above them.

"Love and hate," Grossbart whispered suddenly, his eyes still concentrating on the picture. He glanced at Corman. "That's the bottom line."

"Not exactly the news of the world, Harv," Barnes said. "What happened to the guy?"

"The wagon to Bellevue," Grossbart said.

"Yeah, right," Barnes said testily. "He'll be out cruising the social clubs, hunting for a new wife in . . . what do you think, Corman . . . six months?" He glanced down at the picture. "Meanwhile, the broad is history."

Grossbart's eyes swept the desk again. "Just print up the ones we marked," he said. "The DA wants to have a peep." Then he left the room.

Barnes gathered up the negatives, glanced up at Corman. "So, what can I do for you?"

"The jumper in Hell's Kitchen last Thursday," Corman said, "I was wondering if you'd heard anything. A name, maybe."

"I heard they tagged her," Barnes told him. "But as far as the name, you'll have to call Lang." Something seemed to occur to him suddenly. "But you'd already know that, wouldn't you, Corman?"

"Yeah."

"So how come you're down here?" Barnes asked. "You should be at Manhattan North, quizzing Lang."

Corman nodded, knew Barnes was right, but still wanted to avoid Lang as long as possible, along with the hot, disinfecting shower he always felt he needed after talking to him. "How'd they get the ID?" he asked. "A canvass?"

"The way I hear it, there was some paper on her," Barnes said.

"Rap sheet?"

Barnes laughed. "No. Turns out it was a diploma."

Corman's eyes widened. *Slow decline. Incremental fall.* "Diploma?" he asked.

"That's what I heard. It could be bullshit."

"Where was the diploma from?"

"You're thinking some beautician's school, right?" Barnes asked. "Or one of those second-story paper mills?" He laughed. "I heard it was Columbia."

"Columbia?" Corman said. He saw Julian nodding, stroking his chin, thinking it might be just the thing to advance a little cash on. "Shepherd took some pictures that night," he said. "Would you mind if I had a look?"

Barnes looked puzzled. "Use Shepherd's pictures? I thought you took your own."

"I did," Corman told him. "But I might be able to use a few of his, too."

The puzzled look remained on Barnes' face.

"For something bigger," Corman explained reluctantly. "A follow-up, you might say."

Barnes smiled knowingly. "So that's why you came down here," he said. "You're after some shots."

Corman smiled thinly. "If I can use them, I'll be sure that Shepherd gets . . ."

Barnes waved his hand indifferently. "Yeah. Yeah. Right. You'll see he gets a mention." He shrugged wearily. "Anyway, they're all printed up. But before I hand them over, I want you to take a look at something else." He opened the top drawer of his desk, took out a color photograph. "What do you think of this?" he asked as he handed it to Corman.

Corman lifted the picture, once again angling toward a better light. It was a standard eight-by-ten color photograph of a small windswept cottage on the coast. Tall blades of sea grass, golden in the autumn sun, rose in a radiant wave at the edge of the dune. They looked like thin, glimmering strips of gold. Even their shadows against the white beach sand appeared to glow.

"I bought that little house last week," Barnes said proudly. "What do you think?"

"Nice."

"You can't believe the quiet up there," Barnes said. "Nothing but the sea, you know? Whoosh. Whooosh. Just like that. It puts you right to sleep." He nodded toward the photograph. "But I wasn't just talking about the place."

Corman looked at him quizzically.

"The picture," Barnes explained. "What do you think of the composition?"

Corman's eyes concentrated on the photograph once again. He saw the perfect symmetry of the house and surrounding landscape, the carefully cropped edges that allowed for each blade of sea grass to display its full height. Nothing flowed off the picture, or encouraged the eye to look for more.

"Pretty," Corman said. "Nice."

"It's not a street shooter's thing, I know," Barnes told him. "But I like seascapes, landscapes, stuff like that."

Corman kept his eyes on the picture. It was a vision of some kind, a dream of perfect peace, repose, contentment, a place where all the bills were paid and no one ever tried to take your children from you. But it also seemed strangely isolated, shut away from the general texture of life in a way that made the sea look like a barred window, the beach like a bolted door.

Barnes leaned forward, ran his finger up a single shimmering reed. "See how I handled that shadow? It just throws things into better relief, makes them look brighter."

Corman nodded gently.

Barnes tugged the picture from Corman's fingers. "Anyway, I thought it was pretty good. Technically, I mean."

"Yeah, it is."

"Not the sort of thing you shoot, I know that," Barnes repeated.

"No," Corman admitted. "Not my thing, but still . . ."

"Right," Barnes said quickly as he returned the photograph to his desk drawer. "Anyway, these are Shepherd's," he added as he snapped a plain manila folder from a stack of them on his desk and handed it to Corman. "You'll like them better."

The lounge was on the third floor. It looked like every other lounge Corman had ever seen, square tables with Formica tops and thin chrome legs, a solid wall of vending machines, some that slowly wheeled things to you on a stainless steel carousel, others that simply dropped it into a collecting trench behind a hinged plastic door.

The room was empty, but Corman walked all the way to the far back corner anyway. He sat down, lit a cigarette, then took out the short stack of photographs from the envelope and looked at them one by one.

The first was a long shot which Shepherd had taken from several yards away. It posed the woman as a dramatic center to the surrounding backdrop of empty streets and dark, overhanging tenements. Sheets of blowing rain glistened in the headlights of the patrol car at the curb and in the streetlight above it. To the right, a few feet away from the body, the Recorder stood with his pen and notebook poised for action. His job was to keep a list of everyone who showed up at the scene, all the medical personnel, all the patrolmen and detectives. He was looking almost directly at the camera. Corman assumed that he was scribbling Shepherd's own name down in his notebook. An ambulance stood in the right foreground, and just behind it, a radio patrol car. Lang was off in the far right corner, motioning a man out of the crowd, the one who later turned out to be the witness.

The second shot was a little closer. Now the woman's body stretched further across the rain-slick street. The tires of the ambulance could be seen a few feet away from her outstretched arm, but the rest of it was open, the white and orange body, the flashing hoodlights, the two attendants who leaned against the already open rear door. The unlighted tenements and warehouses loomed larger, and seemed almost to bend toward the woman from above. Lang had disappeared from the frame, but the witness had not. He could still be seen standing in the right background, one hand in the air, talking excitedly to a figure who had been cut away.

The next five shots were in steadily tightening close-ups of the woman herself. The first had been taken only a few feet from her right side, and her long slender body stretched almost across the entire length of the frame. Her fingers seemed to curl around the right edge of the photograph, her feet to press back against its left wall.

The second concentrated on the face, the flattened nose held slightly up, the chin pressed against the rough street, the rain-soaked hair sprayed out in all directions, the puffy, half-opened right eye staring dazedly into the flat gray surface of the pavement.

The third had been taken from the opposite side. The face disappeared behind a curtain of drenched and matted hair, the legs severed at the ankles, her feet stretching beyond the edge of the frame. Her arm was now in full relief, and Corman could see the needle marks which ran up and down it, the cluster of raised purple dots which gathered like a tiny village in the pale valley of her elbow.

The fourth shot was from above. As he looked at it, Corman could easily tell how it had been taken. Shepherd had not used a ladder for this one. He had straddled the body at the waist, bent forward, set his line of vision, and pressed the button. To Shepherd, it must have seemed right at the time, a tight close-up, taken from directly overhead. But now it looked awkward, unsteady, oddly faked, the product of an urge to do more than record. It was as if, just for a moment, Shepherd had fallen victim to a different calling, decided to pump his picture up with a touch of drama, a pinch of trendy grief. He'd tried to find an angle that would weep a little, sputter into art, but he'd only gotten something that looked staged, as if the street had just been hosed by the technical crew, the rain blown by large fans shipped in from Hollywood, the woman about to get up, dry her hair and sprint to the waiting trailer for a line of coke.

The last photograph was taken from even further above the woman's body. It was the one Corman had seen Shepherd take from the ladder. It showed almost the entire body. The head was in the foreground, with the trunk and legs stretching backward, like the stern of a boat shot from some position above the forward deck.

"Those yours?"

It was Grossbart, and Corman didn't have to look up from the photograph to know it. Grossbart had a distinctive voice. It seemed to come from the ground.

"Shepherd's," Corman said. He slid the pictures over to Grossbart.

Grossbart looked at the photographs one by one, concentrating on each in turn. "Why'd he take this one?" he asked after a moment. "What's he trying to do, impress his girlfriend?"

Corman glanced at the photograph. It was the one Shepherd had shot as he'd straddled the body. "He got carried away," he said.

"I don't like bullshit," Grossbart said. He slid the photograph under the others. "Not much of a mystery," he growled.

Corman pressed the tip of his cigarette into the small tin ashtray on the table. "She had a college diploma," he said. "Barnes heard it was from Columbia."

Grossbart was unimpressed. "So? Even smart people get depressed."

"And the Similac," Corman added. "She had cans of it. She was feeding it to the doll."

Grossbart leaned forward very slightly. It was hardly perceptible, just a small inching toward the edge of the table.

"At the same time," Corman told him pointedly, "she was starving."

"How do you know?"

"The way she looked."

"Hypes don't put on much weight," Grossbart said. "You know that." Again there was the slight inching forward, a subtle, stalking movement, silent, cat-like. "What's your point, Corman?"

Corman shrugged. "It's interesting, that's all."

Grossbart did not seem amused. "You trying to make a mystery out of this thing?" he asked. Before Corman could answer, he waved his hand dismissively. "Forget it. This one's not a mystery."

Mystery was common police slang for a murder that would probably never be solved, but Corman knew Grossbart meant more than that. He meant something about the woman, the doll, the dark fifth-floor landing, all that must have finally gathered together in order to get them there. That was the greater mystery, the one that was always less dense and immediate than who did what to whom. It had a mood of aftermath which clung to it like a faint, dissolving odor. While the body lay fresh and soft, the mystery was solid, tense, compelling. But after it had been scooped up, after the blood had been washed away, the walls repainted, sheets changed and carpeting replaced, the intensity of it drained away, and the other mystery settled over the interior space of the room, the street, the mind. It was ghostly, intangible. No one could go at it anymore, drag it down, cuff it, toss it into the paddy wagon. It had become faceless, impossible to contemplate without disappearing into it yourself. Everybody knew that. In Corman's estimation, it was perhaps the only thing on earth that absolutely everybody knew.

Grossbart's right index finger shot out toward the pack of cigarettes on the table. "Mind if I have one?"

"No."

Grossbart snapped up the pack, shook one out and lit it. "Had a hell of a mess on Essex Street this morning," he said. "Guy strung a couple cats onto the clothesline of his building. Just let them dangle in the goddamn airshaft." He looked at Corman. "Why would a guy do that?"

Corman shook his head.

"Something eating him, I guess," Grossbart said. His eyes drifted down toward the pictures. "Some people go out a window, some string up a cat." He shrugged. "The way it is," he added, groaning slightly as he drifted back into his chair.

Corman leaned forward slightly. "I could use a little help, Harvey," he said.

Grossbart looked surprised, as if he thought Corman was about to ask for a handout. He said nothing.

"I need to find out some things about this woman," Corman told him.

"Why?"

"I'm trying to work up a story."

Grossbart shrugged. "It's not my case. You need to talk to Lang."

Corman shook his head.

"You got something against him?"

"The way he is," Corman said.

"The perfect combination," Grossbart said with a slight sneering smile. "Stupidity and corruption."

Corman nodded.

"But the way it is, you got to work with everybody," Grossbart said. "Like a friend of mine said, 'Birth ain't a screening process.'"

Corman smiled.

Grossbart took a draw on the cigarette. "What are you after?"

"Just call it a gig," Corman said. "I want to track her down a little."

Grossbart shrugged. "So go ahead. It's a free country."

"How could I find out who she was?" Corman asked.

"Well, the only guy besides Lang who'd know about her ID right now would probably be Kellerman at the morgue. He'd have to have a confirmed ID before he could release the body."

Corman nodded.

Grossbart looked at him curiously, with a hint of disappointment.

"You never struck me as the grab-for-the-brass-ring type," he said.

Corman thought of Lucy. "Depends on the ring, I guess," he said as he gathered up his things and headed for the subway and the morgue.

* * *

Sanford Kellerman was the assistant ME in charge of the morgue. He was just finishing up an autopsy when Corman walked into the dissecting room. Body parts were scattered here and there, some in jars, some in transparent plastic bags, and the smell, despite the heavy doses of disinfectant, was almost more than Corman could stand.

Kellerman nodded as Corman stepped up to the table. "What can I do for you?" he asked.

"There was a suicide last Thursday night," Corman said. "In Hell's Kitchen."

"The one on 47th Street?" Kellerman asked. "Jumped out the window?"

Corman nodded.

"All the work's been done already," Kellerman said. He picked up a severed hand, dropped it into a transparent plastic bag. Then his eyes shot over to Corman. "You look familiar."

"We've met before," Corman told him.

"Oh yeah," Kellerman said. "I remember now." He sunk his hands deep into the meaty open cavity of the body on the table. "That's right, you're a . . . a . . ."

"Photographer," Corman said. "Freelance."

"Yeah," Kellerman said. "You came down about a year ago."

"To shoot a few faces," Corman reminded him. "I had a death-mask idea."

Kellerman laughed. "Death mask, huh?" He shook his head. "Everybody's interested in the morgue except the people who work in it." He laughed again. "Sometimes I want to get one of them down here to clean out the condensation drains. That would give them a taste of what it's really like. You have somebody crawl up a pipe and scoop out a handful of maggots, that'll be the last of their interest in the morgue." His eyes returned to the body. "So what are you interested in now, more death masks?"

"That woman I mentioned," Corman said. "Did anyone come down to identify her?"

Kellerman nodded. "Surprising, too. Like they say on the street, a zip-top piece."

"She was Jewish?"

Kellerman smiled. "Unless she was trying to pass," he said.

"Name's Rosen. Sarah Judith Rosen." He shook his head at the thought of it. "You know, we don't get many nice Jewish girls down here."

"Maybe she wasn't very nice," Corman said. He took out his notebook, wrote down the name. "Know anything about her?"

Kellerman shrugged. "No. Why, is she somebody's daughter?"

"She was a college graduate," Corman said. "At least that's what they say at Number One."

Kellerman looked at Corman curiously. "So, not only a Jewish girl, but a college girl. The world is getting strange."

"Do you know anything at all about her?"

"Just that somebody's picking her up tomorrow."

Corman felt the tip of his pen bear down on the open notebook. "Who?"

"A funeral home on the Upper East Side," Kellerman said.

"They left a message on the machine. Tomlinson's Chapel." He watched Corman intently. "You think she was some big shot's daughter?"

Corman let the question pass. "She was starving, wasn't she?" he asked.

"Yeah, she was," Kellerman replied. "Very severe malnutrition."

"What was she hooked on?"

"Hooked?"

"The needle marks."

Kellerman shook his head. "She wasn't hooked on anything at all."

"But there were needle marks," Corman said. "I took some pictures of them."

"Those were needle marks, all right," Kellerman said. "But not from shooting dope. They were too big for that."

"What'd they come from?"

"My guess is she'd been selling blood," Kellerman said. "The puncture marks were very large. They looked like they came from the sort of needle they have at those blood-buying places down on the Bowery."

Corman nodded and guessed that selling blood was the way she'd been able to afford the Similac. "When are they going to pick up tomorrow?" he asked.

"Message said one P.M."

"Would you mind if I came by?" Corman asked.

Kellerman looked at him cautiously. "What for?"

"I just want to take some pictures," Corman assured him. "I won't bother anybody."

Kellerman thought about it. "I guess it would be okay," he said finally. "But just be sure you act like you happened by. I don't want the relatives or whatever to think I set them up."

"Okay," Corman said. He looked back down at the body, saw Sarah Rosen's instead, Julian's idea floating in his mind like a small white raft in a stormy ocean vastness.

Once outside, Corman quickly got the number of Tomlinson's Chapel and gave them a call.

The voice at the other end sounded as dead as his customers. "Tomlinson's Chapel. How may I help you?"

"I was wondering about someone who's going to be at your place tomorrow."

"Be at our place?"

"A body. A woman. Sarah Judith Rosen's the name."

"Yes, what about her?"

"I was wondering if you could tell me who's making the arrangements for her."

The voice grew suspicious. "Are you a relative, sir?"

"No."

"And what is your capacity, may I ask?"

"I'm a photographer."

The voice chilled. "I'm afraid we're not allowed to give out information to unauthorized individuals."

"I just need the name of her parents," Corman said.

"I'm sorry," the man replied firmly. "But as I told you, we are not allowed to give out information to unauthorized individuals."

Corman started to blurt another question, but the click of the man hanging up silenced him, as if a label had been stamped on his forehead, blocking him forever: an unauthorized person.

Chapter 11

CORMAN ARRIVED AT JULIAN'S OFFICE A FEW MINUTES later and placed the few photographs he had of the jumper on his desk. "She might be the one you're looking for," he said.

Julian went through the photographs quickly, then glanced up at him. "What's the whole story, David?"

"She jumped out a tenement window in Hell's Kitchen a few days ago."

Julian nodded. "With a doll?"

"She threw it out first," Corman said. "She'd been feeding it Similac."

Julian's eyes drifted back down toward the pictures. "Terrible."

"She graduated from Columbia," Corman said.

Julian's eyes shot up toward him. "Columbia?" he said unbelievingly.

"And she was Jewish," Corman added.

Julian's eyebrows drew together slightly. "From a prominent family?"

"I don't know yet," Corman said. "But I was thinking about that idea you mentioned," he said. "Slow decline."

Julian smiled, let his eyes fall back to the photographs and linger there. "What else do you know about her?"

"Just what I told you so far," Corman said. "I wanted to be sure you were interested."

Julian thought about it for a moment, squinting slightly as he continued to gaze at the pictures. "I'm interested," he said finally. "I need a few more details, but the basic situation sounds promising." He looked back up at Corman. "What's your time frame?"

"For what?"

"Coming up with a proposal."

Corman shrugged. "I hadn't really thought about it."

Julian gave him a pointed look. "He who hesitates, and all that."

Corman nodded. "I understand."

"So I could expect something right away?"

"Yes."

"Good," Julian said brightly, hesitated a moment, then added, "And you might think about hooking up with a writer on this story."

"Writer?"

"For the text."

"I wasn't thinking about a text," Corman said. "Just pictures."

Julian looked doubtful. "Well, a writer might help with the research, too." He smiled gently and began writing on his memo pad. "Here's somebody who might be interested," he said, then handed Corman the paper.

"Willie Scarelli," Corman muttered, reading from the sheet.

"You know him?"

Corman nodded. "We've run into each other."

"He did a piece on that bag lady who froze to death on the Williamsburg Bridge a few years ago," Julian said. "He traced her whole life. Got a TV movie out of it. He might be of service in the current project."

Corman looked up from the paper. "I'd rather work alone, Julian. You know, just pictures." His voice sounded weak to him, his resolve already crumbling slightly.

"Well, that's your decision in the end," Julian said. "But if you change your mind, you can usually find Scarelli at the Inside Track. Sixty-third and Lexington. As it turns out, he loves the ponies."

"All right," Corman said. He pocketed the memo and started to pick up the pictures.

Julian's hand shot toward them. "May I keep them?"

Corman hesitated, without knowing why.

"To help with an initial pitch," Julian explained. He smiled. "One of those corridor conferences we have around here. The pictures could be useful." He glanced back at them. "Very good work, David. Compelling."

Corman drew his hand back from the photographs but felt the uneasy sensation he was letting go of something.

"And get more," Julian added. "The tenement, the neighborhood. Everything you can. Facts. Pictures. The works, right way." He smiled happily. "This could be big, buddy-mine, a new direction for you."

The sky remained overcast, but there were breaks in the clouds from time to time, and as Corman stared up at the tenement's fifth-floor landing, he could see patches of light as they swept back and forth across the dark window like faded searchlights. For a time, he simply stared at the window, as if the morning light might reveal something he hadn't noticed before.

Finally he drew his eyes away and glanced to the left. A young man was standing on the top step of a cement stoop across the street. He wore a black jacket with a gray wool hood, and he kept his hands deep in his pockets as he shifted nervously from one foot to the other. A stream of people moved in and out of the building, nodding to him silently, then rushing up the stairs to get what they needed.

Crack houses operated twenty-four hours a day, just as the legendary opium dens of the old city that had looked down on the teeming crowds of Chinatown. Because of that, Corman was sure a lookout had been posted the Thursday night the woman had leaped out the window. From his place on the stoop, the lookout would have been able to see the blue bundle arc out of the fifth-floor landing, then the woman after it, her arms and legs clawing at the rain.

The man on the stoop eyed him suspiciously, but Corman knew not to flinch. Instead, he nodded solemnly as he walked up to the stoop and lit a cigarette.

The man said nothing. He had large brown eyes set very deep in their sockets and badly pocked skin, scars from what must have been a horrendous case of teenage acne. He moved like a tightrope walker, forever tilting left and right in quick little jerks.

"I'm not a cop," Corman told him.

The man's hands moved inside the pockets of his jacket. "What you want, man?" he asked sharply. His eyes darted up and down the street, catching Corman's face briefly with each sweep.

"I'm just working an angle," Corman said. "About the woman who jumped out the window a few nights ago. Were you around when that happened?"

The man's eyes settled on him stonily, but he didn't answer.

For a moment Corman thought of offering him money, but all he had was a five spot, and he figured the lookout was probably pulling down from six to twelve hundred a day. A five spot would make him laugh. "I just have a couple of questions," he said.

The man considered it a moment, suddenly shrugged. "Go ahead. Just be quick."

"Did you see anybody else around when the woman jumped?"

"I seen some guy talking to a cop," the man said. "Talked to him for a long time, his whole life story, man."

"What's his name, do you know?"

"Simpson's what somebody called him," the man said, then nodded toward the small brick building directly across the street. "I see him come out of that building over there sometimes. Day-tripper, leaves in the morning, comes back at night."

"How about the woman, did you know her?"

The man shook his head. "I seen her a few times." The eyes leaped away again, resumed their frantic outlaw dance.

"Did she have a man?"

The lookout grinned. "A man? Shit. She ain't no slash, man. She look too sick for a man." He glanced down the street and stiffened. "Time's up," he said with a sudden coldness.

Corman stepped back from the stoop. "Okay," he said immediately, turned quickly and saw a car as it moved toward him from the end of the street. The bagman had arrived. "Thanks," he added, then headed back down the street and turned into the alleyway beside the building, following the same route Lang had used the night of the jump. The hole was still exposed, the plywood on the ground before it. Corman crouched down and slipped inside the building.

The entire floor was dark, except for the slant of dusty light which came in from the uncovered entrance. Corman drew his flash out of the camera bag and pressed the button. The darkness drew back instantly, gathered in the far corners of the room, crouched there like a frightened animal. Everything else swam in a hazy, gray light.

Corman moved forward slowly, his eyes combing the bare, cement floor as he walked to the back of the room, then up the stairs, pausing at each landing to illuminate the surrounding interior. Each floor was completely bare, mostly stripped of flooring, ceiling, everything but the steel and cement skeleton of the building itself.

It was the same on the fifth floor, except that Corman didn't need his own light to see it. The windows had not been sealed with wood or cement blocks, and it was easy to see how entirely barren it was, stripped of everything, just like the others.

He walked down the center of the room. Overhead was a cracked skylight and hundreds of brownish water stains. Large flaps of ceiling hung from the supporting beams. Bits of plaster had fallen onto the cement floor, and he could hear his feet scraping dryly over them until he reached the window, leaned against the jamb and stared out toward the surrounding area. Through the misty air, he could see the flat gray expanse of the Hudson, a stretch of rotten wharf, the hazy outline of New Jersey. The rest was what he'd already seen, the tenements across the street, most of them bricked up and abandoned, and an old warehouse of rusting corrugated tin, shaped like a Quonset hut. It had probably once been used as a makeshift World War II barracks for soldiers bound for the European front.

He turned back toward the stairs and glanced at the floor. He was surprised there were no empty crack vials or hypodermic needles. Even if the woman hadn't been a junkie, other people had once used the place as a shooting gallery. If they'd left anything behind, the woman had gotten rid of it.

He took a few pictures on the fifth floor, shot the walls, the window itself, the floor, then did the same on each of the other floors, this time with a flash. When he'd finished, he returned to the window and stared down a moment, his eyes drifting toward the place on the street where her body had come to rest. For a moment, he tried to imagine what she must have felt during the few seconds she'd fallen toward the street, wondered whether she'd felt her skirt lift as the air swept under it, or the cold rain on her face and arms, whether her eyes had taken in the sprinkled light of the surrounding city, or locked themselves instead on the small blue bundle toward which she hurled at terrific speed. He even swung out over the ledge, half his body dangling in the air, as he edged his camera downward, before realizing that without falling with her, he could not capture such a radical descent.

As he drew back, his eyes caught on something, a faint, pale fleck just at the border of his own peripheral vision. He bent down quickly and saw a small white button poised at the very edge of the window, teetering there shakily, as if still trying to decide. He stepped a few feet away, lowered himself down onto his stomach, and angled the camera so that the button seemed to be already half-tipped over the ledge. In his mind, he could see Julian nodding appreciatively at the picture that would result, smiling at the way it worked to sum everything up, a single torn button, just the right touch.

Kellerman looked surprised when Corman walked into his small office just outside the freezer room. "Forget something?" he asked.

Corman shook his head. "That woman," he said, "the jumper. I want to check something else." He took a small square of tinfoil, opened it on Kellerman's desk.

"A button," Kellerman said dryly as he glanced at it. "So what?"

"I found it near the window," Corman explained, "the one she jumped out of."

Kellerman looked up at him. "What's your interest in all this?" he asked, this time more out of curiosity than cautiousness.

"To sell a book of pictures," Corman said unemphatically.

Kellerman looked surprised. "A book of pictures? About some burned-out suicide?" He shook his head. "I guess people'll buy anything, right?"

Corman wasn't interested in discussing the commercial possibilities. "I was wondering if the button came off the dress she was wearing when she took the leap," he said.

"Well, I guess I could help you with that," Kellerman said. He eased himself from his chair and motioned for Corman to follow after him. They walked to the end of the corridor, then turned left into a room filled with tightly packed cardboard boxes. Kellerman snapped a clipboard from a peg at the door, flipped a few pages and drew his finger down a line of numbers.

"There it is," he said. He looked up, scanned the wall of boxes, then headed off to the right. Once again, he motioned Corman along behind him. "It should be over here," he said.

The box had been labeled with a Police Property decal, white background, blue lettering, all of it circling the outline of a badge.

"This is all I took off her," Kellerman said, as he slipped the box from the shelf and brought it over to a long wooden table a few feet away.

Corman pulled the pasteboard flaps open. The dress was balled up in the upper right-hand corner. He drew it out slowly and spread it across the table. It was white, just as he remembered, only with red piping along the hem, the two shallow breast pockets and the deep V-collar. There was a small tear on the front, low and on the right side, near the hem. A few slender threads hung from it. Four small white buttons ran from the waist upward toward the collar. The last one, which should have rested at the point of the V, was missing.

"There's where your button came from," Kellerman said authoritatively.

Corman folded the dress neatly and returned it to the box.

"I don't think the cops are handling this as a case anymore," Kellerman said. "There's no point in them working a suicide."

Corman closed the box, then thought for a moment about what kind of shots might work for the book, a torn dress, a missing button, pictures that would do what Julian wanted, and which he now heard as a kind of frantic chant in his mind: Compel. Compel. Compel.

Chapter 12

CORMAN STILL HAD THE BUTTON IN HIS HAND WHEN HE walked out of the morgue. For a while, he stood on the steps, glancing randomly about while he rubbed it slowly between his thumb and index finger.

He was not sure what he had, if anything, as far as the woman was concerned. At any moment everything could fizzle, and he'd be back on square one, with Julian shaking his head at another idea gone sour, and Trang circling overhead, and finally, Lexie staring at him from across the table, eyes level, mouth fixed, about to speak: *Why should Lucy stay with you?*

He felt a wave of anger pass over him and fired a few questions back at her. *Why did you leave her? What about Jeffrey and his millions? What about crawling into the nearest lifeboat, money? What about the great feminist now comfortably ensconced beneath Jeffrey's rich umbrella, thinking nothing, doing nothing except maybe casting a lustful eye toward the pool man once in a while?*

He shook his head. His bitterness amazed him. And his unfairness. Rage reshaped the world according to its own wounded angles. He drew in a long, deep breath, like a diver trying for the bottom again, reaching for some impossible treasure, something he could bring up from the depths and hand to Lexie on the gleaming beach: *Look what I found for Lucy.*

He started down the steps, then stopped again, thinking of his father. Luther Corman. What a prize. He could imagine him in court, testifying for Lexie, answering her lawyer's final question: *Now, Mr. Corman, in light of your experience with your son, do you think he should retain custody of your granddaughter?* He could see that unctuous, stricken face staring directly at the judge, tragic, mournful, Old Agrippa in a Brooks Brothers suit: *Regrettably, no.* He would say it just like that. *Regrettably, no.* And the judge would feel such pity for him. How could such a dignified and accomplished man have such an immature, wastrel son? Dignified? What about all those smarmy end-runs around the IRS? Accomplished? At what, besides sobriety and, as far as Corman knew, marital fidelity? As a father, he'd hardly existed at all. Lexie had immediately recognized that. "He's like Neptune," she'd once said. "When you reach out to touch him he dissolves." But even in this, Corman thought now, Lexie had been a little off. It wasn't that his father had dissolved, but that there'd never been anything there in the first place.

Again, he shook his head silently, stunned by his own anger, and wondered if perhaps it was the only emotion he knew all the way down to its appalling core.

Corman found Milo Sax exactly where he expected to, feeding a group of bickering pigeons in Hell's Kitchen Park. Lazar had introduced them several years before, when Sax had still been working for the *News.* At that time, Pike had been anticipating an offer from the *Washington Post* and had started grooming Milo as his replacement, but Sax had blown it with a thoughtless reference to the fact that Pike's oldest son had been living with a roommate on Christopher Street for a little too long than was altogether natural. "If my son was a fag, I'd damn well know it," Pike had snapped back, cutting the line of succession in one quick slice. Sax had hung on as a steady shooter for a while after that, but the *persona non grata* status had finally worn him down, and he'd gone freelance for a time, then drifted into idleness. Now, at forty-four, he already seemed old and slightly senile, as if, when he'd hung up his camera, he'd handed over part of his mind as well. He had a small apartment on 47th Street where he continued to live off the dwindling resources the last beats of an ancient trust fund were still able to pump into his hands. It was dank and smelly, and whenever the weather wasn't too wet or cold, Sax usually headed for the park.

"Hello, Milo," Corman said as he sat down on the bench beside him.

Sax arced a fistful of seed over the heads of the pigeons and watched them scurry toward it, gurgling loudly and flapping their wings. "First time I've been able to get out here in a couple days," he said. "The rain's been locking me in."

Corman nodded.

Milo turned toward him. "I heard about Lazar. Best there ever was, Corman. You see him much?"

"I go up when I can."

"I'd go if it didn't bother me so much seeing him like that," Milo said. "You'll tell him I spoke of him."

"I'll tell him."

"He can understand that, my not coming."

"No problem, Milo."

Sax seemed relieved. "So, what are you doing around here?" he asked.

"I took some pictures of that woman who took a leap last Thursday night," Corman told him, "I was wondering if you might have heard anything about her."

"I heard about the jump," Milo said. "The neighborhood buzzed a little."

"You pick up anything?"

"A nut case, so they say," Milo told him, "but who am I to judge?"

"Anything else?"

"They have mostly illegals on that block," Milo said. "Haitians, wetbacks, what-have-you. They keep to themselves. We're all gringos to them."

"If you'd heard anything at all, it might help," Corman said.

"What's your angle?"

"A book."

"Book? On a jumper?"

"How she got to be one, something like that."

Milo shrugged. "Sounds like a real bummer. But who am I to judge?"

"I've picked up a little information on her," Corman said. "Jewish. Graduated from Columbia. Stuff like that."

"Sounds like a real oddball," Milo said. "But who am ..."

"Anyway, Milo," Corman interrupted. "You know the neighborhood, and I was thinking if you didn't know anything about the woman, you might have a few contacts." He offered a slender smile. "The fact is, I don't know how to go about this sort of thing. Investigation, I mean."

"It's not your thing," Milo said. "A shooter. I understand. We're peepshow types. We like to look."

Sax's eyes squeezed together slightly, and Corman could see the glimmer of what he had once been, clever, incisive, always right on the money when it came to how things were. "That's why I came to you, Milo," he said.

" 'Stead of Lazar. I know."

Corman nodded. "So, have you got anything for me on this?"

Milo thought a moment, dug his hands into the small paper bag in his lap and tossed another scattering of seed into the air. "There's a Haitian over there," he said. "Pay-lay-too, something like that. A frog name. Who knows how they spell it. But it sounds like Pay-lay-too. Anyway, he runs this little hole-in-the-wall deli-type place at Forty-seventh and Twelfth. If this woman needed a quick fix of soap, toilet paper, something like that, she'd probably have hit his place." He gave a third desultory toss of seed. "Maybe he can tell you something."

Corman smiled. "Corner of Forty-seventh and Twelfth, you said?"

"That's right."

Corman stood up. "Thanks, Milo," he told him. "I owe you one."

Milo shook his head. "Nah," he said, "I'm just paying one back to Lazar."

The deli was just where Milo had indicated, but before going in Corman took a few exterior shots from various positions across the street. Its cluttered window had the usual assortment of canned goods, along with a small rotisserie where a few cubes of reddish-pink meat turned slowly on a thin metal spit. It had the weary, careless look of a business that had lost faith in itself, was destined to survive only as a memory in an old woman's mind: *And when I was a little girl, I used to buy candy in this shop on our block. There was always a man behind the counter, but I can't remember what he looked like.*

He looked like a fighter, the nose flattened, the left jaw slightly askew, a face that looked as if it had been constructed by someone who hadn't done enough research. The moment Corman glimpsed him, he recognized the slow, lumbering heavyweight Victor had always bet and lost on in the preliminaries. At the bell he'd always plodded to the center of the ring, then stood there, throwing wild, haphazard punches as if he were fighting more than one man. He'd usually gone down by the fourth, his handlers carrying him from the ring like a huge black sofa.

"You're a boxer," Corman said as he stepped up to the counter. The name came to him. "Bowman, right? Archie Bowman?"

Bowman looked at him suspiciously, as if Corman were a bill collector who'd just stumbled on a mark. "Was a fighter," he said in a thin, edgy voice. "Retired in '78."

"I used to see you at this little ring they have in Bensonhurst," Corman told him. "With my brother."

One eyebrow arched upward. "Your brother a fighter?"

Corman shook his head. "No. A gambler."

Bowman's mouth opened slightly. All his teeth were gone, but from the bluish look of his gums, Corman thought neglect had done more damage than the ring. As for his body, it was marvelously preserved, and Corman realized that in a photograph the shiny ebony skin would contrast nicely with the occasional scar, capture the perfect contradiction of vulnerable invincibility. "My brother always bet on you," he said.

Bowman didn't seem to believe him. "I couldn't take the punishment," he said. "You got to be able to take the punishment. Just being in the ring, it ain't enough."

"I guess."

Bowman shrugged indifferently. "I got some posters, though," he said. "I got 'em on my wall. Guys I fought, I got posters of them, too." He shook his head disdainfully. "They never come to nothing. It's like I tell people, you fight some guys, you can say you done it. But these palookas I come up against, they was a dime a dozen." He tapped the side of his head with his index finger. "No mentality, you know. You can't just fight with your hands."

"Some of them didn't look so bad," Corman told him.

Bowman shrugged, unwilling to argue. "You a gambler, too?" he asked.

"No."

"Some people say they ruined the game," Bowman said. "Maybe they did, and maybe they didn't. 'Cause in a way, betting is doing something. It ain't just looking. Your brother fix 'em?"

"I don't know," Corman admitted. "He might have."

"But you was never in on that?"

"No."

"What do you do then?" Bowman asked quickly, firing questions now like short jabs.

"I take pictures."

"Who for?"

"Nobody in particular," Corman told him. "Newspapers sometimes."

Bowman stared at him expressionlessly. "Pictures," he repeated. "How come you doing that around here?"

"Somebody told me I should look up a guy who used to run this store," Corman said. "He's supposed to be Haitian. Got a French name."

"Well, you're looking for old Peletoux," Bowman said. "But he ain't here no more."

"He moved?"

"God took him home," Bowman answered crisply, without mourning. "Me and his wife ... we was—you know—sort of close. She asked me to fill in for him, so I been here the last few weeks. You know, till she gets things settled. Then we're leaving town."

"I see."

"How come you want pictures of old Peletoux?" Bowman asked with a short laugh. "He ain't much to look at."

"I heard he knew a lot about the neighborhood," Corman said. "The people in it."

"That's what you want to take pictures of?" Bowman asked unbelievingly. "The people 'round here?"

"One person," Corman said. "That woman who jumped out of her window last Thursday night." He opened his camera bag, pulled out one of the photographs of the woman and handed it to him. "Early in the morning. About a block from here."

Bowman's eyes lingered on the picture. "Yeah, that got things stirring."

"Did you know her?" Corman asked.

"I seen her. She come in a few times, bought some things."

"Did you talk to her?"

"She didn't do no talking," Bowman said. "She come in, pick up what she wants. She put up the money. Sometimes it come up short. I say, no. So she put something back. Sometimes, it works the other way. She come up with too much money. I always give change, but I never seen her count it."

"Did you ever see her with anyone?"

"No. She was always alone 'cept for that doll she carried around with her. She acted like it was real. Always holding it real close, like she was afraid somebody was going to snatch it from her. She even bought food for it."

"Similac?" Corman asked. "She bought that here?"

"Yeah."

Corman glanced down the center aisle. At the end of it he could see a few cans of Similac nestled among a smattering of other baby products, diapers, baby food, a small box of rubber pacifiers. For an instant he got the same feeling he'd once had in the bar near Gramercy Park where O. Henry had written "The Gift of the Magi" during one long snowy afternoon, the fibrous touch of the Great Man's presence, the soft scratch of his pencil, the sense of what he'd been though. "Would you mind if I took some pictures?" he asked.

Bowman shrugged. "Don't matter to me. I ain't here for long no way."

Corman drew out his camera and headed down the aisle, taking pictures as he walked, one picture at each step, until a single can of Similac filled the neat rectangular window of the viewfinder.

When he'd taken the last shot, he returned to the front of the store. Bowman was watching him steadily as he came up the aisle. "Was she somebody, that woman?" he asked.

"I don't know who she was," Corman said. "That's what I'm trying to find out." He took a slip of paper from his jacket pocket and wrote down his name and telephone number. "If you hear anything about her or find anybody in the neighborhood who knew anything about her, I'd appreciate it if you'd give me a call."

Bowman took the paper and dropped it into the drawer beneath the counter. "These people around here, they don't do much talking. They don't none of them have the right papers, you know? They don't want to be seen. And 'cause of that, they got to be blind, too."

"Still, if . . ."

Bowman grinned widely. "These here pictures, you going to get some money for them?"

"I hope so," Corman said, then heard Pike's voice out of the blue, tossing him another line if Julian's turned to dust, warning him to grab it before it got away, sink his fangs into Groton's death. *In the end, every shooter wants to come in from the rain.*

Chapter 13

CORMAN HAD WALKED THROUGH HALF THE BARS IN HIS neighborhood before he finally spotted Harry Groton in the Irish Eyes. For a moment he lingered just inside the door, feeling somewhat like a steely-eyed vulture as he watched Groton from behind a pane of frosted glass. Then he headed toward him, his eyes watching Groton closely as he neared the small booth where he sat.

Groton was alone, his large hands wrapped around a glass of beer. He had a round face with slightly popped eyes. A thin red netting of broken veins lay across his nose, and his lips were raw and cracked, as if he'd just swept in from the desert wastes. His eyes were blue and heavy-lidded so that he often looked drowsy. He wiped his mouth quickly as Corman slid into the seat across from him.

"How you doing?" Corman asked casually.

"Okay," Groton replied. One of his large furry eyebrows trembled slightly, then collapsed. "What's new?"

"Nothing much."

"You drinking anything?"

"Maybe a short one," Corman said. He walked back to the bar, ordered a beer of his own, then returned to the booth. "Here's to you," he said, then took a quick sip from the beer and returned the glass to the table. "You hang around this part of town a lot?"

"Enough," Groton said. "Used to shoot it some."

"You been shooting a long time," Corman said.

"Since I was eighteen," Groton said. He laughed, but edgily, as if at himself.

"Must have seen a lot," Corman added.

"You writing a book?"

Corman forced a laugh. "Me? No. I'm a shooter. I leave the words to other people."

Groton wagged his finger at him. "That's your mistake, partner."

"You think so?"

"I know so," Groton said. "You know that saying, 'a picture's worth a thousand words'?"

Corman nodded.

"It's bullshit," Groton said with a sudden vehemence. "I'll tell you what a picture's worth. It's worth thirty-five bucks a print. A few bucks more for color." He lifted his glass slightly. "That's what a picture's worth." He took a quick sip from the glass, then returned it loudly to the table. "I never had a picture up from page five. Front page? Forget it. I'm talking page five."

Corman could smell the air souring around him. Groton's self-pity was like a musty odor, and the fact that he probably had a few legitimate reasons for it didn't do a thing to relieve it.

"You shoot blood and guts, you're on the front page five, minimum four times a year," Groton went on irritably. "But you shoot some rich little twit's birthday party at the Met, you're back with the motor pool and the boiler-room jobs."

Corman cleared his throat softly. "I had a shoot a few days ago," he said. "A jumper on Forty-seventh Street."

"East or West?"

"West. Good shots, too, but Pike said no."

Groton shrugged. "When a spade jumps out a window, that's page eight, column one, no shots. That's the way it's always been. Nothing changes."

"She wasn't black."

"Well, these days, even whites end up on the back pages."

"She had a college degree," Corman said. "At least that's what I heard."

Groton leaned back slowly, rubbed his stomach gently, groaned. "Gas," he explained. "Lately, I get real bad gas." He curled one of his large red hands into a fist, pounded it softly against his stomach. "I guess I'll have to get off the sauce," he said quietly, more or less to himself.

"You never worked the news beat, did you, Groton?" Corman asked.

Groton shook his head. "Not me. I got a different gig altogether. Society." He belched quietly. "But even that beat, it has its secrets."

"Like what?"

"Well, you got to know how to shoot it."

Corman cocked his head to the left. If he took over Groton's job, he'd need to know how to play the inside track.

"You got to flatter the rich, that's the secret," Groton said. He laughed. "That's the only secret there is."

"How do you do that?"

"Well, I'll tell you this," Groton said. "You don't concentrate on their fancy clothes and shit." He shook his head dismissively. "That's what the young turks do, dumb fucks."

"You don't?"

"Just enough for atmosphere," Groton told him. "But I'll tell you something about the rich. They don't give a shit about their clothes and their big fancy dining rooms. When it comes to publicity, that's not what matters to them."

"What does?"

"They want to be flattered all right," Groton went on. "Who doesn't? But in a certain way. They want the pictures to make them look like there's something to them besides money. They want to believe that. It's important to them. They want everybody to believe that." He shrugged. "That's why they like to hang out with writers and actors and people like that, and you always need to take pictures of them with that type of people, not just sipping champagne with some leather-skinned old boozer who married a shipping tycoon when Napoleon was a corporal."

It was the sort of tip Corman thought he could use if he ever found himself standing in a fancy ballroom somewhere, staring blankly at a line of giggling debutantes, his camera bag hanging from his shoulder like a ball and chain.

"You eat good on my beat, too," Groton added after a moment. "You know, always scarfing something from the hors d'oeuvre tray."

Corman allowed himself a quick laugh.

Groton turned inward suddenly, as if his mind were taking inventory, recalling, year by year, the motion of his days. "All in all, it's not a bad life," he said finally, as if in conclusion. Then the conclusion fell apart, and a shadow passed over his face. "But it's strictly back page." He belched again, took another sip from the glass. "You live in midtown, don't you?"

"Yeah. Couple blocks away."

"High rent?"

"High enough."

"You're still lucky to have it," Groton said. "There aren't many places left in Manhattan a regular working stiff can afford."

"Yeah, well, I may not be able to afford it much longer."

Groton scratched his ear. "How long you been living in New York?"

"Long time."

"Well, I been here for almost fifty years," Groton said. "But originally, I was from the wide open spaces. Way out west. My father could remember when they still called it Indian Country."

"Is that right?"

"God's truth."

Corman said nothing.

Groton turned inward again, remained silent for a moment, then suddenly smiled, almost impishly. "Where never is heard a discouraging word," he crooned lightly. "And the skies are not cloudy all day."

Night had fallen over the city by the time Corman finally left the bar, nodding quietly to Groton, who seemed hardly to know that he was going.

Near home, the streets were filled with people who only came out after dark, their eyes still dim and puffy with the long day's idleness. A black woman in a blond wig motioned to a couple of strolling West Point cadets. They eased away from her, laughing nervously. For a time, Corman followed them, taking pictures from behind, concentrating on the proud lift of their shoulders as they made their way down the avenue, carefully glancing away from the windows of porno shops, the mocking eyes of the whores who lined their path. He could feel the tension of their besieged rectitude, but as he continued to photograph them, he felt his sympathy slip away, and with it, his interest, found himself concentrating on other faces, bodies, styles of being, the street's engulfing randomness, until he turned onto 45th Street and made his way home.

Once in his apartment, he made dinner, sat with Lucy at the small table, and chatted about her day, the usual round of fourth-grade gossip. He listened quietly but found he could hardly remember what she was saying. It was as if she were already disappearing from his life, dissolving into those tiny dots Seurat had used to portray the parks and beaches of his own dissolving age.

"Maybe we should go to a museum again sometime," he said after a moment.

"Okay," Lucy said.

"An art museum."

"I thought you liked pictures better."

"I like paintings too," Corman said.

"Okay, we could do that," Lucy said. She took a large bite from the hot dog Corman had made for her and munched it energetically. "I like paintings."

Corman wondered if perhaps Lexie would have been more inclined to leave Lucy with him had he been a painter. At least he would have had a little studio somewhere, and she could have gotten the idea that Lucy was being introduced to art, something Lexie would value in a way she could never value the part of life Lucy had come to know by being with him, the streets, the sharp edge of the city, its fierce irony and darkly battered charm.

He thought of the woman, then of the only witness to her fall, the man Lang had interviewed and the lookout had called Simpson. "I have to go out tonight," he said. "Something I'm working on."

"Okay," Lucy replied lightly. "I have lots of homework."

"I won't be gone long," he assured her.

She didn't seem to hear him. Instead she got up and headed for her room, her fingers already digging for one of the small pencils he was perpetually finding among the tangle of grotesquely knotted clothes he sorted for the wash.

"I'll try to be back before you go to bed," he called after her, but she'd already disappeared into her room.

* * *

The building had once had a buzzer system, but it had fallen into disrepair. The front door was slightly ajar, and just inside, the tenants had written their names and apartment numbers across the faded plaster walls. Simpson's name was the third one on the list. His apartment number was 1–C. Before going to it, Corman took a few shots of the names. In a book, the picture would suggest their expendability, tell the world how little they mattered. In the right position, it would add a flavorful detail to the woman's fall, leave no room for doubt as to just how far it was.

Simpson opened his door unexpectedly wide and nodded crisply. "You're the photographer?" he asked matter-of-factly.

"Yes."

"Archie said a photographer was working the neighborhood."

"I talked to him this afternoon," Corman said. He kept his eyes on the man in the doorway, noted the sharpness of his features, the predatory glint in his eyes. In a picture he would come off vaguely menacing, a man you wouldn't want to meet on any terms but your own. "I took some pictures of the store," he added.

"Yeah, he told me," Simpson said. "He said you were doing some kind of book. What about?"

"The woman who fell," Corman said.

"Jumped," Simpson said.

"Yeah, jumped."

Simpson folded his arms over his chest and rooted his feet in place. "So, tell me about this book."

"It's mostly pictures."

"You done something like it before?"

"No, this would be my first one," Corman said, "and I was hoping that ..."

Simpson pressed an open hand toward him. "Whoah, now, slow down," he said. "I got to know a few things."

"Like what?"

"Well, you saw some money, didn't you?"

"For the book? No."

"But you will see some, right?"

"I may."

Simpson smiled cleverly. "Don't start fucking with me. I'm not some goddamned streetfreak."

"I didn't say ..."

"You want a piece of me, I got a right to have a piece of you," Simpson said firmly. "The action. Know what I mean?"

"I don't think there's going to be ..."

Simpson laughed. "You're bullshitting me again."

Corman shook his head.

"Yes, you are," Simpson told him confidently. "Playing me for a fool."

"I was just interested in ..."

"Something for nothing," Simpson interrupted. "Well, you can forget it." He started to close the door. "I got to talk to the cops, but I don't have to do nothing for you without there's something in it for me."

"But I don't have anything to give you," Corman said.

Simpson smiled mockingly and closed the door. "Works the same from me to you, dickhead," he said.

Chapter 14

CORMAN DRESSED QUICKLY THE NEXT MORNING. HE could still see Simpson's door closing in his face, blocking another route to Sarah Rosen and the book Julian wanted out of her. Hastily, he considered his other options, his frantic pace sweeping out to Lucy, rushing her through her morning routine so hurriedly that by the time they reached her school she was tired and irritable.

"May I play at Maria's after school?" Lucy asked as they neared the school gate.

"I guess."

She smiled brightly. "Don't forget to pick me up there," she said, then lunged away from him, sprinting up the stairs, as if in dread of his good-bye kiss.

Corman shook his head helplessly, then walked east to the offices of the *News* on 42nd Street.

As he made his way toward the building's perpetually turning revolving doors, Corman remembered the morning Lazar had brought him over to introduce him to Pike and get him started in the business. They had paused at the doors and Lazar had nodded toward the river, showing him where Nathan Hale had declared his regret at having only one life to give for his country, a line which made him famous, Lazar had said with a slim, ironic smile, despite the fact that he'd simply lifted it from an old English play.

Corman did not pause now as he hustled into the building and went directly to the elevators. Once on the fourth floor, he glanced toward Pike's office and saw him pacing back and forth behind its Plexiglas windows. For a moment he hesitated, standing silently as the elevator doors closed behind him, almost afraid to move. It was as if each step he took now was somehow irretrievable, marked with fatal falls.

Pike was leaning over a light box, staring at several strips of negatives when Corman finally walked into his office. Rudy Fenster stood half-hidden in a rear corner, slumped against a green metal filing cabinet, his eyes darting impatiently about the office while he waited.

"Not bad, Rudy," Pike said finally as he straightened himself. "I might be able to use one of these shots."

Rudy's face brightened with mock delight. "Hear that?" he asked as he stepped away from the cabinet. "Hear that, Corman, one fucking shot."

Pike shook his head tiredly. "What do you want, a private publisher? This is a fucking newspaper. I don't use more than one picture on anything but the lead."

Fenster stepped over to the light box, began gathering up his negatives. "Not good enough, Hugo," he said. "This stuff is still warm."

Pike laughed. "In an hour it'll be cold as death, Rudy. For Christ's sake, take the money and run."

Fenster shook his head determinedly, his fingers still peeling the strips from the light box. "Can't do it."

Pike stared at him wonderingly. "You really going to start playing me against the *Times?*"

"Against whoever I can," Fenster said with a shrug.

Pike grabbed Fenster's hand. "Wait a second, Rudy, let Corman be the judge." He waved him over to the light box. "Take a look at these shots. Tell me how they add up to a lead."

Fenster pulled his hand free and peeled off the last of the strips. "You're king of the butt-fuckers, Hugo," he said disgustedly.

Pike looked at him, stunned. "What did you say?"

Fenster dropped the negatives into a plastic folder. "You heard me."

Pike's eyes turned into small, angry slits. "Get out of my fucking office, Rudy," he cried. "What are you, huh? Van Gogh, something like that? Just get the fuck out of my office."

Fenster hooked his camera bag over his shoulder and started toward the door.

Pike was right behind him, an angry bird swooping at his back. "Get out! Get out! Go slice off your fucking ear!" He slammed the door as Fenster stepped through it, then turned back to Corman, still blazing. "Prima-fucking-donna," he sputtered. "Who the fuck does he think he is?"

Corman stared at him silently, waiting for him to cool. Pike's head rotated slowly back toward the door. Fenster's tall frame could still be seen, a soft blur through the frosted glass.

Pike turned to Corman. "Did I say he was a hack? Did I insult the man? Was I going to buy a goddamn picture? What the fuck's the matter with that guy?"

Corman didn't answer. Instead, he decided to go on to another subject. "I was wondering if you'd heard anything about Groton."

"Yeah, I did," Pike answered gruffly. "He's a dead man." He stomped back to his desk and collapsed behind it. "He came in first thing, told me the whole story, just like he said he would." He glanced out the window beside his desk, stared down toward the swarming ants below, then returned his eyes to Corman. "I knew his father, you know."

"Groton's?" Corman asked, surprised to hear it.

Pike's lips jerked downward. "Rudy's," he said. "From way back, I knew his father." He shook his head. "Tommy Fenster. He was a rewrite man for forty years, as good as there ever was." He thought about it for a moment longer, then returned to Groton, his voice a bit shaky, despite the control. "Harry didn't let out a whimper," he said. "The old guy has balls, I'll say that for him."

"How long's he got?"

"Six months, on the outside."

"Six months," Corman repeated softly.

"You want his job?"

Corman thought about it, remembering the conversation of the day before. "I'm not sure," he said.

Pike leaned forward and turned off the light box. "Groton's willing to take the new guy on a few shoots," he said. "One of them's scheduled for later this afternoon."

"Where?"

"Some wingding at the Waldorf. Big wedding reception in the Grand Ballroom. Three-thirty. You interested?"

"Maybe," Corman said tentatively.

"A little enthusiasm wouldn't kill you."

"It's just that I'm working on something else right now," Corman explained.

Pike's eyes closed wearily. "What something else?"

"The woman who jumped out of the window on ..."

"That's dead meat," Pike said, his eyes still closed. He waved one hand dismissively, rubbed his eyes with the other. "Forget it."

"She had a college degree," Corman said quickly. "She had to come from somewhere or done something, you know, unusual."

Pike opened his eyes and lowered his hands to his desk. "Sounds like you're working a reporter angle more than anything else."

"I need a story to make the pictures worth something," Corman said. He saw Simpson's door closing again. "But, I'm just hitting a lot of dead ends."

Pike's eyes returned to the stacks of envelopes which covered one side of his desk. "It's burying me," he moaned, then glanced up at Corman. "So tell me, you interested in Groton's job or not?" He lifted one of the envelopes and spilled the negatives onto the top of the light box. "Lilies and lace, that's his beat."

Corman could see Groton in his mind, slumped in a velvet chair, his camera bags gathered at his feet like sleeping dogs, his head nodding forward from time to time, heavy-lidded, ponderous, waiting for the bride, the groom, the first blast from the towering pipe organ. "Society shoots," he said, almost to himself, "that's all I'd be doing, too?"

"From morning till night, my friend," Pike said. "You too good for it?"

Corman leaned against the doorjamb and said nothing.

After a moment, Pike glanced up at him. "That's the way it is, Corman," he said. "You don't get cakes and ale." His eyes narrowed. "You want it or not?"

"How long can you hold it open?"

"Like they say, five business days."

"That's all?"

"You got till Monday morning," Pike said firmly. "After that, you'll have to take a number."

Corman drew in a deep breath. "All right," he said. "I'll let you know one way or the other."

"What about this shoot with Groton? The Waldorf?"

"I'll be there," Corman told him. He stood up, started out the door.

"Oh, by the way," Pike said, stopping him. "Even if you come on staff, I don't want to be your social secretary." He picked up a small pink phone message and thrust it toward Corman. "Somebody left this for you about an hour ago."

Corman took the message and read it. "It's from my—what would you call it—the guy who married my wife."

"Before or after you did?"

"After."

Pike seemed to relax a bit. He grinned his old grin. "Just call him Sloppy Seconds," he said.

Fenster was leaning against the wall in the lobby, fumbling through his camera bag, when Corman walked out of the elevator.

Fenster glanced up quickly. "You sell anything?"

Corman shook his head.

"Bastards," Fenster hissed. He eased himself from the wall, pulled the camera bag onto his shoulder and headed for the door.

They walked out of the building together then turned west down 42nd Street. It was a sea of weaving umbrellas. Fenster added his to the jumble and drew Corman under it.

"I hate the city when it rains," he said. He slowed his pace and glanced about aimlessly. "I don't know where I'm going. That stuff about playing Hugo against the *Times,* that was bullshit."

The rain suddenly stopped west of Fifth Avenue. Fenster folded his umbrella and stuck it into his bag. "By the way," he asked, "where you headed?"

"Midtown North."

"What for?"

Corman shrugged, hating the sound of Lang's name in his mind. "Something I'm working on."

Fenster stopped, looked at Corman closely. "Anything big?"

Corman shook his head. "I don't think so."

They walked on silently until they reached Times Square. There was a long bank of public telephones just in front of the old Times Building. Corman left Fenster at the corner while he made the call.

A woman answered immediately. "Candleman and Mills."

"I'd like to speak to Mr. Mills," Corman said. "I'm returning his call."

"May I have your name, please?"

"David Corman."

"Thank you, Mr. Corman. Just a moment, please."

Something from the Brandenburg Concertos came over the phone suddenly, high, metallic, utterly unmusical. Corman drew the receiver from his ear to avoid it.

Jeffrey came on a few seconds later, cutting off the concerto in the middle of a flourish.

"Hello, David," he said in a soft but decidedly serious voice. "How are you?"

"Fine."

"I'm sorry about tracking you down this morning, but I needed to talk to you, and I didn't want Lucy to know."

"What's up, Jeffrey?" Corman asked dryly.

"Well, I was hoping that you and I could meet for dinner."

"I have to be home with Lucy."

"Would a drink be possible? Just a short one?"

"I guess."

"We really do need to have a talk, you know," Jeffrey said, adding a gentle emphasis.

Corman remained silent.

"Would seven be all right?"

"Maybe a little earlier," Corman said.

"Six?"

"Okay."

"How about the Bull and Bear, then," Jeffrey said. "It's a favorite of Lexie's and mine."

Corman's fingers tightened around the phone. It was still hard for him to imagine that Lexie was married to another man, choosing favorite bars, restaurants, songs with him. It seemed strangely doomed in its repetitiveness, as if you could only change your seat on the train, never the direction in which it was moving. "Yeah, okay, the Bull and Bear," he said, then hung up.

"Everything okay?" Fenster asked when Corman joined him again.

"Good enough," Corman said.

The two of them headed west again, down that stretch of 42nd Street the cops called "the Deuce," a wide expanse of cheap souvenir shops, porno theaters and adult bookstores where pimps, burned-out hookers and dope peddlers lounged together in bleak doorways while they watched the other, more prosperous portion of humanity stream by. Corman had spent a lot of time photographing them, trying to capture the way they seemed to envy the ordinary people who rushed past on their way to the bus terminal or the towering offices of midtown, but despised them, too, felt a vehement contempt for their wormy little lives.

"We should be like them," Fenster said as he nodded toward a small knot of grim-faced young men. "You don't butt-fuck one of those guys." He laughed mockingly. "That's what I'm going to say to my kid the next time he asks me what I do. I'm going to say, 'I grab my ankles, Conrad, I take it up the ass.'" His eyes bore in on the men again. One of them nodded toward him and grabbed his crotch.

Fenster stopped dead in his tracks and stared evenly into Corman's eyes. "Did you see that?"

Corman nodded.

Fenster smiled. "Some balls they got, huh?" he said fiercely. "They wouldn't live like us for five fucking seconds." He glanced back at the group of men in the doorway. "They see something they want, they take it. And if there's a plate glass window between them and the goods, they just smash the fucking thing." His face reddened suddenly, his eyes glistening. "You can't be a man in this fucking city unless you're willing to do that. You can't be a man unless you're willing to live like them, tell people to piss the hell off."

Corman started to move down the street again.

Fenster grabbed his jacket, stopping him. "They got the edge on life, Corman," he said. "They got the edge, not us. You know why? Because they know it's all bullshit."

Corman tugged himself free and started walking again.

Fenster followed him, pressing his shoulder against Corman's. "It's the truth," he said. He craned his neck, peering down the street. "Look at this place. You think any of our friends could survive around here?" He stopped again and glared at the long line of cheap movie houses and peep shows. "For Christ's sake, look at this place!"

For an instant, Corman actually looked straight into the eyes of the Deuce, and suddenly glimpsed something that lifted his spirits inexplicably. For years, the new city had been trying to clean it up, but nothing had changed all that much. It was as if the Deuce had the stamp of eternity on it in a way that luxury hotels and climbing real estate prices didn't. In the old city, it had been further south, a world of narrow, crooked streets and dismal courts which some called Murderer's Alley and others called Cow Bay, but whose steamy, sleepless center had been known to everyone by the name of Paradise Square. The fathers of the old city, the ones who'd swilled an imported rum called kill-devil, had done their best to eradicate it. Over the years development had moved it northward, given it a different name, but nothing else had changed because, it seemed to Corman, development was no more than the product of a system, maybe just a mood, while the Deuce sprouted in the chromosomes of everything that lived.

Fenster started walking again. "People are always talking about what they need. I'll tell you what they need. Balls." He quickened his pace, his hands pinching vehemently at the black folds of his umbrella. "A place to be a man, that's what they need."

At the corner of Eighth Avenue, a prophet was shouting loudly into a portable microphone. He had a tangled, black beard and his large body was draped in a long, white robe.

Fenster's face softened as he paused to watch him. "Crazy bastard," he whispered affectionately.

The prophet shouted something else into the microphone, but Corman could not make out what it was. Then the man stepped forward a few paces and looked directly at Fenster.

"No one knows who I am," he whispered ardently.

Fenster laughed under his breath. "Me, neither," he said.

The prophet went back to the microphone, his voice thundering even more loudly.

Corman drew his camera from his bag and began taking pictures while Fenster stood by silently. He was on his second roll a few minutes later when two uniformed policemen suddenly brushed by him and stepped directly in front of the prophet.

"Remember me?" the taller one asked, his face only a few inches from the straggling hairs of the prophet's beard.

The prophet did not answer. He continued to shout into the microphone.

"You got a permit for sound equipment?" the other policeman asked.

Again, the prophet did not answer.

The taller policeman glanced at his partner, then grabbed the microphone from the prophet's hand. "We told you before," he said. "If you don't have a permit for this, we can seize it."

The prophet stepped away, pressed his back against the wall of the building and lowered his hands to his sides. His whole body appeared to grow hard, stony, but as Corman's eyes swept up and down the long, white robe, he could see that beneath it, just at the level of the knee, his legs had begun to tremble fearfully.

Fenster eased himself over to Corman. "Let's get out of here," he whispered nervously. "Situation like this, anything can happen."

Corman knelt down quickly, focused, snapped another picture, moved to the left, shot a second photograph, then a third, a fourth and a fifth. The trembling had become more violent, shaking the lower quarters of the robe like a small wind. Corman leaned forward, focusing closely, reaching for the minutest detail.

One of the policemen began spooling up the long electrical cable that ran from the microphone to the amplifier, while his partner boxed the speakers then swept stacks of pamphlets into a plastic bag.

Corman kept shooting. From the corner of his eye, he could see Fenster shrinking back into the crowd. He made no effort to stop him, but instead concentrated once again on the prophet, his lens sweeping up and down the long, white robe while the prophet continued to stand rigidly at the wall, his eyes straight ahead, his face impassive, his body entirely rigid, except for the trembling in his knees.

Chapter 15

THE HOMICIDE DIVISION OF MIDTOWN NORTH WAS ON the second floor. It was an unsightly bull pen. Each time Corman found himself there, he took a few minutes to concentrate on its disarray, the scattered desks and bulging files, the way everything spilled across the floor so that the room itself looked as if it existed in the aftermath of something violent, the leavings of a storm. As always, it was the people who drew his attention, especially the civilians. They usually looked either miserable or inexpressibly happy, and as he'd watched them over the years, Corman had at last realized that this was because most of them had just received either the best or worst news of their lives, that they'd once again escaped or finally fallen victim to their folly.

Lang's desk was toward the back of the room. He was sitting in a swivel chair. A dirty yellow foam oozed from the cracked arms, and tiny flecks of cigar ash clung to the foam.

"What's up?" he asked as Corman stepped up to his desk.

"It's about that woman," Corman told him, "the jumper. I was wondering if you'd found out anything?"

"Found out? Found what?"

"About her life," Corman said.

Lang looked at him suspiciously. "What's in it for you, Corman?"

"I'm just curious."

"Bullshit," Lang snapped. "What you got, a story idea, something like that?"

"I don't write."

"Costa sold film rights, did you know that?"

"For what?"

"That killing at the Met a few years ago," Lang said. "That opera singer. Shit, man, he got a job consulting for the movie." He laughed. "Fucking Costa, can you believe that? Consulting on a movie?" He shook his head at the absurdity of it. "He couldn't consult on his own eating habits." He laughed again, then stopped, his eyes staring evenly at Corman. "Pictures, then. You trying to sell some pictures?"

"I was wondering about her personal effects," Corman replied crisply.

"You mean what was on her?" Lang asked. "Nothing. Just that old dress and her panties. No rings on her fingers, or in her ears. Nothing. She didn't have anything in her pockets."

"What about in her place?"

"Jesus, Corman, you saw what that was like."

"I heard there was a diploma from Columbia."

Lang nodded. "That's right. A couple Jakes found it the next morning. Framed and everything."

"Do you have it?"

"We gathered it up, yeah."

"Anything else?"

"A few odds and ends," Lang said. He continued to stare at Corman curiously. "Suppose you tell me what this is all about."

"I can't," Corman said truthfully.

"Because it's top secret, that it?" Lang asked mockingly.

"Because I'm not sure myself."

"You expect me to believe that?" Lang hooted. "Let me tell you something, Corman. I've dealt with you freelance shooters for thirty years, and I never met one that wasn't a petty fucking grifter from top to bottom. You telling me you're different?"

Corman said nothing.

Lang sat back in his seat, placed his large beefy hands behind his head and leaned back into them. "Let me tell you a little story. A few years back, a rookie got a call in the Village. Dog loose, you know?"

Corman nodded.

"The guy goes down, sees the fucking dog running along West Fourth Street. It's barking and snarling a little, and a few people are scooting into the shops to get away from it. To the rookie, it sounds bad, so he draws his service revolver, calls the goddamn dog, says, 'Here, boy, here, boy,' and pats his fucking leg." He took a puff on the cigar. "The dog turns, starts coming toward the Jake, still barking and snarling and shit. My guy's beginning to get a little ill at ease, but he knows he can't run from the son-of-a-bitch, not a cop, not a cop in uniform, not from a goddamn dog. So, well, worse comes to worst, and he plugs it. Puts a bullet right in its face. A patrol car shows up right away, and they hustle the rookie into the back seat. Puff, up comes a shooter. Like a genie out of a fucking bottle. He says he wants to take a picture. He says it's for his own private collection. He takes a shot of the rookie and the next day it's on the front page of the *News*. The rookie has his hands in his face. He looks fucking pitiful. The caption says, DOG TIRED." Lang laughed edgily and leaned forward. "So what I want to know is, how are you going to screw me with this angle you're working on?"

"I'm interested in the woman," Corman said. "That's all."

"You got a problem with anything else?"

"No."

"You think I fucked up anything?"

"Not that I saw."

Lang watched him a moment longer, then relaxed slightly. "Okay," he said finally. "Who knows, maybe you can do me a favor sometime. What do you want to see?"

"Whatever you picked up in the building."

Lang shrugged. "Well, we bagged a few items that night," he said, "but everything else got tossed by the landlord. He had some guys come in and sweep everything out. I guess he wanted to seal it up before some other squatter set up housekeeping."

"There was still stuff there," Corman told him.

"Yeah?" Lang said. "How do you know?"

"I went over there."

"You went inside?"

Corman nodded.

"Find anything?"

Corman thought a moment then decided to tell the truth. "A button."

Lang laughed. "A button?"

"Yeah."

"Well, we did better than that," Lang said. He stood up and waved Corman alongside him. "Come on, I'll show you."

Corman followed him downstairs, then into the basement, and finally, through a long, dusty corridor, to a small room in the north corner of the building. The walls were unpainted gray cinder blocks, and overhead, Corman could see the exposed underbelly of the building itself, pipes, electrical cables, the large wooden crossbeams which supported everything.

"If it's not a mystery," Lang said, "we keep everything down here, unless somebody claims it."

"And no one has?"

Lang smiled. "Well, we're not exactly talking about the Queen's jewels." He walked to a large metal filing cabinet, pulled out the drawer, and from it, a single manila envelope. "There you have it," he said as he handed it to Corman. "Her net worth."

Corman took the envelope over to a small wooden desk, sat down and stared at the name: SARAH JUDITH ROSEN. "Where's the diploma?" he asked.

"In the envelope," Lang said. He stepped to the door. "Just be sure to turn out the lights when you're through in here," he added as he left the room.

Corman opened the envelope and scattered its contents across the desk. There were only a few items: a rusty nail file, a compact with a cracked mirror, a pack of matches with two left in place, a small pacifier and a baby rattle shaped like a fat clown. There was an oval rubber change purse, the sort that opened up like a small toothless mouth when the ends are pressed together. Crumpled inside, Corman found a receipt from a blood bank operation on the Bowery.

The diploma was in a teakwood frame. The glass was cracked, and one corner of the frame was splintered. It had awarded Sarah Rosen a bachelor of arts degree in 1988.

Everything else had been inventoried on a police property form, then discarded. The form itself had been folded three times and inserted into the manila envelope. Item by item, it listed the rest of Rosen's worldly goods: a set of toy blocks, along with a plastic pail and shovel, a few infant sleeping suits, one dress, two pairs of jeans, one belt, three pairs of panties, a washcloth and two towels, a pair of sandals, a terry cloth robe, and three dollars and seventy-three cents in cash. There was a notation at the bottom of the list. It said officially what Lang had already told him, that sometime on Saturday the landlord had had the building swept clean of everything else.

Corman let the paper slip from his hand. It fell onto the table, one of its sharp corners piercing the center of the articles spread out around it. It had fallen into an unexpectedly dramatic position, each article at precisely the right angle to another. Corman quickly took out his camera and photographed it. With the right exposure, it would have a sad, haunting quality, perhaps end up as the final picture in Julian's book, stark, graphic, lonely, a life reduced to what it had left behind ... and he hadn't had to move a single thing.

Chapter 16

CORMAN ARRIVED AT BELLEVUE A FEW MINUTES BEFORE Sarah Rosen's body was due to be picked up. It was a massive building, bulky, the sort that always looked overfed. The old city had built it while still reeling in the aftershock of yellow fever, and as he stood at the top of its long line of stairs, it was easy for Corman to imagine the final days of the Yellow Jack Plague, the street cries of "Bring out your dead," the way the people had wrapped the bodies symbolically in yellow sheets before tossing them onto the open lorries that took them to the common burial pit that had been dug at Washington Square. The plague had lasted for many months, and Lazar had often spoken of it, the empty streets and deserted houses, the stricken, feverish looters who'd staggered through the countless abandoned shops, sometimes dying in them, faceup on the floor, their arms still filled with plunder. Only the illustrators of the period had truly flourished, sketching the disaster one line at a time.

Kellerman glanced up as Corman came into his office. "I wasn't sure you'd make it," he said.

"I'm here," Corman answered.

"As far as I know, everything's set," Kellerman told him. "You ready?"

Corman nodded, his mind considering Julian's idea once again: slow decline, incremental fall. "Has anyone else come around to see her?" he asked. "Called to ask about her, anything?"

Kellerman shook his head. "No."

"Father, mother, anyone from her family?"

"Nope," Kellerman repeated, then led Corman into the building, briskly escorting him down the corridor to his office.

Once behind his desk, Kellerman started in on the morning mail. "By the way," he said, slicing open one envelope after another. "How do you want to do this? I mean, if any relatives show up, I don't want them to be disturbed."

"I can shoot from pretty far away," Corman told him.

"Far enough so they wouldn't even see you?"

"Maybe," Corman said. "Where does the hearse pick them up?"

"Back driveway."

"I could set up from across the lot," Corman said. "I don't think anybody would even know I was there."

Kellerman looked relieved. "That sounds good. Why don't you go ahead and get into position? If anything changes, I'll let you know."

Corman walked down the corridor and out into the back lot of the building. An ambulance, orange-striped, with Hebrew lettering across the side, was parked not far away. He stationed himself just behind its rear doors, pulled out his camera, changed the lenses for the shoot, then panned to the right. At the far end of the building, he could see the doors of the Emergency Ward. In the old city, horse-drawn ambulances had raced up to them from Chinatown, bearing the dead from the Tong Wars, or later, piles of bodies, frozen together like stacks of ice cubes during the Blizzard of '88. And later still, Lazar himself had come—stricken, his right arm clinging to Corman's shoulder as the two of them slammed through the red double doors.

It began to rain lightly again. Corman tucked the camera beneath his coat and peeped around the edge of the ambulance.

A couple of female orderlies came out of the building. One of them was crying, and the other one was comforting her as best she could, touching her arm once in a while as she spoke. Corman drew his camera out again. Through the lens he could see their faces clearly. They both looked Filipino, something like that, and the older woman could easily have been the mother of the younger one. They had the same, slightly flattened noses and large, almond-shaped eyes. The young one kept shaking her head frantically, until the older one stopped it by drawing her face up tight against her chest. For a time, they remained locked in that position. Then a man stuck his head out the door and waved them back into the building. They followed his orders immediately, the young one dabbing her eyes as she walked back inside.

Kellerman strode out onto the loading ramp a few minutes later. He was dressed in a long white lab coat, and he was pulling a pair of rubber gloves off his hands. His head made a slow turn until he caught sight of Corman. Then he tapped the face of his wristwatch and nodded crisply.

Within seconds the hearse from the funeral chapel arrived. It was dark gray instead of black, with sleek chrome lines running front to back. It made a wide turn in the lot, moving slowly, its long black windshield wipers sliding rhythmically across the glass, stopped for a moment, then headed backwards until its rear door reached the loading ramp.

Corman lifted the camera and began shooting.

Two men got out of the hearse. They were dressed in black suits. One was tall, black, very broad-shouldered. The other one looked Hispanic. He was short and stocky, with thick legs and small feet. They walked up the short ramp to the rear doors and disappeared behind them.

Corman replaced the lens cap, drew the camera back under his coat and waited.

The doors at the back of the morgue opened suddenly a few seconds later, and Corman jerked himself back to attention and began shooting as a long stainless steel stretcher came out, pushed from behind by the black attendant. The Hispanic walked behind him until they neared the end of the ramp. Then he bolted forward quickly and opened the back of the hearse. The other man maneuvered the stretcher into place, then the two of them loaded the body and returned to their seats in the hearse.

Corman continued shooting, concentrating on the hearse, the two men whose dark outlines could be seen hazily behind the rain-swept windshield. For a time they sat solemnly, then the Hispanic turned toward the other man, said something, and they both laughed.

Corman had taken ten more pictures before Kellerman finally walked through the doors, then slowly down the loading ramp. For a time, they talked through the open window of the hearse, then they shook hands and the car pulled away.

"Well, did you get what you needed?" Kellerman asked as he walked across the cement lot toward Corman.

Corman recapped the lens and tucked the camera beneath his coat. In the distance, he could see the taillights of the hearse as it disappeared around the corner of the building.

"Not much, was it?" Kellerman said. "No relatives. Nothing."

Corman stepped out from behind the ambulance, his eyes still watching the driveway, the traffic on Second Avenue. "You know the address of the chapel they're taking her to?"

"Sure," Kellerman said. "We do some business. They always leave a card." He drew the card from his pocket and read off the address: "247 East 68th Street."

Corman wrote it down in his notebook and glanced back toward the avenue. He could see the little Italian restaurant where it had happened, hear Lazar's voice rumbling through the subdued light, then the sudden halt, the look in his face, the single word he'd managed to say before the left side of his mouth had twisted downward: "Corman."

"So, you like being a shooter?" Kellerman asked.

Corman looked at him. "What?"

"I mean, it must be a killing grind, right?" Kellerman said.

Corman started to answer, but the crackle of his police radio interrupted him. He dialed up the volume and listened. There was some sort of disturbance on Broadway at University Place. A patrol car was requested.

"I think I'll check this out," Corman said quickly.

"Yeah, sure," Kellerman said. He looked faintly envious. "It must be nice once in a while," he said. "Dealing with the live ones."

A small crowd had already gathered at the corner of Broadway and University Place when Corman got there. It formed a kind of jagged semicircle around a taxi and a police patrol car. Two patrolmen stood next to the cab, listening silently as a well-dressed elderly man addressed them.

"I'm not interested in being treated special," the old man declared loudly. "I have never asked for that. But by the same token, I refuse to be abused."

A slightly overweight man leaned idly against the cab. He wore a fishnet T-shirt despite the chilly fall air, and his eyes looked slightly puffed, as if from lack of sleep. "I didn't abuse you, pal," he said to the old man.

The old man's body jerked upward. "I am not addressing you, sir," he cried. "I am not addressing you."

"Okay, okay," one of the patrolmen said to him. "Just tell me what happened."

Corman readied his camera and subtly elbowed himself more deeply into the crowd, searching for a position from which he could get the whole small drama into his lens. By the time he found it, the old man was talking again, while the man in the T-shirt remained silent, his arm draped protectively over the roof of his cab.

"I know the ordinances of this city," the old man said. "I make it my business to know them. And when this ... this ... I don't know what I should call such a person."

"Call me Dominic, pop," the driver said with a laugh.

One of the patrolmen glanced at him irritably. "Don't make it worse, buddy," he said.

The taxi driver shrugged, turned away and idly picked his teeth with a matchstick while the old man continued.

"As I was saying, I know the ordinances," the old man began again, "but that doesn't mean that I want to be treated special. But when it rains, I'm like a great many people. I want a cab." He brushed his nose quickly with his hand, and Corman noticed that he held a leather strap. He followed it downward to where a large seeing-eye dog sat calmly on the sidewalk, its large pink tongue hanging limply from its mouth.

"This man refused to take me," the old man cried with a sudden, wrenching vehemence. "Refused to accept me as a passenger."

The driver's eyes shot over to him. "Not you, pal," he said. "The dog. I don't take no animals in my cab."

"This is a trained dog," the old man shouted. His finger wagged in the air. Corman focused on it and shot.

The driver waved at the finger dismissively. "Yeah, well a trained dog gets fleas and shit just like any other dog."

The old man's face lifted in offense. "This dog does not have fleas, sir," he declared.

The driver's face tightened. "How the fuck do you know? You couldn't fucking see them if it did!"

The old man's body stiffened. He seemed on the verge of lunging toward the driver. "I was blinded by the Japanese, sir," he screamed. "On an island called Iwo Jima. I don't suppose you've ever heard of it."

The driver laughed. "I seen the movie with John Wayne," he said. Then he winked good-humoredly at the crowd, which only stared back at him resentfully.

"Yes, well I was not with John Wayne, sir," the old man fired back. "I wasn't making movies. I was protecting this country!"

"All right, all right," one of the patrolmen said. "Let's everybody calm down here, okay? Let's just everybody cool it."

The second patrolman moved closer to the driver, motioned him forward, then whispered something into his ear.

The old man drew in a deep breath. "Anyway," he said, "I asked this gentleman ..." His hand swept out, reaching for something. "This gentleman ..."

A man in jogging clothes leaned his shoulder into the searching hand. "When the cabbie refused to take him, he asked me to get the cabbie's license number," he said to the patrolmen. "And when the cabbie saw me doing that, he started cursing me."

The driver turned away again, his eyes moving along a line of small square windows across the street. "I used to take them in, the blind people," he told the second patrolman, "but I always ended up with fleas all over the car. It's like every time I picked one of these people up, it cost me twenty bucks to fumigate the fucking cab."

His eyes turned from the patrolmen and began to search the crowd imploringly. "Can you blame me? Huh?" he asked. "What would you do in my place?" He looked directly into Corman's camera, his eyes narrowing intently. "What would you do in my place?" he demanded. For a moment he stared fiercely at the camera. Then, suddenly, his whole body slumped back against the cab, as if defeated, and as he did so, Corman felt his sympathies shift miraculously toward him and away from the old man. It had happened in an instant, so that Corman recognized the shift must have come from some separate quarter of existence that lay beyond the teachable forms of right and wrong, a world of ancient traces, basic as the primordial ooze.

It made him think of Sarah Rosen, the way her body had been starved down to its glistening fundamentals, perhaps even in the way her mind had finally come to concentrate with a single, sacrificial intensity on the ancient devotion of her motherhood. For an instant, he could see her standing at the tenement window, her white arms wrapped around the blue-eyed doll, her eyes fixed on the unrelenting rain, her body trembling like the prophet's robe. The air seemed to chill around him, as if a wintry blast had unexpectedly swept through the city, and he felt himself ease back into the crowd, away from Sarah and her ledge, toward a safer place, where the purest urges were seeded with protective dross, the stars were fixed, lakes had bottoms, and things fell back to earth because they had to.

Chapter 17

"DO YOU THINK SHE HAD TO?" CORMAN ASKED. HE STILL felt oddly shaky, as if the sudden shift in his sympathies had rocked his own foundations.

Grossbart looked at him questioningly. "What are you asking?"

"About the woman, the one who went out the window."

"Is that why you wanted to meet me?" Grossbart asked. "The woman?"

"Just to talk about her," Corman said. Only a few weeks before, it would have been Lazar across from him now, the calm face watching him in the shadowy light of some bar in the Village.

Grossbart glanced out the window of the pizzeria. The heat from the ovens had misted the glass, but people could still be seen hurrying across Sixth Avenue, most of them headed for a place that sold safari clothes and had a stuffed rhinoceros in the window. "What have you found out about her?" he asked when he looked back at Corman.

"Nothing much," Corman said. "They picked up her body today. I took some pictures."

"Pictures? Why?"

"Something I'm working on."

Grossbart looked at him pointedly. "Have you come up with anything?"

Corman shook his head. "Not much."

Grossbart looked at the wedge of pizza which was turning cold on Corman's plate. "You going to eat that?" he asked.

"No."

"Mind if I do?"

Corman slid the paper plate across the table toward him.

Grossbart took a small bite of the pizza, grimaced. "Jesus."

"It's never good here," Corman said.

Grossbart let the piece slide lifelessly back onto the plate and wiped his fingers with a napkin. "I heard about the button," he said. He shook his head. "But you got to understand something, Corman. Something like that, all it does is make you look like some kind of hotshot amateur detective. And, between me and you, that's not the way to impress the people downtown, or the guys on the beat. They work with pros." The napkin shot up to his mouth and wiped the grease from the lips. "Besides, that button stuff, that's bullshit. She could have pulled it off. It could have fallen off. Christ, anything."

"It seemed strange," Corman said.

"I know the feeling," Grossbart said. "But in this case, my guess is a lot of things went haywire for this girl. Simple as that." He turned to the window, wiped a path through the mist with the sleeve of his jacket and pointed eastward. "When I was a rookie, a woman over there in Brooklyn killed her two sons." His eyes flashed back to Corman. "Seven and four, that's how old they were. This woman, she found the tallest building in Brooklyn. Now at that time, there weren't that many tall buildings in Brooklyn, but she found the tallest one, and don't ask me how, but she got to the top of it, and one by one she dropped the two boys off, then went off herself." He leaned back in his seat, nodded toward the pizza. "At the bottom of the building, they looked like that, all three of them." He glanced back up at Corman and stared at him intently. "She was a middle-class woman, a good Catholic, happily married as far as we could find out, the whole *schmeer*. So I asked myself, 'Christ, what happened?' On my own time, I started checking around. Nothing. Then the ME's report came in. Turns out the woman had a brain tumor the size of a golf ball. The guy at the morgue, he even showed it to me. A little black ball, nothing. I looked at that thing, and I said to myself, 'There's the murderer.'" He lifted his hands, palms up, fingers spread. "Simple."

Corman shook his head doubtfully. "Sarah Rosen didn't have a brain tumor."

"Well, there's all kinds of people, Corman," Grossbart said. "Some are lucky. That's just the way it is. Others, it's like they're made up of some different kind of substance. Velcro, something like that. Trouble sticks to them." He smiled. "Just petty stuff sometimes. When they're on the ramp, the fucking train takes forever."

"It would take a lot of trouble for someone to end up like she did," Corman said.

"Some people are born drowning," Grossbart said. "They bob around a little, gasp for air, but basically, they're drowning."

Corman leaned forward. "If I were trying to run down the story of this woman, where would I begin, Harvey?" he asked. "Like I told you back at Number One, I'm new at this. I could use a few tips."

Grossbart shrugged. "Well, you could start with the neighborhood."

"I did that. They're all illegals. They won't talk about anything."

"Didn't Lang have a guy?"

Corman shook his head. "He thinks I'm a millionaire, hit me up for money."

"Which you don't have much of, I take it," Grossbart said.

Corman wondered what it was that made him look so strapped, and realized that if Grossbart had noticed it at all, then Lexie would see it written across his face in bright, pulsing neon.

Grossbart pulled himself to his feet. "Well, I don't know what else to tell you. You're working a case now, so you learn how it is. Either you get something direct, or you stumble on to a new lead, or . . . you just come up a crapper."

"I can't do that," Corman said, surprised by the edge of desperation he heard in his own voice.

Grossbart looked at him a moment, then took the napkin from the table and unnecessarily wiped his fingers again. "You know what I say, Corman, not just to you, to everybody. I say, 'Hey, you looking for a mystery, some big tragedy? Look in the fucking mirror.'" He smiled thinly and let the napkin float back to the table. "Nobody has to go any further than that."

Corman smiled tentatively and thought of Lucy. "I do," he said.

Chapter 18

A SHORT FLIGHT OF STAIRS LED UP TO THE SECOND-floor landing of the Inside Track. Corman paused at the bottom of them, slapped some of the rain from his hat, then headed up.

There was a small counter just inside the door. The man behind it nodded politely as Corman walked in. Corman nodded back and began to make his way to the right toward a room filled with small tables and chairs.

"That'll be five dollars," the man behind the counter said.

Corman turned to him. "Five dollars?"

"Entrance charge," the man explained.

Corman hesitated for an instant, then reluctantly reached for his wallet and counted out the money.

The man took the money and handed Corman a small booklet.

"What's this?" Corman asked.

"The racing program," the man told him matter-of-factly. "Good luck, sir."

Corman walked toward the room to the right, searching through the crowd for Willie Scarelli. He found him near the front windows, sitting with another man, both of them going over the same racing program Corman had been handed at the door.

"Who do you like in the first?" Scarelli asked. He was dressed in dark navy-blue pants and a red blazer. A cigarello hung from the corner of his mouth, and while he went over the program, he chewed its white plastic tip determinedly.

The other man frowned. "Where'd they get these wheezers?" he said. "Off a truck to the glue factory?" He shook his head despairingly. "Every year, more of these cheap claimers in New York."

"Yeah," Scarelli moaned. "Shit." He circled something in the program, then thought better of it, crossed it out, put another one around something else.

Corman touched his shoulder. "How you doing, Willie?"

Scarelli looked up. "Corman?" he said, obviously surprised to see him. "I didn't know you followed the ponies."

"I don't," Corman told him. "I was looking for you."

"Well, pull up a chair," Scarelli said. He nodded toward the other man. "This old fart is Darby McMillan. He pretends inside knowledge."

Darby continued to stare at the racing program. "Glad to meet you," he muttered. He puffed irritably at a white meershaum pipe, grunting under his breath from time to time, as his eyes went down the program.

Corman took a seat.

"Be right with you," Scarelli said. "Soon as I decide what to play." He glanced toward Darby. "What about Forest Drive," he said. "What do you think?"

Darby's eyes swept the form. "I think he's being ridden by a douchebag," he said.

Scarelli's face tightened as his eyes returned to the program. "Eddie Sheen. Yeah, not the go-jockey for that fucking stable."

"Look at the guy on Ginger Snap," Darby said. "Another douchebag apprentice." He shook his head. "With these old nags, you got to have a rider with some balls."

Scarelli considered it for a moment. "Yeah, you're right."

"Fuck the first," Darby said. "I'll just place some recreational doubles. We can still play Ginger Snap in the fourth."

"You gonna play any exactas in the first?" Scarelli asked.

Darby laughed. "Exactas?" he said. "Fuck. I'd be more willing to bet that two of these old whores won't make it to the eighth pole."

The two men laughed together, then went on to the fifth race, comparing jockeys, horses, trainers, stables.

They were still doing it when a voice suddenly sounded across the room: "Ladies and gentlemen, please rise for our National Anthem."

Chairs scraped loudly across the floor as the people in the room got to their feet, then stood silently as the anthem swept over them. Darby placed his hand over his heart, while his eyes roamed about the room, catching for a moment on a tall young woman who chewed the end of a swizzle stick while she stood in place. "Oh, Sweet Jesus," he moaned under his breath.

"Well, let's do it," Scarelli said when it was over. He sat down quickly, glanced at one of the television sets that hung from the paneled walls, then handed a roll of bills to Darby. "Just spread it around on some doubles," he said. "And include that fucking apprentice in some of them. Who's to say, lightning might strike."

"Okay," Darby said. He reached for his wallet with one hand and thrust his other one palm up toward Scarelli. "I'll always put myself out for a two-dollar bettor."

Scarelli nodded. "Don't forget my change," he said with a wink.

Darby turned and walked toward the betting booths at the back of the room.

Scarelli took a sip of ale then wiped his mouth with a napkin.

"So, what'd you want to see me about?" he asked, as he glanced toward Corman.

"A story," Corman said. "At least, a possible story. A guy I know—in publishing—he thought you might be interested."

Scarelli leaned back in his seat. "Well, absolutely," he said. "You know me, I'm always looking for a story. What's yours?"

Corman dug into his camera bag and came out with the picture. "Take a look at this," he said as he handed it to Scarelli.

Scarelli eyed the photograph casually. "Looks like somebody gave her a good beating," he said.

"She jumped out of a window." Corman pointed to the small mound of cloth that could be seen near her outstretched hand. "Threw a doll out with her."

Scarelli continued to stare at the picture. "Is this that jumper from Hell's Kitchen?"

Corman nodded.

"I heard a little something about that," Scarelli said. His eyes drifted over to Corman. "Saw some video on it, too."

"They were there."

"Network?"

"Local."

Scarelli's eyes settled on the picture again. "What do you know about her?" he asked.

"I've found out a few things."

"Like what?"

Corman labored to put everything in order, arrange the facts so Scarelli would be drawn in by them. He decided to start small, build toward a big conclusion.

"Well, first of all, she's white," he said.

Scarelli laughed. "Like everybody else who has a say in anything."

"It turns out she graduated from Columbia," Corman added.

"When was this?"

"Eighty-eight."

"So she was young when she took the leap."

"Yeah."

"Twenty-three, four, something like that," Scarelli said. "Can't tell much from the picture." He grimaced as he looked at it again. "Jesus, it did a job on her nose." He looked back up, as Corman fingered the edge of the photograph. "Is this a drug thing?"

"What do you mean?"

"Bright, promising youth tragically destroyed by drugs, that sort of thing?"

"I don't think so."

"I got to know so," Scarelli said. "Because if it is, it's dead in the water. Shit, man, you got Broadway heavies iced by that stuff, big-time basketball players. Ivy League's small potatoes compared to that."

"She wasn't a junkie," Corman assured him.

"Okay," Scarelli said. "Shoot. What else you got?"

Corman could feel the room closing in around him. In his mind he saw Trang grinning happily as he and Lexie toasted each other behind the beaded curtain of a dark, Oriental den. Quickly, he riffled through his other pictures, found the one he wanted and pressed it toward Scarelli.

"What's this now?" Scarelli asked, without reaching for it.

"Take a look," Corman said.

Scarelli reluctantly took the picture and stared at it without enthusiasm. "What the fuck is this?"

"A button."

"She throw that out, too?" Scarelli asked in mock horror. "Ain't life a fucking tragedy?"

"Look where it is."

"By a window," Scarelli said. "So what?"

"It was on the ledge of the window she jumped out of," Corman told him.

Scarelli glanced toward him. "I repeat, Corman, so what?"

"That button came off her dress," Corman said.

"Yeah?" Scarelli asked teasingly. "What about it? You're thinking murder, right? Some bastard heaved her out, and in the process, ended up with a button in his hand."

"It's possible."

"Yeah, great, but who did it?"

"I don't know."

"Was she a hooker?"

"No."

"So we're not talking some Shriner with a mean streak?"

"No, nothing like that."

Scarelli thought about it for a moment. "What was her name?"

"Sarah Rosen."

"Jewish girl," Scarelli mused. "Could have been a twisty little thing." He smiled. "That's something, at least."

"She was starving," Corman said. "She'd been selling blood to feed the doll. There were empty cans of Similac all over the place. She was living in a burn-out."

Scarelli handed Corman the picture, leaned forward and dropped the side of his face into his open hand. "Could it be that this kid just got a screw loose somewhere along the way?"

Corman glanced at the picture hopelessly. "Maybe."

Scarelli grinned impishly. "Well, that's the way it is with a lot of things, right?"

"So, you're not interested at all?" Corman asked.

Scarelli hedged a moment. "Well, that's not exactly what I'm saying."

"What is?"

"What you need is a suspect, Corman," Scarelli told him. "It doesn't have to be that solid. You can finesse that sort of thing."

"Finesse?" Corman asked. "Finesse what?"

"The mystery element," Scarelli said. He took a swig from the glass. "A mystery element's what I need. If I had that, I could invest some time." He shrugged. "The rest is nothing to cheer about."

"Okay," Corman said.

Scarelli leaned back and looked at him carefully. "Now as far as this mystery thing is concerned. Come clean, okay? You got anything or not?"

"Just the button."

"That's it?"

"Yeah."

"Well, it's early," Scarelli said almost to himself. "These things take time."

"I don't have any time," Corman told him.

"You don't?" Scarelli asked. "How come?"

Corman didn't feel like going into his own troubles. "Nothing," he said. "It doesn't matter."

"Well, I'll tell you this," Scarelli said. "If you get something good, I could run with it mucho pronto." He laughed. "You know what they call me in the trade? Deadline Scarelli. You know why?"

Corman shook his head.

"Because I'm a professional," Scarelli said. "I get my stories in when I say I'll get them in. Nothing stops me. Booze, women, forget it. Some movie star butt-naked wouldn't matter to me if I was working a deadline." He glanced toward the television monitor that faced him from across the room. "Not even the ponies."

Corman leaned toward him. "If I came up with a suspect, something interesting, how long would it take for you to get a deal?"

Scarelli kept his eyes on the monitor. The horses were at the starting gate. "The track's pretty wet," he said to himself. "Have to watch a couple races to figure out the bias."

"A day?" Corman asked insistently. "A week?"

Scarelli looked at him. "With Deadline Scarelli?" he said with a wink. "The fall of a sparrow, my man, the blink of an eye."

The bell rang at Belmont, sending the horses slogging across the wet track. Scarelli's eyes immediately swept over to the television monitor. "The blink of an eye," he repeated absently, his own eyes locked on the horses' flight.

Chapter 19

GROTON WAS SITTING IN ONE OF THE ENORMOUS HIGH-backed chairs which dotted the lobby of the Waldorf. Plush carpet spread out in all directions. Two huge porcelain vases rested on either side of the lobby, both of them overflowing with sprays of silk flowers. As Corman strolled across the lobby, it was hard for him to imagine that the place itself had once been a potter's field, and after that, the site of a women's hospital. Much was buried under the marble floor, deeply buried. Except for still surviving photographs, it was all beyond recall.

Groton had taken a chair near one of the vases. He looked as if he'd been sent down to make sure no one used it for an ashtray.

"You the guy they sent?" he asked as Corman came up to him.

Corman nodded and sat down.

"So you talked to Pike?"

"Yeah."

Groton took a long drag on his cigarette. "He tell you the problem?"

"Yeah, he did."

"I told him he could do that," Groton said. "It's nothing to be ashamed of."

"No."

Groton shrugged. "Even before I knew, you know, for sure, I said to myself that I was going to take it like a man. What else can you do?"

Corman smiled quietly.

"Nobody's problem but mine, anyway," Groton added. "I never connected, you know? You got a kid, right?"

"A daughter."

"That's good," Groton said with a casual nod. "Somebody to do the crying for you." He crushed the cigarette vehemently into the stainless steel ashtray beside his chair, lit another, glanced at his watch. "They'll be having us in pretty soon."

"Having us in?"

"Inviting us to the party," Groton told him. "You wait until everything's set up. That's the way it's done." He thought a moment. "And another thing, there'll be a shitload of food spread around. Don't eat any of it until you're invited to. They usually invite you, but wait until they do. A beat like this, you got to have manners." He took another long drag on the cigarette and let his eyes drift from Corman's shoes to the hat that still rested unsteadily on his head. "And spruce up a little for this kind of gig," he added. "Brush the dust off your jacket. It's not like the street. These people, they're what you might call fashion-conscious, you know? I mean, you don't see a chauffeur in a sweatshirt, right?"

Corman nodded.

"And another thing about the food," Groton added. "Don't eat too much. Don't make like it's your meal of the day. Just a nibble, to be sociable. But don't gobble the stuff. You look like an asshole, you do that."

"Okay."

"These are just the tips of the trade," Groton said. "That's what you want, right?"

"Yeah."

Groton glanced about, chewed his lip, turned back to Corman. "You got to get along with the society reporters, too," he said. "Whoever it is, you got to make like they're top notch, really know how to move with the upscale crowd, you know? One thing you notice, they get to believing that they're really one of the bunch, not just people who tell the rest of the world what the rich are doing, but one of the group themselves. That's bullshit, and the shooter never falls for it. It's the writers who get sucked into that, but you got to play to it, anyway."

"All right," Corman said, then listened as Groton continued on with the rules of the game. He tried to imagine what Lazar would have said in the same situation. But Lazar had never been in the same situation, had never had anything to think about but his camera. He'd lived in a small furnished room just off Times Square, had slept in his clothes, listening for the next voice on the police radio, and leaped up the instant it called to him. He had lived with only the streets as his companion, lover, wife, child, everything. He had nursed the streets, loved them, pitied them. They were in his eyes, mind and heart. He had grown old in his devotion; it had become a state of grace.

"Never more than one glass of champagne," Groton said. "They see you swilling the good stuff, they might mention it to somebody. And I don't mean to some greaseball from the City Room. These people don't know him from the shoeshine boy. They don't know the people who work at the paper, they know the people who fucking *own* it." He tapped the side of his head with his index finger. "You got to remember that."

Again, Corman nodded, and for the next few minutes the two of them sat silently while people swept past them, heading for their rooms or in the opposite direction, toward the large revolving door which led to Park Avenue.

Stuart Clayton came up slowly, his long, slender body draped in an elegant blue double-breasted suit. "You ready, Harry?" he asked.

Groton pulled himself to his feet. "Anytime, Stuart," he said. "Hey, by the way, you know David Corman?"

Clayton's eyes shifted over to him. "I don't think so."

"He's a freelance shooter," Groton said. "He may be taking over my job."

"Really?" Clayton said. He offered Corman his hand, shook it, looked back at Groton. "I didn't know you were leaving the paper."

"In a couple of weeks," Groton said, adding nothing else.

"Retirement?" Clayton asked.

Groton shrugged. "I guess that's what they call it." He headed off toward the ballroom. "Let's get going."

They walked to the ballroom immediately, and for the next few minutes, Corman strolled about, taking in the surroundings, the long tables, filled with hors d'oeuvres, the fully stocked bar, the enormous flower arrangements which stood here and there throughout the room. In the old city, the Fifth Avenue mansions had had ballrooms of their own, sleek marble corridors where the Fricks and the Vanderbilts ate, laughed and made deals across glittering ice sculptures of slope-necked swans. Now they gathered at the Waldorf, the Plaza, the Pierre, their ranks swollen by the well-dressed security men who lined the floral walls, glancing about apprehensively while they spoke softly into the little microphones that winked from their lapels.

It was late in the afternoon by the time the last of the guests had drifted out of the ballroom, but Groton was still shooting, his body craning for this shot, stooping for the next one. There was an obsessive quality to it which Corman found alarming. It was as if Groton were trying to get one last shot of everything he saw, repeatedly taking one picture after another until he'd photographed every face in the room a hundred times, every square inch of carpeting or wall space, every petal of every flower.

Finally Corman caught up with him and touched his shoulder. "Clayton left a long time ago," he said.

Groton crouched at the edge of a table, focused on a small porcelain tureen and snapped the picture.

"Everybody's gone," Corman added softly.

Groton straightened himself, turned to Corman. "Everybody but us," he said.

"Time for us to go, too, Harry."

Groton nodded reluctantly. "Yeah, I guess so," he said with a sudden weariness. He slung the camera over his shoulder and headed for the door.

The rain had started again by the time they reached the wide entrance to the hotel. Up the avenue, a fountain was spurting its white frothy torrent. For a moment, Groton watched it expressionlessly.

"It wasn't a bad party," Corman said, to lighten the atmosphere.

Groton said nothing, his eyes still on the distant fountain.

"Well, I got to go," Corman said after a moment. He turned up his collar and stepped out from beneath the wide sheltering canopy.

Groton's eyes darted over to him, intense, wondering, as if he'd just heard something he could not possibly believe or any longer doubt. "I got two more shoots," he said urgently. "And that's it."

Corman glanced back toward him, felt the rain drumming on his hat.

"One on Wednesday, one on Friday," Groton added.

Corman smiled. "Maybe I'll come along."

Groton's face brightened very briefly, then sank again. "Up to you," he said.

The Bull and Bear was only around the corner from the Waldorf, but by the time Corman got there he was drenched. A slender stream of water spilled over the brim of his hat as he took it off, shook it gently, then hung it up beside the table which Jeffrey had already taken.

"I don't think it's ever going to let up," Jeffrey said amiably.

Corman eased himself into a chair and glanced at the speckled marble table which separated him from Jeffrey.

"Care for a drink?" Jeffrey asked.

"Scotch."

"Any particular kind?"

Corman gave him a chilly smile. "Why don't you order for me, Jeffrey."

Jeffrey looked at him glumly. "I didn't mean that to sound pretentious."

Corman glanced away and said nothing.

"I guess we've started off badly," Jeffrey said.

"Looks that way."

Jeffrey offered a tentative smile. "So, shall we start again?"

Corman looked at him and nodded.

"Well, *is* there any particular brand you'd prefer?"

"I usually settle for the house brand," Corman said. "If you know a better one, order it."

Jeffrey nodded for the waiter. He appeared instantly. "A Glenlivet for both of us," Jeffrey said to him.

The waiter vanished.

Jeffrey tested another smile, didn't like the feel of it and grew solemn. "I hope this can be a profitable talk, David," he said hesitantly.

"Me, too."

"I understand that Edgar spoke to you."

142

"That's right."

"About Lexie."

"Lucy."

"I mean, Lexie's concerns."

"Yeah, he talked to me," Corman said. He tugged his collar down, felt a trickle of rainwater make a jagged dive down his back.

"And I understand that you're meeting Lexie on Saturday night?"

Corman nodded.

The waiter returned, placed the drinks in front of them and disappeared again.

Jeffrey lifted his glass. "Cheers," he said.

Corman nodded and drank. "So what's on your mind, Jeffrey?"

Jeffrey shifted uneasily in his seat. Behind him, a lighted tickertape machine was running off the closing prices from the New York Stock Exchange. American Telephone and Telegraph was up an eighth, but things didn't look good for the steel industry.

"Lexie is quite unhappy these days," Jeffrey said softly, casting an eye about quickly to make sure only the anonymous strangers in the Bull and Bear were in earshot.

"She is?"

"Yes," Jeffrey said. "Particularly about Lucy."

"What's the problem?"

"Well, she's worried about a great many things," Jeffrey said. "I'm sure Edgar mentioned a few of them."

"She doesn't like my apartment," Corman said coolly. "Lucy's school, she doesn't like that."

"She wants the best for her, David," Jeffrey said sincerely. "She really does. She wants to protect her."

"From what? Me?"

Jeffrey laughed nervously. "You? Of course not."

"The bottom line is that she gave me custody," Corman said bluntly.

"That's true."

"And now she wants custody herself."

"Yes," Jeffrey admitted. "I think that's what she wants."

"And you're here to persuade me."

Jeffrey looked at him, puzzled. "What?"

"I said, you're here to persuade me," Corman repeated.

"Persuade you to what?"

"To give Lucy up."

Jeffrey's face relaxed. He laughed. "Well, no," he said. "Not exactly."

Corman watched him, confused.

"I'm not here to try to get Lucy," Jeffrey said, still chuckling to himself. "Just the opposite."

"What?"

"Well, as you can see by my hair, David," Jeffrey said, finally bringing his laughter to an end, "I'm not getting any younger." He shifted his head to the right, so that the abundant gray could catch the light. "And, as you know, I already have three children by my first wife."

Corman nodded. He had never met Jeffrey's first wife, but he had seen her picture from time to time in the society pages of the paper. She had the look of a woman who had once been beautiful, but whose skin had now dried to a wrinkled crisp, her lips curling down, sagging, along with what was left of her self-esteem.

"I'm fifty-three, David," Jeffrey announced. "And to tell you the truth, males in my family are notoriously short-lived."

Corman stared at him expressionlessly.

"My father died when he was sixty-three," Jeffrey added. "And his father was even younger, fifty-eight." He shook his head. "Those are biological facts, and in my estimation, they are very good predictors of one's own life span."

Corman leaned toward him and stared at him intently. "So what are you getting at?"

"Well, the fact is, when I married Lexie, I didn't bargain for the possibility of a second round of parenthood."

"So you don't want Lucy?" Corman asked.

"Well, that's not exactly it."

"What is?"

144

"I want to ease Lexie's mind," Jeffrey said. "About Lucy's surroundings."

"How could you do that?"

"I'd like to help with some of the expenses," Jeffrey told him.

"What expenses?"

"Yours, David," Jeffrey said. "And Lucy's. The rent, maybe a private school for Lucy, things like that."

Corman felt his lips part involuntarily and closed them.

Jeffrey leaned forward slightly, fidgeting with the napkin. "I'm a wealthy man," he said. "I have everything but time. That's the one thing I'm not rich in." He took another drink of scotch. "I believe that these are my last years, David, and I want to live them well. I care about Lucy. I really do. And I certainly care about Lexie. I want both of them to be happy, but I don't want both of them in my house." He shrugged. "I'm being very frank. I hope you don't mind."

"Not at all," Corman said.

"I'm being selfish, I admit it," Jeffrey added. "Lexie is a beautiful woman, and I want her to myself." He lifted the glass again, downed the rest of the scotch. "So there you have it."

Corman's eyes drifted up to the ticker-tape scoreboard. If he had money, he realized that he would keep it in a nice little country bank where nobody cared if Ecuador could pay its bills.

Jeffrey called for the waiter and ordered another scotch. "So, what do you think?" he asked. "About my helping out a bit. Just between the two of us, of course. Lexie couldn't know, and neither could Lucy for that matter."

Corman actually found himself thinking about it. "How would I explain where the money came from?" he asked, after a moment.

Jeffrey shrugged. "A rich uncle?"

"I don't think so, Jeffrey."

"Use your imagination," Jeffrey said insistently.

Corman shook his head. "No."

Jeffrey looked at Corman intently. "Does that mean you won't allow me to help you?"

"I don't see how it could be arranged."

Jeffrey eased himself back in his chair, his face now very stern. "David, I have to tell you, Lexie is very, very concerned about the way you live. She's very concerned about the effect it will have on Lucy."

Corman listened and said nothing. He wondered how it must feel to see the world as Jeffrey saw it, a place where no prize game was so rare it couldn't ultimately be sighted through the cross hairs of his checkbook. And yet, there was another side to him as well, and as he watched him, Corman could see it as if in pentimento behind his face. He was scared, as Corman thought Joanna's husband must be scared, his eyes forever drifting down toward the lump in his groin. Jeffrey had the same, faintly panicked look, time breathing down his neck, sucking up his days, whispering incessantly that he was dying, dying, dying, that he could not afford a single moment's loss. "I wish I could help you out, Jeffrey," he said.

Jeffrey looked at him oddly. "Help me out?"

"In this situation," Corman explained. "With Lexie."

Jeffrey nodded peremptorily, then looked at Corman solemnly. "Well, I think you should know that she's getting more and more adamant about this whole thing," he said. "And I honestly think that she might sue for custody."

Corman's fleeting sympathy for Jeffrey's mortality withered instantly. "She left Lucy," he reminded him sternly. "Winning her back won't be easy."

"She left under difficult circumstances," Jeffrey said. "And 'left' is a little strong. She never really abandoned Lucy." He smiled tentatively. "She had to find herself. When she did, she fell in love."

"With you."

"Yes," Jeffrey said. "But I understand that in matters of fidelity, you had your own problems."

"Proving that won't be easy," Corman said.

"It's an old story anyway, David," Jeffrey said dismissively. "And we both know it. The real question now is what would be best for Lucy. Lexie has one idea. I have another. And I guess you have a third?"

"That's right."

"Which is for her to stay with you."

"Yeah."

"In the same apartment, on the same street, going to the same school," Jeffrey said, as if he were ticking off the descending circles of Hell.

Corman nodded.

Jeffrey shook his head. "It won't do, David," he said wearily. "It really won't. Lexie is becoming obsessed with this whole question, and I'm sure you have a very good idea of what that's like."

Corman watched him silently, half-contemplating his offer once again. He was not really sure why he'd refused it so quickly. Was it pride? If it were pride, then it was wrong. Why should Lucy be deprived of things because he was too proud to provide them in any way he could, even this way, a discreet arrangement between two worldly gentlemen, arrived at in the muted elegance of the Bull and Bear while the stock prices streamed silently above them like a lighted pennant.

"David," Jeffrey said sincerely, "Lucy's a very bright little girl. She's not being served by that school, and you know it. What's to gain by keeping her in it? What's to gain by staying in that apartment, on that street? What's to gain for either one of you?"

Corman realized that he absolutely did not have an answer, and he could feel the lack of it at the very center of himself, a dull, dead space that insisted upon its right to exist without a conscious reason, purpose or claim on anything.

"I could understand how you would feel if it were a question of losing her," Jeffrey went on. "But that's what I'm trying to avoid."

Corman shook his head. "I can't, Jeffrey," he said, then repeated it. "I just can't." He got to his feet immediately. "I don't know why."

Jeffrey stared at him imploringly. "Please think about it," he said.

"I can't," Corman repeated as if it were part of an addled litany. "I can't." He pulled on his coat and his hat, and felt the clammy chill that had gathered in them. "No. No. No."

He picked Lucy up at Maria's and then the two of them walked the short distance to the apartment. Lucy sometimes ran ahead of him, her body moving in a zigzag pattern along the sidewalk, her bright yellow rain-slicker perfectly visible despite the slightly foggy air. As he continued to walk at some distance behind her, Corman realized that he liked the way she ran in the streets, the way her head was always turning left and right, as if she were searching for something, an oddly torn window shade or dark, mysterious alley, something with a story that could not go untold.

Once in the apartment, she quickly completed her homework while Corman struggled with dinner in the small kitchen, whipping up a quick meal from a mound of hamburger meat, a small scattering of frozen french fries, the few remaining leaves of lettuce which had managed to survive for one more day.

They ate together quietly, savoring the simple relaxing calm more than the food, then sat down on the sofa. Lucy took a copy of *The Secret Garden,* a luxury edition Lexie had given her, and began to read aloud.

He listened silently while she nestled beneath his arm. He relished her voice and looked forward to its changes, just as he looked forward to the day when she would leave him. Because of that, it seemed to him that loneliness was not the issue, that the fact that he would miss her was not enough to keep her with him. If Lexie went through with the custody suit, he would fight for Lucy with an animal rapaciousness, but he also knew it was not her presence he would be fighting for. His life would be easier without her. As to love, he would always love her, and be loved by her. Even love was not the issue with him, but he was not exactly sure what was.

"What's this word?" Lucy asked suddenly.

Corman glanced down toward the word she was pointing to. "Obtuse," he said.

"What does it mean?"

"Stupid," Corman told her. "That's the usual meaning."

"You mean like dumb?"

"Sort of."

"Like retarded?"

"No, not like that," Corman said. "Dense. You know, hard to get through to."

Lucy nodded. "Oh," she said. "Like someone who doesn't get it."

"That's right."

Lucy smiled then went on reading.

Corman eased himself back into the sofa, closed his eyes and tried to relax. Her voice curled around him, very soft and youthful. He drew her in more closely, wrapping his arm around her shoulder, squeezing gently but steadily until she finally stopped reading and glanced up at him.

"Let go," she said, jerking her shoulders right and left to loosen his grip.

"Sorry," Corman said quickly.

She looked at him accusingly. "Are you listening?"

"Yes."

"Are you sure?"

"Yes."

"Tell me what I read."

"Just keep going," Corman told her sternly.

She gave him a doubtful glance then began reading again.

He kept his arm delicately around her shoulders, but didn't try to draw her more firmly into his embrace. He didn't want to hold her down, tie her up or crush her. He wasn't sure what he wanted for her, or even what he could provide. Jeffrey had been right about everything, just as Lexie would be right when she took the stand, made her point and rolled off the figures in a city where nothing mattered quite so much as the figures. He could hear her now. It was a husky, solid voice. It would be persuasive. He knew it would. He couldn't even deny that most of the facts were on her side. He had left a steady job to pursue one that was not only unstable, but in his way of doing it, ineffable. He worked too many days, too many nights, wandered sleeplessly even when at home. He provided too little of himself, or anything else for that matter. Those were the facts, and there was no way to change them or even give them a gloss that wouldn't look self-serving. If it went to court, the most obvious fact would also be the most damaging one. It was simple, straightforward: there was no way he could actually prove he was a good father.

And yet? And yet?

It struck Corman that at the center of every conclusion there was always a lingering "And yet?" It haunted every fixed idea, troubling, discordant, a quavering at the core.

He shook his head silently, still listening as Lucy continued to read beside him. He tried to think of all the other fathers who'd listened to their children read while just beyond the door the wolves had howled through the night, war, fire, plague, poverty, all the bad faith of the age. He doubted that any one of them would have been able to prove how much he loved his children, worked for them, and taught them. Not even a thousand expert pictures could prove what he had done.

And yet?

Chapter 20

"NEED A LIFT TO SCHOOL?"

Corman turned around, reflexively reaching for Lucy's hand, then tilted the umbrella slightly upward to find a face to go with the voice behind him.

Victor stood in a long black leather coat and shimmering red scarf. "I'm the rider in the rain," he said grandly, then stretched his arms toward Lucy in a perfect portrait of the outlaw in his pride.

Lucy smiled excitedly. "Hi, Uncle Victor." She ran to him and leaped into his arms. There was something in Victor's wildness that had always drawn her to him.

Victor held her tightly in his arms, kissed her softly and whispered something in her ear, then lowered her back to the sidewalk, his eyes drifting up to Corman as he released her. "Hello, brother," he said.

"Hello, Victor." Corman stepped toward him, and they shook hands.

"I thought I might give you a ride this morning." Victor nodded toward a small black sedan. "As you can see, I brought my wheels."

"Yeah, great," Lucy said brightly.

Victor opened the door, watched as she scrambled in, then turned to Corman. "Good to see you, David."

"You too," Corman said. He walked to the passenger side and slid into the car, the umbrella resting awkwardly between his legs.

Victor pulled away from the curb, sped around the block, then stopped in front of Lucy's school. "This close enough?" he asked her jokingly. "Or should I drive you to the classroom?"

Lucy leaned forward and kissed him on the cheek. " 'Bye, Uncle Victor. Thanks for the ride."

"Nice kid," Victor said as he watched her dart up the stairs. He turned to Corman and smiled teasingly. "You don't deserve her."

"When did you get back?" Corman asked.

"Early this morning. The red-eye from Las Vegas." He inched the car back into the traffic, moving down the street toward Ninth Avenue. "It was a pretty good game. Some moderately heavy hitters."

"How'd you do?"

"A living," Victor said. He stopped at the light on the corner and drew in a deep breath. "So, how have you been?"

"Okay."

The light changed, and Victor turned left onto Ninth Avenue, heading downtown. "You going anywhere in particular this morning?" he asked.

Corman shrugged.

"Well, do you have time for breakfast?"

"Yeah."

"Good for you, David," Victor said, then smiled the charming, open-faced smile that Corman knew had pierced a thousand unprotected hearts.

They parked near a small diner in Chelsea. It was shaped like a stainless-steel railroad car, long and silver. Coils of neon spun around, throwing pinkish light. Beyond the large windows, the Hudson spread out like a field of gray slate.

"The weather's better in Las Vegas," Victor said as he glanced briefly out the window, turned back and motioned for a waiter.

Corman looked toward the river and the 23rd Street pier which stretched over it. The old city had used it as a makeshift morgue for the scores of young women who'd died in the Triangle Fire. Daughters, he thought, so many daughters.

"You've never been to Las Vegas, have you?" Victor asked.

Corman shook his head. They'd left the bodies out till dawn, some charred beyond recognition, some merely broken by the fall, their skirts still smelling of the smoke that had driven them to the windows of the building's upper floors.

"Two coffees," Victor said when the waiter stepped up to the table. He looked at Corman. "Want anything for breakfast?"

Corman shook his head again, without turning from the river. He imagined night falling over the city, the black, gutted ruin of the Shirtwaist Factory building illuminated by searchlights as the bodies were brought down from the upper floors by block and tackle, small gray bundles swinging slowly in the still smoldering air over Greene Street. The shooters had remained on through the night, wandering wearily among the distraught relatives, or back and forth from the pier, bowed, silent, their boxy black cameras and spindly tripods hung over their shoulders as if they were going through some hallowed shooter's version of the Stations of the Cross. Far from lilies and lace, incremental falls. Lazar had always thought of it as their finest hour.

"Just two coffees, then," Victor told the waiter. He glanced back at Corman, waited a moment, then spoke. "How do you like my new car?"

Corman turned toward him, blinking the old city from his mind. "Nice," he said.

"I got it in Florida. But don't worry about it. I don't hustle people who can't afford to lose." He looked at Corman pointedly. "I have a few rules. How many people can say that?"

Corman didn't answer.

Victor watched him a moment, then broke it off with a smile. "We're a lot alike, David. At least in one respect. We're both major disappointments to our father." The smile turned slightly bitter. "He must think God hates him."

Corman nodded.

"Have you been out to see him lately?" Victor asked.

"Not in a while."

"He probably misses you."

"You, too."

Victor shook his head. "I doubt it." He grew silent a moment, his eyes concentrating on the plain paper napkin which rested beside his coffee.

"He's been sick lately," Corman said.

"Anything serious?"

"The usual complaints."

Victor's eyes drifted up from the napkin and settled on Corman. "To play it safe, that's all he ever wanted us to do." He smiled ironically. "Edgar is his pride and joy." He shrugged. "What can I say? People don't get what they deserve in this world, David, they get what they settle for."

"He had big plans for all of us," Corman said.

"Big plans," Victor said dismissively. "That's what the average bourgeois always has. Instead of love, honor, conviction. Big plans."

In his mind, Corman saw his father curled in a beach chair beside the pool, his body wrapped in the bright Connecticut air, a pair of binoculars hanging like a heavy black amulet from his neck. "He's become a bird watcher," he said.

Victor laughed. "The last refuge of a bullshitter. What's his goal in life now, to spot the yellow-throated turkey buzzard?"

"It's how he spends his time," Corman said. "Mostly by the pool, when it's warm enough."

Victor took out a pack of cigarettes and offered one to Corman. "No, thanks."

Victor took one for himself then returned the pack to his jacket pocket. "Maybe I'll get out to see him." He shrugged. "I still like the trees."

Corman nodded, remembering them, the great cradling branches of the oak, the deep green tent of the weeping willow by the pond. Lucy had only the metal igloo of the climbing dome in Central Park, the layer of black rubber beneath the slide, only cement, asphalt, granite fissures filled with glass. "It'd be nice to have a summer house," he said.

Victor thumped the end of the cigarette against the side of the pack. "Summer house?" he croaked. "You're getting soft."

"Maybe."

"How's the photography coming?"

"I haven't sold anything lately."

Victor looked surprised. "Anything? You mean, not anything?"

"Not in a while."

Victor lit the cigarette and waved out the match. "Why?"

"Most things don't sell," Corman told him. "That's just the way it is."

"The artistic life," Victor said. "It's a tough business. But then, you knew that when you started, right?"

"Yes."

The waiter brought the coffees then disappeared behind the counter at the far end of the room.

Victor took a sip, his eyes watching Corman thoughtfully from over the rim of the cup. "You giving up, David?" he asked, as he lowered the cup to the table.

"On what?"

"The adventurous life."

"It's never been that adventurous."

Victor took another drag on the cigarette, then crushed it into the ashtray. "Just make sure you keep your edge. That's all you've got. It's all anybody's got. People should spend their time sharpening it, instead of flattening it out."

Corman said nothing.

Victor looked at him solemnly. "I mean it, David. You lose that, and you're nothing. Just a shutterbug with bills to pay."

Corman let him go on about it for a few minutes after that, watching his face, the glint in his eyes, the way his fingers moved constantly, first drumming lightly on the table, then ceaselessly massaging the fork, spoon, cube of sugar, anything they settled on. A picture would reduce him to a caricature of the middle-aged hustler, the rogue male on parade, childless, wifeless, the nomadic habitué of countless resort hotels. And yet, as Corman remembered it, he had never been entirely wrong about anything. *How many people can say that?*

"The edge is all there is," Victor concluded finally. "It's the thing you have to nurture." He waited for Corman to respond.

Corman took a sip of coffee and said nothing.

"So, how's Edgar?" Victor asked after a moment.

"The same."

"Frances still the typical neurasthenic?"

"More or less."

Victor shook his head. "Pure bathos, those two."

Corman's eyes drifted toward the table where two sets of initials were carved inside a jagged heart. It struck him that if the world made sense, only the most courageous natures would risk such public declarations. The rest would move about as Victor did, never tying their lives with such exquisite jeopardy to anyone, victimized by nothing but the cowardice of solitude.

"So what do they do, Edgar and Frances?" Victor asked, with a slight laugh.

"They manage," Corman said.

Victor laughed again. "Manage? Is that the goal? To manage? Christ. The last time I saw Frances, she was boiling. I mean it, a blink away from humping the doorman."

Corman turned away slightly.

"And she'd be better off if she did, too," Victor added flatly.

Corman looked back toward him. "Do you ever think about Mississippi?"

Victor stared at him wonderingly. "What?"

"The way you lived in those days," Corman said.

Victor's face softened slightly. "Sometimes," he said quietly. Then he smiled. "In fond remembrance."

"I remember all your stories."

Victor looked pleased. "Really?"

"Yes," Corman said. "I think they made a difference."

"In the world?"

"In me."

Victor studied Corman's face silently, his eyes narrowing very slightly before he spoke. "What's the matter, David?" he asked solemnly. "I can tell something's wrong."

Corman shrugged.

Victor leaned forward and touched his hand. "I'm your brother. What is it?"

Corman drew in a long, slow breath. "Lexie wants me to let Lucy live with her and Jeffrey out in Westchester," he said.

Victor brought his hands together on the table. "When did she tell you?"

"She told Edgar. He passed it on to me."

"Is he representing you?"

"If it goes to court."

"Will it?"

"I don't know," Corman said. "That's up to Lexie."

"So she's just asking you, is that it?"

"That's what Edgar thinks."

"What are you going to say?"

"I'm not sure I have much to say," Corman told him. "My work is off. Trang's going to evict me. Lucy's school is lousy. I know what they could give her."

Victor started to speak, drew back, then began again. "I don't know what to tell you, David. You know how I live. On the lam, more or less. I stay with a woman for a month, two on the outside. Kids are things I see on milk cartons. You know, the Missing."

Corman nodded.

Victor shook his head slowly. "Mississippi. Why'd you bring that up? Christ, that was another world." He picked up a fork and raked his index finger across the prongs. "It should have lasted. You could have come down when you got old enough, left the old man, worked with me in the Great Cause."

Corman smiled. "I dreamed of that."

Victor drew in a deep, faintly resigned breath. "But it died before we did," he said, then smiled knowingly. "Most things do, right?" The smile withered. "And nothing stinks like a dead cause, you know?"

Corman nodded. "How long will you be in New York?"

"A few days," Victor said. "I was thinking of taking Lucy out tonight. Maybe pick her up at school. Dinner and a show, something like that. Any objections?"

"No."

"Still don't think I'm a bad influence?"

"No more than most."

Victor laughed sharply, then grew serious. "I wish you luck on this one, David. I know what she means to you."

Corman said nothing.

Victor let his eyes linger on him for a few seconds, then he took a final sip of coffee and motioned for the check. "I guess you'd better get to work."

"Yeah," Corman said, then quickly drained the last of his coffee, too.

They walked out of the diner together and got into the car.

"Where do you want me to drop you?" Victor asked as he hit the ignition.

For a moment, Corman wasn't sure himself, then he remembered the picture he'd taken in the basement of Midtown North, the small crumpled receipt. "A blood bank on the Bowery," he said.

Victor's eyes shot over to him. "Christ, David, you're not ..."

Corman shook his head. "No, not me," he said. "Just something I'm working on."

Chapter 21

THE BLOOD BANK OPERATED OUT OF A CRAMPED storefront off the Bowery on East 3rd Street. Several men were scattered among the short, jagged rows of metal chairs that crisscrossed the front of the building. Some of them munched the plain sugar cookies distributed after the blood had been taken. Others were still waiting, their fingers holding idly to small cards with hand-lettered red numbers.

"Thirty-seven," someone called from the back of the room.

Corman turned toward the voice and saw a tall man in a slightly soiled lab coat. He wore large, black-rimmed plastic glasses and cradled a clipboard in the crook of his left elbow.

"Thirty-seven," he repeated. His eyes darted left and right, surveying the crowd. "Thirty-seven."

A very thin old man eased himself to his feet, then walked shakily past Corman, nudging him slightly with his shoulder as he made his way down the aisle toward the tall beige curtain that divided the room. He had an oddly crumpled look, as if his body had been snatched up, crushed in a large hand then tossed back to earth.

"Your name Sanderson?" the man in the lab coat asked him.

The old man grunted, shifted on his feet, then reached listlessly for the clipboard.

The man in the lab coat drew it away from him. "Just a second, please," he said sharply, then adjusted his glasses. "Have you been hospitalized recently, Mr. Sanderson?"

"No."

"How old are you?"

Sanderson shrugged. "Somewhere 'round sixty, I guess."

The man in the lab coat looked doubtful, but wrote it down on the form anyway. "Are you on any form of medication?"

Sanderson grinned. "Just my old standby," he said.

The other man scribbled something on the form.

Sanderson waved his hand impatiently. "And it's 'no' to all the rest of them questions."

The man in the coat nodded, made a few checks on the paper, then escorted Sanderson behind the curtain.

Corman walked to the front row, shoved his camera bag beneath one of the chairs and sat down. For a moment, he stared about, trying to get a fix on the room by concentrating on the details: a Coca-Cola wall calendar, its pages a month behind, the soda machine next to it, a small table filled with uneven stacks of medical pamphlets, the poster of an earnest physician urging regular checkups on the listless men who muttered obliviously a few feet away. One by one, Corman envisioned the individual frames, trying to find a way to get beyond the obvious social ironies and clichés.

"Excuse me."

Corman glanced around and faced the man in the lab coat.

"May I help you?" the man asked.

Corman reached into his pocket, brought out the small yellow receipt and handed it to him.

The man glanced at it peremptorily and gave it back. "What about it?"

Corman pocketed the receipt. "Do you recognize the name?"

"Yes."

"She died last week," Corman said.

"Was she a relative of yours?" the man asked.

"No," Corman said. "I'm a photographer. I'm working on a story about her."

The man thought for a moment, his eyes squeezing together slightly. "I do remember her," he said finally. "Probably because she was white, a woman. We don't get that down here."

"Did you ever talk to her?"

The man nodded. "We try to be cordial to people," he said. "We usually talk to them a little during the procedure. Like a hairdresser would, at about that level. We don't give counseling or anything like that. That's not our function."

Corman took out his notebook. "Do you remember anything she said?"

The man shrugged. "Not really."

"Do you remember when you saw her the last time?"

"Whenever that receipt was dated," the man said. "Not since then."

"How often did you see her?"

"No more than once a month," the man said firmly. "We can't accept blood more often than that. It's against the law."

Corman remembered the outstretched arm. "She had a lot of needle marks."

"Maybe she was a junkie."

Corman shook his head.

The man didn't argue the point. "She could have been selling blood all over the place. We're not the only one, and some of them don't keep very good track of who's been in and out."

"Do you remember anything in particular about her?"

"She had a doll with her," the man told him, as if suddenly recalling her with more detail. "She treated it like a real baby."

"Was she alone?"

"Yes, always," the man said.

"Did you notice if she talked to any of the other people?"

"As far as I can remember, she always sat alone." He nodded toward the left corner of the room. "Over there, in that chair by the window. That's where she sat until we called her number."

Corman glanced at the chair. It was made of gray metal and one of the hinged supports was bent, throwing it off balance. "And you never saw her with anybody?"

"No."

Corman felt the little notebook go slack in his hand, like a small bird that had just died. "Do you know anything at all about her?"

"Only what she wrote on the form."

The bird's eyes fluttered. "What form?"

"The one they have to fill out."

"Do you still have it? Would you mind showing it to me?"

"No," the man said. "Wait here." He turned and disappeared behind the curtain.

Corman waited, his hand pumping rhythmically at the notebook as his eyes circled the room once again, looking for shots, noting a few more details, an old shoe lodged between two chairs, a plastic spoon on the windowsill, the fact that someone had started to paint the radiator blue, then abandoned the project halfway through. More cliché images. As pictures, they would fit perfectly in a light blue, tear-shaped frame. The chair the woman had always sat in would do the same. He took a few pictures of it anyway, hoping that after he'd developed them, Julian would not be able to see their grim melodrama.

"Here it is," the man said as he came out from behind the curtain a few minutes later. "It's just a simple form, not much on it."

Corman took the paper from the man's hand and stared at it intently. The woman had answered its few questions in a tiny, cramped handwriting that used up only a small amount of the space provided. The longer words were broken up into their syllables as Corman remembered being taught to do in elementary school. The spelling was crudely phonetic.

"Strange, I know," the man said, "but she still fit the test for informed consent."

Corman looked at him. "Which is?"

"That she was correctly oriented as to space and time." The man answered matter-of-factly, as if he were reading it from a script.

"And that's all she needed to know?" Corman asked.

"It was all *we* needed to know about her. All the law requires."

Corman glanced back down at the form. She'd signed her own name and listed the name and address of someone to contact in the event of an emergency: "Burneece Taylur Ate Nyn Grow-ve." He studied the writing for a moment, then glanced back up at the man. "Bernice Taylor? Eighty-nine Grove Street?"

The man gave a quick look at the form. "Probably," he said.

Corman copied the name and address down in his notebook, then scanned the form a final time, his mind concentrating on the oddly shattered words, the spelling of sounds. He remembered something one of his professors had once told him, that writing was the voice of the absent person. If that were true, then this was as close as he had gotten to Sarah Rosen's voice. In a picture, her handwriting on this single form would have to represent its final days, cracked, disjointed, primitive, as if she had been striving for something beyond the words themselves, the meaning in pure sound.

Corman glanced at his notebook, checked the address, then walked into the building's cramped vestibule. A line of small black buttons crawled down the wall to the left of the door, each just ahead of a name and apartment number. There was a B. Taylor listed beside the buzzer marked 3–B. Corman pushed the button, waited, then pushed again. There was no response, so he walked across the street, took out his camera and snapped a few pictures of the building.

It was a rundown brownstone, one of the few left in the West Village, but still elaborated with those soft touches the builders of the old city had insisted upon, a bit of carved stone here and there, flower boxes at each window. Corman concentrated on the large windows on the third floor and wondered if Sarah Rosen had ever sat behind them, or whether she'd simply scribbled Bernice Taylor's name and address from a phonebook according to her own mad scheme.

He took a few additional pictures, focusing on the street, the glistening wet pavement and bare dripping trees. The rain would drench the photographs nicely, give them a mournful, watery fatalism, hinting symbolically at some kind of death by drowning or burial at sea. If the light was just right, they might even go a step further, suggest oceanic tragedies, tearful destinies, a picture worth a thousand banal words.

He took a final shot, this time of the line of shutters on the fifth floor. Then he returned the camera to the bag, tugged his hat down further over his face to protect it from the rain and headed toward the train.

At the end of the block, he noticed a small delicatessen, felt his late-morning hunger and decided to go in.

An old man rested on a metal stool behind the counter. He watched Corman listlessly and smiled only after he bought a muffin. "Nothing but rain," he groaned.

Corman glanced out the window while he waited for his change.

Across the street, an old woman emerged from her building, tugging a small brown dog behind her. As she stepped out onto the sidewalk, the dog flinched violently, drew back and flinched again, snapping its head back and to the side.

"It's blind," the old man said, his eyes watching the dog. He shook his head. "It can't see the rain, so it don't know what's hitting it. I told her to put it to sleep." His lips curled down disapprovingly. "'For Christ's sake,' I told her, 'you can't have much of a life if you don't know what's hitting you.'"

Corman picked up his change and walked outside. The rain was beating down heavily, tapping loudly against the store's striped metal awning. He took out the muffin and ate it slowly, his eyes drifting back toward the brownstone. The window boxes on the third floor hung heavily in the gray air, and for an instant, Corman thought he saw something move just behind the shutters, and reached for his camera, then realized it was only the finger of a limb as it raked its bony tip across the closed white slats.

It was almost an hour before he saw someone go up the stairs of 89 Grove Street. She was a tall, slender woman with close-cropped blond hair, and she moved very quickly through the rain.

Corman headed toward her quickly, making it to the bottom of the landing just as the woman got to the top.

"Excuse me," he said, then offered a quick, uneasy smile the woman did not return. "I was wondering if you were Bernice Taylor, by any chance."

The woman eyed him silently, with a certain icy wariness, as if already calculating her moves if he should suddenly lunge toward her. "I'm Bernice Taylor," she said in a voice that sounded as if it had slid off the blade of a knife.

"My name's David Corman. I've been looking into someone's life, and your name's come up."

She seemed to guess his business. "Candy's not here," she said. "She moved out a month ago."

"I'm not looking for Candy," Corman said. "Somebody else. Maybe you've heard of her. Sarah Rosen."

Her small eyes squeezed together. "Sarah Rosen? You mean Dr. Rosen's little girl?"

"Her father's a doctor? Do you know his full name?"

Bernice shrugged. "I always just called him Dr. Rosen. Maybe I knew his name one time, but I can't recall it now." She waved her hand. "Anyway, he wasn't a real doctor," she added. "Just one of those teacher-type doctors."

"A professor?"

"Yeah. College professor. Columbia," Bernice said. "Why are you asking about Sarah?"

Corman saw no reason to blur the issue. "She's dead," he told her. "I was hoping I could talk to you about her."

"When'd she die?" the woman asked.

"Last Thursday."

Bernice's face remained passive. "You a friend of hers?"

"I never knew her," Corman said. "But I'm trying to find out what she was like." He anticipated her next question. "She was selling blood at this place on the Bowery. She listed you as her next of kin."

The woman's eyes widened. "Me? Next of kin?" She shook her head. "I haven't even seen Sarah since she was five years old."

"Would you mind talking to me, Mrs. Taylor, or is it Miss or . . ."

"Just Bernice," she answered dryly. "Yeah, okay. I'll tell you what I know." She turned, opened the door and headed up the stairs. Corman followed behind her until they reached the third-floor landing.

"I was living in this same place back then," she said as she fumbled for her keys. "I guess that's how Sarah had the address." She swung the door open and walked inside.

It was a tiny studio, but everything had been arranged in a neat, orderly fashion that made it look larger than it was. Two orange overstuffed chairs rested by the front window, ashtrays balanced on the right arms. A large hoop rug stretched between them, sending out swirls of steadily lightening yellows from its dark brown center, so that from where Corman stood it looked like a huge yellow eye, its dark pupil staring sightlessly toward the faded ceiling.

She moved directly to one of the orange chairs and motioned for Corman to take the other.

"So, you knew Sarah when she was a child," Corman began, as he leaned back into it.

"Yes."

"For how long?"

"When her mother got killed, her father needed somebody," Bernice said. "That's when I come by."

"Her mother was killed?"

"That's what Dr. Rosen said. Hit by a car. Right on the street." She reached under her chair, drew out a pack of cigarettes, and lit one.

"What year was that?" Corman asked.

"That must have been in 1973, something like that."

"And you worked for Dr. Rosen after that?"

"That's right."

"For how long?"

"Couple of months," Bernice said. "Up until November." She inhaled deeply, then let it out in a quick angry burst. "Then he let me go."

Corman looked up from his notebook. "Why?"

Bernice smiled bitterly. "Guess I wasn't good enough to watch over his precious little daughter."

"In what way not good enough?"

Bernice shifted slightly in her seat, threw one long bony leg over the other and rocked it edgily. "He had a check done on me. That's when he found out I had a record. If he'd asked me, I'd of told him about it. I'm not ashamed of what I did. But Rosen had his own way of doing things."

"What way was that?"

"On the sly, you might say," Bernice said. "He never came clean on anything. You always felt like you were talking to somebody he'd sort of made up, not the man himself." She shrugged. "Anyway, he had a check done, and I came up with a record, so that was the end of that."

"And this was only about two months after he hired you?" Corman asked.

"Yeah, about that. Two months, I'd say. Not much longer. She was five years old, I think. Went to this private school over on the East Side. Every morning the car came for her. The car was always coming for her. Dr. Rosen wouldn't let her out on the street. Not even for a little walk. Wherever she went, the car took her."

"Did you talk with her very often?"

"I would have talked to her," Bernice said. "I didn't have nothing against her. But she never seemed that interested. One time—this was just before I was let go—Candy, that's my little girl, she got sent home from school, so they called me to come get her, and I had to leave, so I took Sarah with me, because I knew Rosen wouldn't want her left alone in the house. So, anyway, I took her home with me, and when I picked Candy up, we all went to the park near the school, and they played together for a while." Her face grew more concentrated as the memory returned to her. "Sarah was real quiet. She sat real close to me. She wouldn't do much. Candy was about her age, but tougher, the way she's always been, and Sarah didn't want to play with her. I guess she was afraid. Anyway, it took forever for Candy to get her in the swings. But after she got in it, she swung a little. Not too high, sort of dragging her foot." She dropped the cigarette into the ashtray, lit another. "That's about the only time we really had together. The very next day, that's when Rosen found out about me, and that's when he let me go."

"What did he find out exactly?" Corman asked.

"What I did to Harold."

"Harold?"

"Candy's daddy," Bernice said. "I shot him one night. Everything was setting him off, and I got tired of it, so when he started in on me, I shot him. The bullet went right through his arm. Didn't even touch a bone." She shrugged. "I just got three years, and even that was a suspended sentence, but that didn't matter to Rosen. With him, a record was a record."

"And that's why he fired you?"

"That's what he told me," Bernice said. "He said he'd hired this guy. Told me his name. Walter Maddox. He said this Maddox guy had checked up on me, and it came out I had a record, and he didn't want anybody like that around." She shrugged. "He was nice about it, I guess, gave me a whole month's pay."

Corman nodded and wrote Maddox's name in his notebook.

"So really, as far as Sarah was concerned, I didn't know much about her," Bernice added. "Didn't have time to learn much."

"Did you get some sense of her?"

Bernice thought a moment. "Well, there was this one thing she did that made me wonder."

"What?"

"She bit through her lip one night," Bernice said. "Almost all the way through it. Her bottom lip."

"Why?"

Bernice shook her head. "She did it in her bed. Maybe while she was sleeping, I don't know. There was blood all over the pillow, I remember that. Dr. Rosen said it had to be thrown away. He didn't want it washed."

"Did Sarah ever talk about it, mention a bad dream, anything?"

Again, Bernice shook her head. "She was very quiet, but very jumpy, too. The slightest little movement and she'd flinch."

"Flinch?"

"Yeah," Bernice said firmly. "Like everything was about to jump her somehow, fly out at her, something like that."

"But you never knew why?"

"I always wondered, but I wasn't there long enough to find out," Bernice said, then shrugged. "That's about all I know." She glanced at her watch. "Got to change into my uniform," she said. "I'm waitressing now."

Corman fixed his eyes on Bernice Taylor. Backlit by the window, her face gave off an eerie sheen that reminded him vaguely of Sarah Rosen's skin. He reached for his camera again. "Would you mind if I took a picture?" he asked.

Bernice grinned coyly. "Nobody's asked for my picture in a long time," she said, then stood up and posed grandly by the shutters, the cigarette still dangling from her hand.

Chapter 22

WALTER MADDOX WAS IN THE YELLOW PAGES UNDER private investigators, his address listed as 345 West 57th Street. To Corman's surprise, he agreed to see him immediately.

On the way uptown, the connecting door of the subway suddenly opened and a large man stepped into the crowded car. He was wearing a flannel jacket that was two sizes too big and baggy gray trousers, torn at the pockets. A tangle of Rastafarian curls hung about his ears, and when he spoke, Corman could make out two gold teeth.

"I smell bad, but I'm hungry," the man shouted over the grinding roar of the subway car. Then he banged a tambourine against his leg and began to sing: "I shot the sheriff."

The crowd shifted away from him. Scores of faces buried themselves in newspapers, magazines, a dance of fiddling fingers. Corman reached for his camera and began shifting right and left as he angled for a shot.

"I'm gonna be riding this line for the next month," the man said loudly. "Break you guys in." He thrust out a half-crumpled Styrofoam cup. "I smell bad, but I'm hungry," he repeated. Then he stepped forward, elbowing his way through the crowd. When he got to Corman, he stopped and held his cup out. "God bless the givers," he said.

Corman lowered the camera and shook his head.

The man edged the cup forward, his dark eyes staring intently into Corman's face.

Again, Corman shook his head.

The man inched the cup forward until it nearly rested on Corman's chin. "I smell bad, but I'm hungry," he repeated emphatically.

Corman sat back slightly and started to put his camera away. He could feel the man staring at him, resented the little pinch of fear it caused and felt relieved when he finally moved away.

Maddox's office was a good deal more luxurious than Corman had expected. There were no splintered wooden desks or rickety filing cabinets, no battered gray hats hanging from pegs beside the door or empty whiskey bottles collecting dust on the windowsills. Even Maddox himself looked as if the lean years were well behind him, his body draped in an expensive, double-breasted suit. He wouldn't do for the kind of hang-dog gumshoe Julian no doubt would prefer, and Corman wondered if there might be a way to shoot him that would give him a somewhat less prosperous aspect, make him look more like the weary tracker of a million hopeless lives than the beaming petty bourgeois who sat behind his desk.

"Glad to meet you," Maddox said exuberantly as he rose and shook Corman's hand. "Photographer, that's interesting. What sort of stuff do you shoot?"

"Anything that comes up," Corman said. "Accidents, crime scenes, just about ..."

"Crime scenes," Maddox interrupted. "Interesting. Do you have many contacts at NYPD?"

"A couple," Corman said. "Barnes down at the photo lab, Harvey Grossbart in ..."

"My God, Harvey Grossbart," Maddox said. "He was in uniform the first time I saw him. Any promotions lately?"

"No."

"Hasn't made it to Division Chief yet?"

Corman shook his head.

Maddox looked faintly disappointed. "Why not?"

"Bad luck," Corman guessed. "Integrity."

Maddox laughed and motioned for Corman to take a seat opposite his desk. "So, what can I do for you?"

"A book I'm working on," Corman said. "A woman. Jumper. Went out the window in Hell's Kitchen last Thursday."

Maddox nodded thoughtfully, and as Corman watched his face grow steadily more solemn, he realized that his first impression had been slightly off. Maddox hadn't lost his curiosity yet. The varied ways in which human beings drove themselves or others nuts still interested him enough to wipe the wide, self-satisfied smile from his face.

"Her name was Sarah Rosen," Gorman said. "I think you did some work for her father."

"Professor Rosen," Maddox blurted immediately. "I did a lot of work for him."

Corman reached for his notebook.

Maddox's eyes swept down at the notebook, then back up to Corman. "All of it confidential, of course."

"It would be off the record," Corman told him. "I'm just trying to find out a few facts."

Maddox wasn't yet willing to give him any. "Well, what facts do you already have?"

"I know you did a background check on a woman named Bernice Taylor."

Maddox nodded. "That's right. Clean except for this one rap."

"Shooting someone."

"Her husband, boyfriend. Anyway, a worthless little prick."

The harshness of the language seemed odd coming from Maddox's round, cherubic face, but Corman could see the stripped-down soul beneath the business suit.

"His name was Harold, wasn't it?" Maddox asked. "Harold something?"

"That's right."

"She shot him in the arm," Maddox added. "A through-and-through." He shrugged dismissively. "She didn't hurt him much."

Corman nodded.

Maddox leaned back in his seat and spread his legs widely. "I did a lot of that kind of work for Dr. Rosen. He was about as close as I ever got to a steady customer."

"You checked on other people?"

Maddox nodded. "Quite a few. Tutors for his daughter. Math. Science. Anything. I checked on all of them. Once, when he was having his place remodeled, I even checked on the architect." He laughed. "Rosen was the type of guy that liked to keep tabs on things, know exactly what he was dealing with."

"Did you ever meet his daughter?"

"Just to say 'hi' on the way to Rosen's office," Maddox said. "Sarah, like you said. Black hair. Brown eyes. Not a beauty, but pleasant-looking, am I right?"

Corman nodded.

"I have an amazing mind, don't I?" Maddox asked, half-jokingly. "It drives people crazy, the way I can remember details from years back."

"Is this a common practice?" Corman asked. "Doing so many background checks?"

"Well, it's not uncommon," Maddox said. "But I'd have to say that Dr. Rosen was a little excessive."

"In the number of people he had checked?"

"That, and in the depth he wanted. You couldn't just come up with a quick fact-sheet, born here, worked there, blah, blah, blah. He wanted more than that. He wanted to know about what was going on inside of them, in their heads, what their personalities were like, that kind of thing." He smiled broadly. "And that was okay with me. It took a lot of time, and I worked by the hour." He shrugged. "Of course, I never really came up with all that much for him. The business with Bernice Taylor, her record, that was about it, and he didn't even use that."

Corman looked at Maddox intently. "Didn't use it? What do you mean? He fired her."

Maddox shook his head assuredly. "No, he didn't."

"She said he did."

"Fired her?" Maddox asked wonderingly. "When?"

Corman flipped back through his notes. "November 1973."

Maddox shrugged. "Well, he must have fired her for something else, then," he said confidently. "Because I had that report on Rosen's desk a long time before November." He thought about it again, as if checking his facts, then shook his head determinedly. "No, believe me, if he had fired Bernice Taylor for having a criminal record, he would have fired her in August. That's when I submitted the report."

"Before she was hired," Corman said.

"Of course," Maddox replied. "That's the way Rosen always worked. The background check was what cleared the way."

Corman nodded.

"Have you spoken to anyone but Bernice?" Maddox asked off-handedly, as if trying to test Corman's investigative skills gently, without accusing him of not having any.

"No," Corman admitted. "Who do you suggest?"

"Well, are we talking about a quickie here?" Maddox asked. "Cut and paste?"

"I'd like to get some information as soon as possible," Corman told him.

"Then if I were you, I'd start with her husband."

"She was married?"

"As far as I know," Maddox said. "Rosen asked me to do a background on him before they were engaged. I did, and after that I assumed they got married. Anyway, it. was the last business I got from the old man."

"Do you remember the fiancé's name?"

Maddox smiled confidently. "Of course. Oppenheim. Peter Oppenheim."

"Does he live in New York?"

"As far as I know."

"What did you find out about him?"

"Very much a steady type," Maddox said. "All the right schools. Andover. Yale. Good family, lots of connections. A dream come true as far as Rosen was concerned. They were colleagues, you might say. Both of them at Columbia."

"Oppenheim teaches there too?"

"He was when I did the background."

"When was that?"

"Five years ago," Maddox said. "And everything was fine as far as Rosen was concerned."

"He seemed pleased? I mean, with Oppenheim?"

"Pleased?" Maddox said. "As pleased as he ever got. I think he actually smiled when I told him his future son-in-law was about as clean-cut a guy as God ever made. And to tell you the truth, Dr. Rosen didn't exactly have what you'd call a smiling face."

Corman regretted that he didn't have a picture of that face. He glanced at his watch, and realized that he still had time to get one.

Chapter 23

ONCE IN POSITION, CORMAN TOOK ONE PICTURE, THEN another. After that he simply watched the entrance to the Tomlinson Chapel on East 68th Street. It had a small arched doorway with modest stained-glass windows and two marble columns on either side. Corman kept a close eye on it as he waited across the street, lingering under the awning of an apartment house while the rain swept up and down. He'd already been there for several minutes before the doorman approached him.

"Excuse me," the doorman said. He straightened himself slightly, showing off the buttons of his uniform. "May I help you?"

Corman continued to watch the front of the chapel. A limousine had pulled up in front, and he could see a man in a black raincoat as he got out and headed into the building.

"Excuse me," the doorman repeated. He tapped Corman's shoulder. "I asked you a question."

Corman looked at him. "What?"

"This is not a bus stop," the doorman said. "Are you waiting for someone who lives in this building?"

"No," Corman said. His eyes drifted back toward the chapel. The long black limo had already pulled away from the curb.

"Then I'd like for you to move on," the doorman said firmly.

Corman glanced at him. "Move on?"

A thin smile slithered onto the doorman's face. "It makes people nervous."

Corman looked back toward the chapel, its door now tightly closed.

"I said, it makes people nervous," the doorman repeated emphatically.

Corman looked at him. "What does?"

"People just sort of hanging around the building. People they don't know."

"I'm a photographer," Corman told him.

The doorman chuckled. "Is that supposed to impress me?" He placed his hand on Corman's shoulder and squeezed very slightly. "No trouble, please. Just move on."

Corman felt like resisting. He didn't move. "What's wrong with me standing here?"

The doorman looked surprised by the question. He gave him a very small shove. "I mean it." He was an overweight, middle-aged man with wispy strands of gray peeking out from under his cap, but he looked hardened rather than weakened by his age, the sort of man who'd been pummeled, come back for more, then taken it again on the chin, the jaw, the eyes, until all the features had finally merged into a kind of doughy mass, slack and puffy, but still strong despite all that. Corman had met such people before, the type who knew exactly where the line was in them because they'd faced so many others who'd crossed it without a thought.

"I mean it," the man repeated.

"I was just watching the chapel across the street," Corman said innocently.

The doorman didn't feel like discussing it. "Look, pal, when you pay rent in this place, you can stand here till hell freezes over, but until then ..." He gave Corman another small shove.

Corman thought of Lucy, Lexie, and his picture in the paper, sprawled across the sidewalk, the doorman grinning above him. He could read the caption: News stringer roughed up by doorman. He stepped away from him and put up his hands. "Okay, okay," he said. "I'm going."

The doorman eased off slightly. "Good."

Corman nodded, strode out from under the awning and headed across the street to the chapel. He could feel the doorman staring at him all the way, watching for a quick move, the pistol that might come from nowhere and turn his big hard fists into paper cups.

Once across the street, Corman took a few close-ups of the chapel's stone facade. He focused on the small details, the carvings on the wooden doors and the swirling pastels of the stained glass windows. Then he took a few more shots of the entire exterior.

Inside, the chapel was modest, and as he stepped into its small dark foyer, he was struck by how slightly seedy it looked. There was a small square foyer, decked with slightly faded flowers, a brown wooden table with a few assorted vases and a signboard which listed the various rooms, along with the people who were in them. The memorial service for Sarah Rosen was scheduled for Room Four.

Corman glanced around, found the stairs and headed up them. There was a wooden lectern just outside the room. Someone had placed a leather-bound register on it. Corman searched his pockets for the little notebook which seemed to be a part of him now, the one in which he could write down the facts, then hand them over to Julian or Willie Scarelli. He quickly opened the register. The page was blank. He sank his notebook back into his jacket pocket and stepped quietly into the room.

Sarah Rosen's plain mahogany coffin rested in front of a short wooden altar. It was closed, and someone had laid two sprays of red roses on top of it. The man in the black raincoat sat alone in the front pew, his head erect, facing the coffin.

Corman took a seat in the back and waited for the ceremony to begin. Several minutes passed, then suddenly, as if on a signal, the man in the raincoat rose silently and began to make his way down the aisle.

Corman stood up and watched him approach. He could tell that Dr. Rosen's eyes had fastened on him, but it was too late to retreat, and so he simply stood in place as the old man made his way up the aisle.

Dr. Rosen's head was lifted high, chin up, his face strangely shadowed, as if stage makeup had been applied to darken the deep furrows of his brow. He stared intently at Corman as he approached, then stopped dead in front of him.

"Who are you?" Rosen asked.

His face was so near to Corman's that he could gather its details immediately, the white, carefully trimmed Vandyke, the gold-rimmed glasses that looked as if they'd been imported from another age, the dark, hooded eyes. In a modern version, it was the face of Lear, Creon, King David's face when he first glimpsed Absalom hanging by his hair.

"Who are you?" Rosen repeated, when Corman failed to answer him.

Corman lifted his shoulders nervously. "Nobody," he said.

"Nobody?" the old man said. One of the hoods lifted. "You don't have a name? I made it clear that this was strictly a closed memorial."

Corman glanced away, then said, "My name is Corman."

"Did you know my daughter?"

"No."

"Then what are you doing here?"

"I'm a photographer."

"A photographer? Why are you here? What was Sarah to you?"

Corman realized he couldn't exactly answer that question, but struggled to do it anyway. "It's just that . . . that I was there the night she . . ." He stopped.

Rosen's body stiffened. "You took pictures of her?"

"Yes."

"On the street?"

"It's my job," Corman said weakly.

Rosen looked at him hatefully for a moment, then suddenly his hand shot up and slapped Corman's face.

Corman remained before him, frozen, his face still hot and trembling from the blow.

Rosen lifted his hand again, then held it trembling in the air, its gray shadow resting like a veil over Corman's face.

"I'm sorry," Corman sputtered. "I didn't mean to . . ."

Rosen's eyes narrowed spitefully for an instant, then darted away. For a moment he stood entirely still. Then he bolted forward abruptly and fled the room.

Corman sank down in the wooden pew, felt himself give over to the inevitable, rose again, walked into the street and headed east, toward what he thought now the only opportunity he still had.

Chapter 24

THE CONCIERGE WAS SMARTLY DRESSED, AND HE DID everything but click his heels as Corman walked through the large glass doors.

"May I help you?" he asked.

"I'm here to see Harry Groton," Corman told him.

"And your name?"

"Corman."

The concierge began to finger the buttons of the console behind his desk. "That's 20–B, isn't it?" he asked.

"I don't know," Corman said, glancing back outside. The bare limbs of the trees weaved slowly as the rain and wind lashed them. They looked forlorn, forsaken, forest exiles walled in by the cityscape, their slender uplifted branches entangled in a net of rain.

"Mr. Groton?" the concierge said into the black receiver, "Mr. Corman to see you. Yes. Thank you." He looked at Corman. "You may go up: 20–B. Turn to your right when you step out of the elevator."

Groton's apartment was near the end of the corridor and Groton himself was already standing in the door, his body wobbling slightly as he offered Corman a quick wave.

"Didn't think you'd make it," he said. "Haven't had a guest in a long time. Forgive the mess."

"Don't worry," Corman said. "I'm used to mess."

Groton waved his hand groggily. "Ain't it the truth."

Corman pulled the camera bag from his shoulder and let it drop to the floor.

"Want a drink?" Groton asked.

"Do we have time?"

"Sure. What the fuck."

"Okay," Corman said. "Thanks."

"Sit down anywhere," Groton told him. His hands swept out from his sides in a gesture of resignation. "I'm a man of simple tastes."

Corman took a seat in a small wooden chair and let his eyes take in the room. Groton's sleeper-sofa was still out. It sagged at the center, and a large rumpled pile of bedding spilled over the right edge and gathered on the uncarpeted floor below. The curtains were frayed at their edges, and there were no photographs on the walls.

"Two sixteen a month," Groton said. "That's what I pay for this place." He shook his head. "Shit, they'll probably get close to fifteen hundred for it when I . . ." He stopped, catching himself. "When it's vacant."

Corman smiled. "At least."

Groton pulled two paper cups from a stack of them on a small table. "Scotch okay?"

"Yeah."

"What? Two fingers?"

"Yeah, that's good."

Groton smiled. "Can't get tight," he said, wagging his finger scoldingly. "Them's the rules. Can't get tight if you got a shoot."

He handed Corman a glass. "You look like shit," he said, then lifted his cup. "To shit."

Corman turned toward him. "How many have you had, Harry?"

Groton waved his hand. "Not enough." He walked uneasily over to a chair, slumped down in it and took another sip.

"When's the shoot?" Corman asked.

Groton started to answer, then looked as if he'd misplaced something, and said nothing.

"Did you write it down?"

Groton nodded. "Somewhere." He stared about blearily. "Where the fuck could it be?"

"What was it on, a piece of paper?"

"Yeah," Groton answered dully. "Some piece of paper, somewhere."

"It's at the Plaza," Corman reminded him. "That's what you said yesterday."

"That's right," Groton said, suddenly remembering. "The Plaza. Pomegranate, something like that. Some fruit name. At four-thirty."

Corman looked at his watch. "That's in fifteen minutes."

"Fifteen minutes," Groton said without concern. "Yeah, that's right. Fifteen minutes."

Corman glanced at the cup which tilted back and forth unsteadily in Groton's hand. He'd poured himself a good deal more than two fingers.

"You going to make it?" Corman asked.

Groton grinned childishly. "Nope," he said quietly. He shook his head. "Nope. Nope."

Corman shrugged. "Don't worry about it," he said. "I can handle it."

Groton looked at him softly. "Would you do that, Corman? Would you mind? I mean, to tell you the truth—" He thrust his hand out, and a wave of scotch washed over the front of his shirt. "Shit," he hissed angrily. "Shit." He began to slap at his shirt, sending small amber drops across the floor. "Shit. Shit."

Corman grabbed a handful of Kleenex from the box beside the bed, rushed over, bent down and began wiping the scotch from Groton's shirt.

"I'm entitled, right?" Groton asked brokenly. "Just one time?"

Corman nodded quickly. "Yeah, you're entitled. Don't worry about it." He could feel Groton's fingers toying with his hair. He drew them out and lowered the hand back into Groton's lap. "You're okay now," he said.

"Right, right," Groton said. He sat up slightly, his chest thrust out, chin held up. "Just fine," he said determinedly. "No problem."

There were no "fruit names" listed among the people who had rented ballrooms in the Plaza, but one of the families was named Pomeroy, and Corman thought it was a safe guess that that was the one Groton had meant. It was a wedding reception, and he managed to rush up the stairs to the designated room just as Stuart Clayton was glancing nervously at his watch for what Corman figured was probably the thousandth time.

"Where the hell is Groton?" Clayton asked as Corman mounted the last step.

"He came down with something," Corman told him. "He sent me instead."

"Sent you?"

"Yes."

"Why you? This is not a blood-and-guts shoot. No offense," Clayton said, "but I've never worked with you. And you can't just work with anybody on this kind of thing. This is serious business."

"I know how to handle it," Corman assured him.

Clayton eyed him suspiciously. "You do, huh? Well, let me ask you something. How many of these shoots have you done, anyway?"

"Ten, twenty," Corman said, lying through his teeth.

Clayton wasn't buying it. "Really? When? Where? Give me some details."

"In Boston," Corman replied, grasping for straws. "I worked in Boston before I came to New York."

Clayton still looked doubtful. "Where in Boston?" he demanded. "What rooms? What affairs? Jesus Christ, we're not talking about the Ramada Inn here. We're talking about the Plaza-fucking-Hotel."

Corman knew his bluff had been called and made a do-or-die grab for the job.

"Look," he said firmly. "Groton's sick. He sent me. If you've got a problem with that, fine. I understand. So, go get somebody else." He turned and started to leave.

"No, wait," Clayton said quickly. "Sorry. Don't take it personally. It's just that ..."

"Forget it," Corman said, cozying up again. If he was going to replace Groton permanently, he'd have to get along with Clayton, and he didn't want to ruin any chance of that on his first solo shoot. "Just relax," he said easily. "Believe me, I'll do a good job for you."

"Okay," Clayton said. "We'll forget all about this little dispute. We'll just go to work, okay?"

Corman nodded. "If you want anything special," he said, "just let me know."

Clayton smiled halfheartedly. "Good, thanks." He slapped his hands together softly. "Well, as they say, we're into the arena."

Corman forced out a small laugh, then followed Clayton into the ballroom, walking slowly behind him, making sure he kept the lead.

It was over in less than two hours. Corman stood in the corner, munching a small cracker while Clayton worked the room, methodically pumping the last Pomeroy hand just one more time.

"Well, that's it," Clayton said, as he walked over to Corman, snapped off a bit of what was left of the cracker and chewed it slowly. "What'd you think?"

"It was okay," Corman said.

One of Clayton's light green eyes seemed to reach out toward him like a small, searching probe. "But did you enjoy it?"

"Yeah," Corman said lightly. "It was fun."

Clayton laughed. "You think so?" He laughed again. "Well, anyway, you did a good job. Really. Not bad at all. Maybe we could team up again sometime."

Corman nodded.

"Would you like that?" Clayton asked.

Corman offered him a quick smile. "Yeah, sure. Why not?"

Clayton looked pleased. "All right," he said. "But if we're going to work together from time to time, I want to make a few things clear." He turned and began to stroll out of the room, waving Corman up beside him. "You know what they call this beat?" he asked.

Corman shook his head.

"The snoot patrol," Clayton told him. "That's what they call it, all the so-called 'real' reporters." He stopped, studying Corman's eyes. "Real reporters," he scoffed. "What bullshit. The editorial writers, the critics, the political reporters with their noses stuck two feet up some Congressman's ass." He laughed. "And they have the balls to turn up their noses at this beat?" The laugh thinned into a derisive chuckle, then trailed off entirely. "They're lost, Corman. Take it from me, they're completely lost." He continued on, sailing gracefully over the littered carpet. "Because what they don't understand is that in this city, what the rich do is the only real news there is." He looked at Corman earnestly. "I'm talking about *human news*. I'm talking about the human fucking spirit."

They moved out of the room, down the stairs. At the side of the Palm Court, Clayton stopped again, his eyes lingering on the wide dining room. The band was playing softly, the piano in the lead, the accompaniment no more than a swaying presence in the background. "The people in editorial, international, all those people," he said, "they think they've got the inside track on how things work, on what people are really like." He shook his head. "But I'm a student of psychology just as much as they are, and let me tell you something, if you want to know what people are like, you have to study the ones who have everything. You don't study the hustlers, the scroungers, the ones who have nothing. They're lost in bullshit. You can't learn anything from them."

Corman nodded.

"But if you study the rich," Clayton went on, "I mean study them very closely, if you do that, you can really find out what people need, what people miss." He looked at Corman and pointed to his chest. "I'm talking about in here. You know what I mean?"

"I think so."

Clayton began walking again, strolling quietly among the potted palms, a lean white skiff cruising over tranquil waters. "That's what makes this beat worthwhile," he added in conclusion. "The insight."

Clayton picked up his pace suddenly. Corman trailed after him, just a single step behind, his eyes following the smooth gait and uplifted shoulders, the high, straight back. He wondered where Clayton had gotten all that style, whether he'd been born with it, or just soaked it in over time, like a tan.

Once outside, Clayton stopped at the bottom of the stairs. Several limousines were lined up in front of the hotel. One by one they came forward and people got out of them, then either rushed under the great awning or ducked beneath the doormen's large black umbrellas.

"Very elegant," Clayton said musingly as he watched. "The way they keep out of the rain. And very, very serious." He glanced toward

Corman. "You want to see something different?" he asked, as if it had just occurred to him.

"Different?"

"I always go to a certain place after one of these assignments," Clayton told him. "I usually go by myself. But I was thinking that you might want to come along."

Corman thought of Lucy, of keeping her, of giving Lexie some bit of encouraging news about his work, of how important Clayton had suddenly become to all of that. "Yeah, okay," he said.

"Good," Clayton said happily. "Follow me."

They walked east to Lexington Avenue, then north into the Sixties, finally stopping at a noisy bar, crowded with people who were gathered in tight circles around tiny marble tables.

"A lot of the 'real' reporters hang out in this place," Clayton said after the two of them had found a table. "This is their real beat, Corman. Not the 'corridors of power' they're always talking. No way. This is their real beat. You know why? Because it determines the way they see things, the way they report things. It determines what they are." He looked at Corman piercingly. "You understand what I'm saying?"

"I think so."

"Good," Clayton said. He ordered a fancy brandy for both of them, sniffed it when it came, then lifted his glass toward Corman. "Fuck 'em all," he said with a smile.

Corman smiled back, drank, rolled his glass a little nervously between his hands and smiled again.

Clayton watched him for a moment, then nodded toward a man in a tan jacket who stood at the end of the bar. "He's probably carrying three thousand dollars' worth of cocaine in his left coat pocket." He smiled. "Not exactly a Colombian with a buzz-saw, is he?"

"No."

"Customers look different, too," Clayton added.

Corman nodded.

"But they're customers, all right," Clayton said. "Do you know why? Because they need an up, a thrill." He gave Corman a long, penetrating glance. "But why they need it, that's a separate question."

Corman felt obligated to bite the hook. "Why do they need it?"

"Because the deepest thing any of them have ever experienced is a dose of aggravation," Clayton answered matter-of-factly.

Corman laughed.

"I'm serious," Clayton insisted. "Listen, aggravation is the only really safe form of excitement left on the Upper East Side."

Corman glanced about. Everywhere around him, people were laughing, talking, showing off their clothes. They looked no different than most people of means, and long ago Corman had come up with the simple nightmare truth that if a camera followed anyone around for twenty-four hours, that person would look ridiculous, no matter who he was. Pope. General. Average guy. All in the same boat. Ridiculous because no one ever fully appreciated how small he was. Only the camera appreciated that.

Clayton leaned over toward him. "Take it from someone who knows, Corman, these are the only really worthless people in the world. They don't have power like the rich. They don't run things. And they don't have any purpose, like the working people do. They don't make anything. Their whole lives, not so much as a goddamn doorknob." He laughed. "You know what they produce, Corman? Self-esteem. It's the basic goal of their whole productive process."

Corman nodded silently.

Clayton turned away from him, watched the bar for a moment, then returned to him. "Were you in the war?"

"No."

"Too young for it?" Clayton asked.

"I'm thirty-five."

"Yeah," Clayton said. "You just missed it." He shook his head. "I did two tours as a combat reporter. What I saw every day, you can't even imagine. Not in your worst nightmare. A real shit-storm." He looked at the crowd and laughed under his breath. "Sometimes, I feel like calling down some NVA fire on a place like this. Just a little strafing run down Third Avenue on a Saturday night, give these people a taste of how little they're made of."

Corman allowed himself a quick, nervous little laugh.

Clayton's eyes shot over to him. "Don't suck up to me," he snapped.

"Was I doing that?"

"You've been doing it all afternoon."

Corman shook his head wearily. "Christ."

Clayton smiled. "That's what we all hate, right?" he said. "How much we have to swallow, just to get by."

Corman said nothing.

Clayton eyed him intently. "What do you want from me?"

"I was hoping to do a good job."

"Why?" Clayton said. "And hey, don't tell me it's because you love your goddamn craft."

Corman looked at him squarely. "But I do."

"Maybe the streets," Clayton said. "But wedding receptions? Bullshit. It's something else. What?"

"I need a job."

"Groton's job?"

"Yes."

"What was wrong with Groton?" Clayton asked bluntly. "Is he finally wearing down?"

Corman decided not to lie. "He's dying."

Clayton didn't seem to care one way or the other. He glanced about restlessly, his eyes shooting from one knot of people to the next. "That's the real tragedy," he said. "To think you know so fucking much, when you know absolutely nothing." He looked back at Corman. "So, you're tired of free-lancing?"

"I'm having a few problems," Corman said.

"Like what?"

"Money."

Clayton looked surprised. "Money? There's just yourself, right?"

"I have a daughter."

Clayton nodded. "Oh. Well, that puts a different spin on it."

"Yeah."

"With a kid, you need something steady."

"It would help."

They sat silently together for a few more minutes, then paid the check and walked out. The rain had stopped. Clayton kept his umbrella tightly beneath his arm as the two of them walked west, along the almost deserted crosstown streets.

"I'll get a cab here," Clayton said when they reached Fifth Avenue. "You need a lift?"

"I think I'll walk," Corman said.

Clayton stepped off the curb and lifted his arm as a wave of headlights rushed toward him from up the avenue. A taxi swerved out of the traffic, stopped and waited as Clayton got in. "Say hi to your kid," he said quickly as he ducked inside.

Chapter 25

IT HAD BEGUN TO RAIN AGAIN BY THE TIME CORMAN reached Seventh Avenue, only harder this time, with gusts of wind driving the thick gray drops against the lighted windows. At first, he tried to go on despite it, then gave up and ducked under the doorway of a small coffee shop to wait it out.

He'd expected it to trail off almost immediately, but for several minutes the rain continued to fall in long wet sheets. Across the street, he could see another small restaurant. It had a French name and a dark-blue awning. From time to time people moved in and out of it, huddled briefly under the awning, then either signaled for a cab or rushed down the street, shoulders hunched beneath their umbrellas.

Corman took out his camera, stepped back into the shadows slightly and began taking pictures. He was still taking them when a large, well-dressed man came out, a woman holding tightly to his arm. The man was laughing, his face was so bright and youthful that for an instant, Corman didn't realize it was Edgar. When he did, he shrank back quickly, put away his camera and pulled his hat down over his face.

Edgar gave the woman a long, lingering kiss, then stepped out from under the awning and hailed a cab. The woman rushed over to it when it stopped, kissed Edgar again and got inside. Her hand shot out the window and waved back at him as the cab lurched forward and pulled away.

For a few seconds, Edgar lingered on the sidewalk, smiling sweetly as he watched the cab move away from him. Then he turned back toward Seventh Avenue, his eyes sweeping the opposite street until they stopped, hung like two frozen circles in the air.

Corman nodded but did not move toward him.

Edgar stood stiffly, his arms at his sides, the rain pelting him mercilessly. He seemed unable to move, as if his indiscretion had suddenly encased him solidly within a tomb of ice. For a few more seconds he stared into Corman's face with a calculating intensity, then walked quickly across the street and joined him in the cramped doorway.

"No bullshit story, David," he said determinedly. "You won't get anything like that from me."

Corman said nothing.

"I don't know what shook me up there for a minute," Edgar added. "I mean, it's an old story, right?"

Corman waved his hand. "Forget it, Edgar."

Edgar shook his head. "No, I don't want to do that," he said. "I don't want to forget it." He drew in a long, slow breath. "I'm tired of keeping everything to myself. It can kill you, doing that." He paused a moment, as if to gather the whole story together in his mind, then went on. "I've known her for five years. It's not just some little trinket on the side. It's better than that."

"Edgar ... "

He put up his hand. "Love makes it better, that's what I'm telling you." He seemed embarrassed by his own statement. "I'm no philosopher, not like Victor, with big ideas to justify every fucking thing he does. I don't know if love makes it okay. I'm not saying that. But I know it makes it better."

"You don't have to ... "

"I know, I know," Edgar said. "Believe me, I know. But to tell you the truth, I want to talk about this." He smiled. "I'm glad you're here. I really am." He took Corman's arm and eased him toward the door of the coffee shop. "Come on, let me buy you a cup of coffee."

They took a small table in the back and ordered two coffees. Edgar glanced at the bowl of pickled green tomatoes, the place setting on its white paper napkin, the speckled Formica surface of the table itself while he searched for the words. Finally, he seemed to find them. "She's a little chunky," he said happily. "I guess you could tell that."

Corman nodded.

Edgar laughed. "When it hits her, her whole body trembles, and there's this long thing that sweeps over her. I don't know what you'd call it. A peace. You know what I mean? A calm."

His eyes were very bright, cheerful, childishly amazed. "And she starts to laugh, David, right out loud. It just comes over her, this uncontrollable laugh." He shook his head. "Jesus Christ, it brings tears to my eyes."

Corman pulled out his cigarettes and offered one to Edgar.

Edgar hardly seemed to notice. "You know what she makes me feel?" he asked emphatically. "She makes me feel like I'm doing something good, comforting somebody, making her life better." He lifted his hands upward. "How often do you get to do that in life? I mean, do it in a way that you see it right in front of you? How often does that happen?"

Corman didn't answer, just let him talk.

Edgar stared him straight in the eye. "I can't be with her on Christmas, you know? But, David, about once every two weeks or so with her, I'm goddamn Santa Claus."

Corman smiled and lit his cigarette.

Edgar studied Corman's face. "I hope you're not laughing at me," he said.

"I'm not."

"Good," Edgar said, a little doubtfully. "Because you're not saying much."

"Just listening," Corman said.

The coffees came. Each of them took a quick sip and returned the cups to the table.

"Her name's Patty," Edgar said. "Patty Lister. She lives down in Tribeca. A little studio all done up in this sort of Victorian style, doilies everywhere, little framed pictures."

Corman nodded again. He could see the place just as Edgar described it, a room out of time, from a lost age.

Edgar grabbed him by the wrists. "You know what it is, David?" he said. "This thing with Patty? I'll tell you what it is. It's fucking beautiful." He laughed. "It's fucking gorgeous. The sex? Let's face it, strictly double-vanilla. But, Christ, it makes my heart sing."

Corman tugged gently at his hands, but Edgar refused to release them. Instead, he tightened his grip. "Remember when we were kids? You know, before Dad made it in the ad game?"

"Yes."

"We had some pretty lean times," Edgar went on. "Chipped plates. That's what I remember. All the time at dinner, these fucking chipped plates. You remember them?"

"I guess."

"Well, I remember them very well," Edgar said. "And when I was about fifteen, I said to myself, 'When I get out of this goddamn place, I'm going to make sure I never have to eat off a chipped plate again.'" He sat back slightly, his eyes fixed rigidly on Corman. "And that's what I've done, what I've achieved. My wife doesn't have to eat off chipped plates. I don't either. And Giselle? Christ, she's never even seen one." He stared at Corman hungrily. "That's something, isn't it?"

"It's something," Corman admitted quietly. "Yeah, it's something, Edgar."

"But there're other things," Edgar added quickly. "Things you forget." He watched Corman silently for a moment, as if trying to find something more to say. Finally, he gave up, released Corman's wrists and sat back in his chair. "So, as the saying goes, 'What's new with you?'"

"Nothing much."

"Anything new on the money front?"

"Not yet."

Edgar's face turned grim. "You need something to break, what with Lexie on the prowl."

Corman nodded.

"I'm supposed to call her tomorrow, set everything up. The meeting, I mean."

"If you could delay it a little . . ."

"I don't think so," Edgar said. "She's not in the mood."

"No, I guess not."

Edgar looked at Corman very intently. "David, I hope you know, it's not like you're alone in the world."

"I won't take money, if that's what you mean."

"Call it a loan," Edgar said. "For Lucy. A loan to her. She'll pay me when she gets to be a rocket scientist."

Corman shook his head. "Jeffrey offered. I said no to him, too."

"Jeffrey?" Edgar said unbelievingly. "Offered what?"

"Lots of things. Money."

"Money?"

"To pay for a different apartment," Corman told him. "A school for Lucy. Stuff like that."

"He offered to pay? Jeffrey? Himself?"

"Yeah."

"Jesus," Edgar groaned. "Lexie must be burning the bed." He looked back at Corman awkwardly. "I mean . . . bad choice of words."

"No, you're right," Corman said. "She probably is. She knows how."

Edgar thought a moment, his eyes on the coffee cup. "Look, David, you have to face facts," he said when he looked up again. "When you have your meeting with Lexie, you're going to have to . . . "

"I'm working on something," Corman said quickly.

"But it's not coming through," Edgar said. "Something needs to come through."

"It will," Corman told him. "I hope."

Edgar shook his head determinedly, wagged his finger. "Not hope. That's your first mistake. Fuck hope. Hope and two bucks, that's what bets the Lotto. We're talking about keeping Lucy."

"I'm doing the best I can."

"Well, you have to do better," Edgar said. "What about that other thing, that permanent thing you were talking about?"

"It's shooting society."

"So?"

"I don't know, Edgar."

"What? You don't know what?"

Corman looked at him pointedly.

"A compromise?" Edgar asked. "Is that what you mean? That it's a compromise? If that's what you mean, say it."

"It's a compromise."

Edgar glared at him fiercely. "It's a fucking living," he cried. "That's what it is."

"That much, yes."

"As if it's shit. What kind of attitude is that?"

"It's my attitude."

"It's a living, for Christ's sake," Edgar said loudly. "Compromise? Let me tell you something. If you look at things a certain way, everything's a compromise. Food's a compromise. A roof over your head. Shirt, shoes. Everything."

"Some are worse than others."

Edgar shook his head. "No. That's where you're wrong. They're all the same."

"And that's an argument to make one?"

"You're goddamn right it is," Edgar bawled. "Absolutely."

"Come on, Edgar."

"I mean it," Edgar said. "Christ, David. Don't be a kid. You can't afford it."

Corman leaned toward him and stared at him intently. "Why do you want me to keep Lucy?" He paused a moment, unsure. "Or do you?"

"I do."

"Why? Is it just because I want to, and you're my brother, lawyer, whatever?"

"No."

"Then why?"

"You're her father."

"Lexie's her mother."

"Lexie's a space cadet."

"No, she's not," Corman said. "And you know it."

"Jeffrey's a twit."

"That's not true either," Corman said. "But I'm not talking about them. I'm talking about me. Why should Lucy stay with me? Why would she be better off?"

Edgar shook his head, as if defeated. "I can't answer that, David. I really can't. Maybe you were right the first time. Maybe it's because you're my brother. I love you. When you love somebody, you want them to have what they want. You want Lucy. So, there. I want you to have Lucy. Maybe it's just that simple."

Corman slumped back into his seat. "That's not good enough, Edgar. Not for me. Not for Lucy."

"Well, what are you looking for?" Edgar asked. "A compliment? You want me to say what a great father you are?"

"No."

"Good," Edgar said bluntly. "Because there are problems." He looked at Corman fervently. "We're talking about very basic things here, David. Support. How basic can you get?"

"It always comes down to that."

"Out of the dreamworld, yes, that's what it comes down to," Edgar said. "Support. Protection. How well you can provide these things." He leaned toward him. "Listen, I see Patty, right? Okay, maybe to some people that's wrong. But let me ask you a question. Does it take anything out of Giselle's mouth? Does it mean the rain comes through the roof?" He shook his head. "No. So really, when it comes down to it, who gives a shit? It's something anybody can understand. Nobody's hungry. Nobody's out in the . . . the . . ." He glanced toward the window. "Nobody's out in the fucking rain." He shrugged. "Out of the dreamworld, that's the way it is."

Corman remained silent for a moment, staring into Edgar's exasperated face, then glanced away from him, toward the front of the restaurant. The rain had slackened. "I'd better go," he said. "Before it starts up again."

Edgar nodded wearily. "I wish I could have been more help."

"Don't worry about it."

"It's you I worry about," Edgar said.

"I'll find a way," Corman assured him.

Edgar pulled himself to his feet. "As always," he said. "Whatever I can do, I'll do."

Corman offered him a consoling smile. "I know."

They walked outside and stood for a moment in the doorway.

"At least let me give you a ride home," Edgar said after a moment.

"All right, thanks."

The ride was very short, and at the end of it Edgar suddenly draped his arm around Corman's shoulders. "Thanks for listening to my bullshit, anyway," he said. "I mean, about Patty."

Corman nodded.

Edgar's face softened suddenly. "I really feel like I have a brother, someone at my side, you know? I hope you can feel that way, too."

Corman smiled thinly then realized that he had never in his life felt more entirely alone. "Absolutely," he said.

As he stepped off the elevator, Corman noticed Mr. Ingersoll standing at his door, quietly reading a piece of paper someone had taped to it.

"Oh, sorry," Ingersoll said quickly, when he caught Corman in his eye. "I wasn't meaning to . . ."

"What is it?"

"Looks like an eviction notice," Ingersoll said. "From Trang. The asshole."

Corman began to read the notice.

"Slope-headed bastard," Ingersoll hissed. "Ever notice his teeth? Like they've been filed down or something." He shook his head. "Slope-headed bastard. Some right he's got. How long's he in this country? Two years? Three? Five at the most? What right's he got to . . ."

"It says I have ten days," Corman said.

Ingersoll looked at him sadly. "To show cause, right? To show cause why they shouldn't kick you out?"

"Yeah."

Ingersoll stared at the notice sourly. "Back when, in the old days, the Depression, they used to try to kick people out, put their furniture on the streets. But it wasn't that easy. They had hell to pay then. You took your life in your hands, you fucked with people's homes."

"Times have changed," Corman said. He pulled the notice from the door and waved it in the air. "Do you have any idea when they put this up?"

"I saw the little slope-headed bastard prowling around," Ingersoll said. "Maybe around eight, something like that."

"Around eight," Corman repeated to himself, hoping Lucy hadn't seen it.

"Some right, he's got," Ingersoll said irritably. "Did he build the bridges, that little gook? The buildings? The goddamn skyscrapers? Did he build them?" He waved his hand. "He was wading through a rice paddy when we built this city." His lips curled downward bitterly. "New York, New York," he sang coldly. "What a wonderful town."

Lucy and Victor were sitting in front of the television, polishing off a bowl of popcorn, when Corman walked in.

"Uncle Victor said I could have butter," Lucy told him.

"Gives it flavor," Victor said. He looked at Corman pointedly, all but plastered the eviction notice to his face. "I hope everything is all right," he said.

"Everything's fine," Corman said crisply. He could feel the paper beneath his arm, hanging there, a strange crinkly growth. He quickly stepped over behind the sofa and touched Lucy's hair. "What are you watching?"

"Some movie about a stolen bird," Lucy said. She looked over at him. "We had Japanese food."

Victor laughed. "She's a real sushi expert now."

"Then we saw a show," Lucy said.

"Which one?" Corman asked.

"*Cats.* It was pretty good. But there wasn't much of a story."

Victor grinned happily. "Lively, though." His eyes swept back toward the television.

Corman glanced at the screen. It was a colorized version of *The Maltese Falcon.* Humphrey Bogart was talking out of the side of his mouth to a bemused and unflappable Sydney Greenstreet. Both of them looked as if their faces were covered with pink icing.

"It's about your bedtime, isn't it?" Corman said to Lucy.

"It's almost over," Lucy protested. "Can I just see the end?"

"Okay," Corman said. He looked at Victor and forced a smile. "You want to stay and see the end, too?"

"Sure, why not?" Victor said. He put his arm around Lucy's shoulder and squeezed. "Should I see the end of it with you?"

"If you want to," Lucy said with a shrug, her eyes fixed on the screen again.

"Maybe I will, too," Corman said wearily. He pulled a chair over from the dining table, sat down, and watched the movie as if he were actually interested in it. For a time, he was able to follow the action, but his mind began to drift, and soon everything seemed strangely funny, Trang's teeth, Edgar's affair, the endlessly falling rain, absolutely everything, as if it were all one big joke that thundered through space, raising the rooftops. Then suddenly, he thought of Sarah Rosen, saw her face amid the throng, staring vacantly and chewing her lip as the punchline finally came home.

Chapter 26

HE WOKE UP SWEATING, DAMP SHEETS KNOTTED AROUND his waist, his hands cold, clammy and trembling slightly, as if he had spent the night cold turkey. He stood up and walked to the bathroom, avoiding his own face in the mirror as he washed himself and brushed his teeth.

When he'd finished, he awakened Lucy but hardly spoke to her as she ate her breakfast at the small folding card table that served as the apartment's dining room.

On the street, he maintained the same silence, marching her to school at a rapid pace, an irritable guard escorting a prisoner.

She gave him a quick kiss at the school gate, then hurried away.

It was still early, so he walked to Eighth Avenue, ordered a coffee at a small diner there, lit a cigarette and reconsidered what Scarelli had told him several days before: his only hope was a mystery.

It was raining steadily again when he finally finished the last of his coffee and walked outside. The traffic on the avenue was barely moving, the cars inching forward heavily, as if continually blown back by the gusting winds. To get out of it, he retreated under a wildly flapping canopy and waited for the squall to pass, his eyes sweeping up the street while he calculated what he could save, along with what, in order to do that, he would have to lose. Everything passed through his mind, some things quickly, others suspended for a great while, Lucy more than any other, but after her, Sarah Rosen and the mystery. He saw her suddenly from a different angle, one that hadn't been captured in any of his photographs, and in which it was hard for him to figure out his own exact position. It was as if he were lying near her on the wet pavement, her face lifted toward him, poised on its shattered chin. The dead eyes stared directly into his, the torn hand growing large in the foreground as it reached across the slick paving stones to where his own eyes seemed to look back at her—staring, he realized with a sudden chill, from behind the rain-streaked, sightless pupils of the doll.

It was nearly ten o'clock when he got off the Number 1 at the 116th Street stop, then pressed through the crowds of students who were hurrying down Columbia Walk toward their classes. He stopped at the entrance to Low Library without really knowing why, then glanced down the stairs and across the esplanade that swept toward Butler Library. The rain had left small puddles in the brown grass, and as his eyes moved from one to another in that quick, darting motion Lucy had noticed and called "connecting the dots," he thought of the old days again, when he and Julian had vied for Lexie like two contending swains. They seemed like pages from a book he'd liked once, but no more, had no desire to read again.

He turned quickly, walked inside, then down a corridor to a room marked RECORDS. "I'm trying to get a little information," he said to the woman he found behind a large wooden counter.

She looked up from a stack of computer sheets. She wore glasses with pink tinted lenses, a style he'd even noticed on a few shooters in recent weeks.

"About a former student," he added. "She graduated in 1988."

"What do you need to know?"

"Her major. Maybe get a look at her transcript. Anything might help."

"Some things require written requests," the woman told him.

"Just give me the stuff that doesn't."

The woman snapped the sharpened pencil from her ear. "What's the name?"

"Rosen. Sarah Judith Rosen."

The woman wrote it down, disappeared into another room, and reappeared with a sheet of yellow legal-sized paper.

"That's all I can give without some other kind of authorization," she said. "It's not very much."

Corman took the paper. "Thanks," he said as he began to read it.

It told him even less than he'd expected, certainly not enough to put a charge in Willie Scarelli. Rosen had graduated in 1988, as he already knew. Aside from that, the paper gave him only one additional fact. She'd majored in English Literature.

Corman looked up once he'd finished. "One more thing," he said. "Do you know where I might find a professor in the Philosophy Department. His name is Peter Oppenheim."

She reached for a directory, flipped through the pages and glanced back up at him. "Jay Hall, 308," she said.

Oppenheim was a short, somewhat stocky man, balding as he neared forty, and he looked at Corman as if he were a workman who'd been summoned to repair something in the office, recaulk the windows, shore up the sagging floor.

"Yes?" he said when he glimpsed Corman standing at the door.

"I'm looking for Professor Oppenheim."

"I'm Professor Oppenheim."

Corman took a short, tentative step into the office and adopted the diffident, somewhat formal tone he remembered from graduate school. "I was wondering if I could have a word with you."

"About what?"

"Sarah Rosen."

Oppenheim's face betrayed nothing. "Are you with the police?"

"No," Corman answered immediately, then realized how odd the question was. "Have you talked to them?"

"No," Oppenheim said. "But I know what happened to Sarah, and I thought there might be questions about her death."

"From the police?"

"The authorities," Oppenheim said. "Whomever they might be." He turned from his desk, as if to get a better view of Corman's face. "Who are you?"

"My name's Corman. I'm a photographer."

"What did you have to do with Sarah?"

"I was there after she ... I'm a freelance ... I took some pictures."

"Pictures?"

"I didn't sell them," Corman said. He took another small step into the office, noting the photograph of Einstein above Oppenheim's desk. He remembered the ones he'd tacked to the wall of his own office—

Shakespeare, Dante, other leading lights—and wondered whose face he'd hang now if he still had an office of his own. Lazar, perhaps. Lucy, without doubt.

"Would you mind talking about her?" he asked tentatively.

Oppenheim considered it a moment. "Have you talked to her father?"

"No."

"He knows her best," Oppenheim said a little stiffly.

"I plan to see him when I can," Corman said casually, as if it were just a matter of making an appointment. "But for now, I'd like to . . ."

"Strange as it may seem," Oppenheim said curtly, "I barely knew her." He shrugged. "We were only married a few months. It was hardly a marriage at all." He looked at Corman quizzically. "Has she been buried yet?"

"Her father didn't tell you?"

Oppenheim shook his head, smiled bitterly. "Her father never told me anything."

"There was a service yesterday," Corman said. "On the East Side."

Oppenheim nodded. "Did anyone show up?"

"Dr. Rosen," Corman said then added dryly, "Me."

"That's what I would have expected," Oppenheim said. "Knowing Dr. Rosen." He indicated the chair in front of his desk. "Well, sit down," he said. "I suppose I can give you a few minutes."

Corman took his seat, then listened as Oppenheim began immediately, without waiting for a question.

"Sarah and I didn't really choose each other," he said. "That was Dr. Rosen's choice. I didn't realize that at the time. I'm not sure Sarah did, either. But, in any event, he introduced us when Sarah was a junior here at Columbia. He wanted her married before graduation. He told me as much several weeks later, when Sarah and I became engaged."

"Told you when to marry her?" Corman asked.

"Well, let's just say he made his preference quite clear," Oppenheim said. "And I went along with it. So did Sarah." He looked at Corman knowingly. "I hadn't had a lot of experience, if you know what I mean. The marriage sounded good to me. Sarah was rather mysterious, difficult to know. Perhaps I found that somewhat alluring." He sighed softly. "And she was young, and you know how it is, sometimes a man my age ... he ..."

"How long were you married?"

"Only a few months," Oppenheim said. "After we lost the baby, she fell apart."

"She lost a baby?" Corman asked.

"Well, not exactly lost," Oppenheim said tensely. "Aborted."

"When was that?"

"About the middle of her senior year."

"What happened?"

"She was pregnant," Oppenheim said, "and her doctor advised her that there was some risk involved, and after that, she decided that she'd rather not take that risk."

"He advised an abortion?"

"A therapeutic abortion, yes," Oppenheim said. "It was for her own safety. You can ask the doctor, if you like. Dr. Walter Owen, East Seventy-Sixth Street."

"What happened after the abortion?" Corman asked. "You said she fell apart."

"It was her last semester," Oppenheim replied. "She had only a few courses to complete the degree, but I wasn't sure she was going to make it. It was as if pieces of her mind were falling away. I'd come home and find her by the window, always by the window, looking out, like a cat." He shrugged. "I tried to talk to her, but she didn't really seem to be there." He shook his head. "I knew she was in trouble, but I didn't know how bad it was until Dr. Maitland called."

"Maitland?" Corman asked. "From the English Department?"

"That's right," Oppenheim said. "You know him?"

Corman nodded.

"Well, Sarah had written a final examination for him," Oppenheim said, "and he couldn't make heads or tails of it. He said it was very strange, and that he didn't know what to do about it."

"About what?"

"About Sarah's grade, her graduation. He didn't want to stand in her way, cause her more strain. We met, all of us, Maitland, Dr. Rosen and myself. It was all very cordial. In the end Maitland agreed to accept the paper, and that was the end of it."

"And so she graduated?"

"Yes," Oppenheim said. "She was quite mad by then. You could tell that by what she'd written on the examination." He looked at Corman pointedly. "Not of this world, I'll tell you that, not of this world at all."

"Do you have it?"

"No," Oppenheim said. "Perhaps Dr. Maitland does. Would you like for me to check?"

Corman shook his head. "No, that's all right," he said. "I'll do it myself."

During the next few minutes Oppenheim moved on through his brief experience with Sarah Rosen, her deterioration and disappearance, and Dr. Rosen's odd refusal to look for her, while Corman listened feverishly, prowling through Oppenheim's words like a cat through the night, scratching for the mystery he could drop on Scarelli's table like a dead mouse from a vulture's beak.

When he rose to leave, Oppenheim shook his hand and looked at him worriedly. "Are you all right?" he asked.

Corman drew his hand away, realizing that he'd begun to sweat again, as if boiling slowly just beneath the skin.

"Perhaps you're coming down with something," Oppenheim added.

Corman shook his head then darted away, glancing back down the corridor furtively, as if Oppenheim had discovered his nasty little secret, caught him sneaking out of some house of ill repute.

Chapter 27

CORMAN EASED HIMSELF DOWN IN THE CHAIR OPPOSITE
Julian's desk and waited while Julian finished up a phone call with one
of his writers.

"At the most four cities," Julian said. "New York, of course. Boston,
Washington. That's ... yes ... yes. No, nothing on the West Coast. It's
between Baltimore and Philly. We may sneak Atlanta in, but nothing
on the West Coast." He listened for a moment, glancing at Corman. "I
understand, Bryan. Yes. I understand." A short, mocking laugh broke
from him. "Promises were made? Really, Bryan, isn't that from *Death of
a Salesman*? Are you playing Willy Loman now?" He looked at Corman
and winked. "What? What? Bryan. Bryan, listen. Bryan, when was the
last time you couldn't have Chateaubriand whenever you wanted it? In
all honesty, Bryan, when was the last time?" He waited for an answer,
then drew the phone from his ear, looked at it unbelievingly for a
moment, then shifted his eyes over to Corman. "He hung up."

Corman said nothing.

Julian shook his head and returned the phone to its cradle.
"Everybody feels badly used," he said. "That's the poison in the air." He
glanced at the phone again, then returned to Corman. "Well, I hope
you're in better spirits than he was this morning."

Corman handed Julian a plain manila envelope. "Some pictures," he said.

"Great." Julian took the pictures out and began to flip through
them. He looked up when he'd finished. "What about text? What have
you found out about the woman?"

"She graduated from Columbia in 1988," Corman told him. "She
was an English major. Her father is Samuel Rosen, and she evidently
had an abor—"

Julian's eyes brightened. "Did you say Samuel Rosen? Dr. Samuel Rosen? The scholar?"

"Yes."

Julian nodded thoughtfully. "Good. Very good. What happened? I mean, she certainly strayed a bit far from the old professor's nest, didn't she?"

"Yes, she did."

"Any idea why?"

Corman shook his head. "Not yet, but I ..."

"Maybe he laid the academic pressure on a little thick," Julian suggested. He smiled excitedly. "That could be it, Corman, some kind of 'Rappaccini's Daughter' scenario on the Upper East Side." He seemed hardly able to keep from licking his lips. "Gothic. Very Gothic."

"Maybe," Corman said. "I don't know."

Julian looked slightly irritated. "Well, that's what we have to find out, David." He sounded as if he were talking to a small child, explaining the facts of life for the tenth time. "A story to go with the pictures."

Corman reached for an answer, something that would satisfy him briefly. "I talked to Willie Scarelli," he said.

"Good," Julian said brightly, as if pleased that Corman was finally getting a handle on how things were really done. "Is he willing to work on the text?"

"He's thinking about it."

"He's a good choice for this sort of thing," Julian said. "He's got a good, steady track record. Nothing made of gold, but steady. With a man like that, lightning could strike at any time."

Corman nodded.

"The only thing," Julian said. "It might complicate things financially."

Corman looked at him quizzically.

"Well, now we've got two people involved," Julian explained. "Maybe three."

"Three?"

"Scarelli's agent," Julian said. "I'm sure he has one. Which means there'll either be more money expected of us, or the three of you will have to split whatever we offer." He smiled. "Agents these days take about fifteen percent." He looked at Corman knowingly. "I don't suppose you'd thought of that."

"Not really."

Julian returned the pictures to the envelope. "Well, that's the sort of thing we'll deal with when the time comes." He handed the pictures back to Corman.

"You don't want to keep them?" Corman asked.

Julian shook his head. "No, not now. I know enough to start the wheels turning."

Corman tucked the envelope into his camera bag, then drew the bag over his shoulder.

"The Rosen connection," Julian said. "That's the real ore in this book. Check that out carefully." His eyes squeezed together intently. "I have a feeling that if you got deep enough into that household, you might really hit the jackpot." He gathered up a stack of papers and thrust them under his arm. "That's the real task, to get deep."

Corman looked at him, baffled. "How do I do that?"

Julian stood up quickly and glanced at his watch. "Sorry to rush you, David, but I have a meeting."

"How do I do that?" Corman repeated.

"Ask Scarelli," Julian said hastily as he darted out the door. "He knows the game very well."

Scarelli rolled the coffee cup between his two open hands. "So he said to ask me, huh?"

Corman nodded. "That's right."

"And I could tell you how to get deep, that's what he said?"

"Yes."

"Get deep," Scarelli said with a short laugh. "What bullshit." He sat back and smiled knowingly. "He wants the smut, that's what, the ground-in dirt. He's changed the angle on you, Corman."

"What do you mean?"

"He's not after the girl anymore," Scarelli said. "It's the old man he wants turning on the spit. That's where he smells the blood. Don't you get it?"

"Not exactly."

Scarelli stuck the cigar back into his mouth and chewed the tip, sending a swirl of gray ash over the table. "It's an exposé, a hatchet job, on the old prof. Take it from me, that's what your buddy has in mind, a freak-piece on the old man, Frankenstein with an Ivy League literary angle."

"So he's not interested in Sarah?"

"Maybe at first he was," Scarelli said. "But not anymore." He leaned forward, staring at Corman pointedly. "The woman's just the bait now. It's the old man they want to see dangling from the line. They need a villain for the piece. Some poor bastard they can wag their goddamn fingers at, say, 'Hey, you. Fuckhead. You did it!'" He shrugged. "I've seen it a thousand times." He laughed. "I've even pulled it off for them, you know, for a day's wage." He blew a column of smoke across the table. "Speaking of which, has money been brought up in all these heartfelt communications?"

"You mean, how much?"

"Well, I'm not talking about the denomination of the bills, Corman. Are we talking some little shit sum here? Fifty thousand, some little pissy thing like that?"

To Corman it sounded like a fortune. "I have no idea," he said.

Scarelli sat back and stared at him. "That's because you're an amateur, Corman. But me, I'm a pro. Deadline Scarelli, just like they call me." He balanced the tiparillo carefully on the glass edge of the ashtray. "Money talks, bullshit walks."

"Does that mean you're walking?" Corman asked.

"No, it means you are," Scarelli said. "Because the way this is shaping up, I think I'll pass, let you go it alone." He shrugged. "You got nothing on the old man, precious little on the woman. it doesn't add up to much, and that's a problem. Especially when you start talking money." His eyes drifted up. "Which, I take it, you don't care much about."

"I care about it."

"But not enough," Scarelli said. He smiled and rolled one shoulder. "Fucking rain, gives me an ache." He massaged the side of his arm. "No offense, Corman. but I've saved myself a lot of time and money by being a good judge of character, and when I look at you, I see the type of guy that ought to have a board hanging over his chest, saying 'No sale.'" He smiled. "Not 'Loser.' Not that. Just 'No Sale.'"

"That doesn't sound so bad," Corman told him.

Scarelli laughed. "See what I mean?" he said as he stood up and headed for the door.

For a while Corman remained at the table studying the well-heeled habitués of the Inside Track as he calculated his next move. With Scarelli out, it was up to him now. If there was a mystery, he alone would have to find it.

Dr. Owen looked at him from behind his desk. "You're a reporter, my secretary said."

"Photographer," Corman told him.

"But for one of the newspapers, is that right?"

"Yes," Corman said. "I'm working on a story."

"About obstetricians?" Owen said with a wry smile.

Corman shook his head. "Sarah Rosen."

The name registered instantly in Owen's mind. "I see."

"You remember her?"

Owen nodded. "A bit, yes. She was my patient for a time."

"During her pregnancy."

"Brief as it was, yes," Owen said. "She was about two months pregnant when I first saw her."

"And you did an abortion not long after that?"

"Yes," Owen said with sudden hesitation. "That was a long time ago." He looked at Corman curiously. "There were no complications that I knew of. Why are you interested in Sarah?"

"She killed herself last week."

"She was a friend of yours?"

"I never knew her," Corman said. "I'm just trying to find out a few things."

"Like the details of her abortion?"

"That, and how you felt about her. What you saw. Anything."

"There's such a thing as doctor-patient confidentiality," Owen said.

"I know," Corman told him. "But I thought you might just answer a few questions. Sarah's not alive anymore."

Owen watched him cautiously. "I can only tell you this much. The abortion itself was therapeutic." He stopped. "Well, maybe one other thing. I didn't recommend it."

"You didn't?"

"No. I didn't think it was necessary. The risk was not great in her case."

"What kind of risk?"

"I thought you only wanted a few details."

"Just what the problem was," Corman said quietly. "I'd like to know that."

"She had a very slight heart problem," Owen said offhandedly. "Nothing terribly serious at all. Millions of women have them and experience no difficulty in giving birth." He shrugged slightly. "Still, it was my duty to make her aware of it. I didn't advise the abortion, but Dr. Rosen insisted."

"Dr. Rosen?" Corman asked. "How about Sarah?"

"She agreed to it," Owen said. He thought a moment. "If we can talk, as they say, 'off the record'?"

"Okay."

"Well, the whole situation struck me as rather strange," Owen said. "I called Sarah and asked her to drop by the office. I told her that there was something I wanted to talk to her about. I expected her to show up as most women do, either alone, or with the male party, husband, lover, whatever. But Sarah brought her father with her instead."

"Had you ever met him?"

"No," Owen said. "But he later said that he'd done some checking before directing Sarah to me. I don't know what kind of checking that was. A few phone calls to the AMA, perhaps, something like that."

"So he selected you for Sarah?"

"That's what he told me, yes."

"What happened at the meeting?"

"Well, I tried to tell them about the heart problem as casually as I could. It wasn't something she needed to be alarmed about, really. Just notified, that's all."

"But she was concerned anyway?"

"Her father more than she. He was quite adamant. He didn't want her to take the risk of having the baby, no matter how slight that risk might be."

"How did she react?"

"She was very quiet. She seemed to have very little will of her own, if you know what I mean."

"He dominated her?"

"I would say so, yes."

"And he wanted the abortion?"

"Absolutely," Owen said firmly. "There was never any question in his mind that that was the appropriate thing to do. Even though I told him several times that the birth would probably go just fine."

"What did he say?"

"He was very sharp at that point," Owen replied. "Even haughty. 'Probably?' he said in this very stiff way he has, 'I don't care for probablies, Doctor.'" He lifted his shoulders helplessly. "And that was the end of it. I scheduled the abortion for the following week, and when it was over, Sarah and Dr. Rosen walked out of my office. I never saw them again."

"She never came for a follow-up appointment?"

"No," Owen said. "I had my secretary call her several times. We left messages on her machine, but she never called back." He stopped, and looked at Corman curiously. "You say she killed herself?"

Corman nodded. "She jumped out a tenement window down in Hell's Kitchen."

Owen did not look surprised. "Well," he said dryly, "something in her was dead already."

Corman left Owen's office a few minutes later, glanced at his watch and realized that it would soon be time to pick Lucy up at PS 51. He tried not to think of her, the school, Lexie's righteous cause, and so let his mind drift toward less threatening worlds. For a time, he thought of Lazar, but found that his mind continually returned to Lucy, circled awhile, then went on past her, finally settling on Sarah Rosen, her body sprawled across the wet street, as if in some indecipherable way everything now came back to her, fell precipitously toward her body like the rain.

Chapter 28

CORMAN WAS STANDING AT THE DOOR, WATCHING LUCY take off her raincoat, when the phone rang. It was Pike.

"Hey, Corman," he said. "I got a call from that little fag who writes the society column. What'd you do, buddy, blow his joint?"

Corman didn't answer.

"Anyway," Pike went on. "He likes your work. Says you'd be great for his beat when Groton leaves."

"I did my best," Corman said.

"Well, this call is just a friendly reminder that Groton has a shoot late tomorrow afternoon," he added. "If you're interested, meet him at his place."

"Okay. When?"

"Six o'clock, sharp."

"I'll be there," Corman assured him. He hung up and turned to Lucy. "I may be getting a steady job," he said and instantly thought of Julian, the faint hope he offered that there might still be some way out.

Lucy shrugged. "That's good, I guess."

"I'd be home nights."

Lucy glanced up at him and smiled. "It doesn't matter," she said. "Even when you're gone, it's like you're here." She darted into her room and did not come out again until Corman called her to dinner, scooping out a portion of something he called "Whatever," a mixture of whatever vegetables and meat were still left in the refrigerator at any given time.

"Are you going out tonight?" she asked, as she drew her fork tentatively to her mouth.

Corman nodded and took his seat at the table. "An old professor of mine, if I can get in touch with him."

Lucy looked puzzled. "Are you going back to school?"

Corman shook his head. "No. It's about something else. Some pictures I'm working on."

"Mama's thinking about going back to school," Lucy said.

"Really?" Corman said. It was the first he'd heard of it. "To study what?"

Lucy shrugged. "I don't know." She began circling her fork in the food. "She said you were a great teacher."

"I'm glad she thought so," Corman said. He glanced over at his answering machine. The red light was blinking madly, but he didn't feel like listening to his messages yet.

"I guess I'll never have you, huh?" Lucy said.

"I guess not," Corman said. He nodded toward the listlessly circling fork. "It's to eat, not to play with."

Lucy took a minuscule amount of food onto the fork then brought it slowly to her mouth. "I have lots of homework," she said after she'd swallowed. "I guess I can't watch TV or anything."

"Homework first," Corman said. "You know that." To set the right example, he took a large bite of Whatever and chewed it, faking enjoyment as best he could.

Within a few minutes, dinner was over. Corman began clearing the table, while Lucy sat at the small desk in her room, groaning audibly about her homework, but continuing to do it anyway. He washed and dried the dishes, then picked up the few things that had remained scattered across the room long enough to attract his attention: pieces of newspaper, an old cigarette pack or two, junk mail.

The red light of the answering machine finally annoyed him enough for him to listen to the messages. There was only one, from Joanna, telling him she'd be at one of their usual places at around midnight and hoped he'd drop by. Her voice seemed calm, and it was impossible for Corman to judge what she wanted or whether Leo had gotten bad or good news from the tests.

Lucy peeped her head out the door of her room when the message ended. "I guess you'll be seeing Joanna, too," she said teasingly.

Corman faked a smile. "Finish your homework."

When she'd gone back into her room, Corman clicked off the machine, then looked up Dr. Maitland's number and dialed it.

A man answered immediately, and Corman recognized the deep, resonant voice that he remembered first from the lecture halls, then from the short, earnest conversations along Columbia Walk.

"Dr. Maitland," he said. "It's David Corman."

"David?" Dr. Maitland said brightly. "My God, I thought you'd fallen off the edge of the world."

"Just to Forty-fifth Street," Corman said.

Maitland chuckled. "Well, that's not too far," he said. "But it's been a long time since I've heard from you."

"Yes, it has," Corman said. "As a matter of fact, I was wondering if I could meet you for a few minutes."

"Of course," Dr. Maitland said.

"Tonight?" Corman asked hesitantly.

Dr. Maitland laughed. "You always were a fast starter, David," his voice hinting subtly that it was the finish line that had always given him problems.

"West End Cafe?" Corman said. "Around nine?"

"I'll be there," Dr. Maitland said. "Just be sure you are."

He was, and as he waited for Dr. Maitland, sitting silently in his old haunt, the darkened booth in the rear corner of the cafe, he thought of all the leisurely times he'd spent there, all the high, purposeful talk he'd listened to, with Lexie across from him, boldly holding forth on whatever popped into her mind. It was the sort of memory that had a well-defined potential for bitterness, but quite unexpectedly, Corman found that he still felt a distant fondness for the Lexie of his youth, the one who'd been so brazen, so full of high mockery. She'd had the mimic's gift for lampooning people, especially her professors. She closed her eyes with mock portentousness as Dr. Berger did. She rolled her eyes and sputtered like Dr. Wilkins. She delivered orotund pronouncements, then sank into obfuscation. She did all of this while Corman and the other students around her teared with laughter. No doubt about it, she'd reigned like a comic queen in those days. It was the years after college that had given her trouble. After graduation, she'd simply put her life on hold, drawn in close to the fire, while everyone else had finally gotten up, swallowed hard and ventured out into the jungle. He couldn't imagine why this had happened or whether he'd been in any way responsible. He only knew that her edginess had slowly worn down and that a kind of decomposition had set in. There were even times, toward the end, when it seemed almost physical, as if while sitting across from her at dinner, he half-expected to see her face crack like dry ground or a handful of iron gray hair suddenly come loose from her scalp and float down to her shoulder.

Maitland came in a few minutes later and stared around, squinting in the darkness, until he caught Corman's eye. Then he moved heavily through a barricade of crowded tables until he reached the booth in the rear corner. He was a large, potbellied man now, not exactly old, but getting there fast. His hair had thinned considerably since Corman had last seen him. It had gotten grayer too. He looked more weathered than before, but still robust, energetic, full of quick responses.

"Hello, David," he said as he slid into the booth.

Corman nodded and smiled.

Maitland turned toward the bar, ordered two beers on tap, then looked at Corman. "So, what have you been doing since you left Columbia?"

"I taught for a while," Corman said. "That private school you wrote the reference for."

"Oh yes, I remember," Maitland said. "How'd that turn out?"

"It was okay."

"But you're not there now?"

"No."

"Somewhere else?"

"Not a school," Corman said. "I'm working as a photographer. Freelance."

Maitland looked surprised. "Photographer? I didn't know you were interested in that."

"Newspaper work mostly," Corman explained. "Off and on." He thought of the stack of pictures that lay piled like dead fish in his camera bag. "It's not what you'd call secure."

"Well, what is?" Maitland said. He smiled. "Except tenure, of course."

Corman nodded.

Maitland watched him for a moment, as if trying to put him in another category. He seemed vaguely dislocated, as if the fact that Corman was no longer a student or teacher had shifted him into a hazier world that was hard for him to get a grip on. "I always thought you'd stay in teaching," he said finally.

"So did I," Corman told him.

"I suppose you like your new work?"

"It's interesting," Corman said. "You learn a lot."

"Well, that's all that matters, I suppose," Maitland said. He smiled, a little indulgently, like a grown man who was going along with a child's view of the world, letting Corman believe in the tooth fairy or Santa Claus or anything else that got him through the night. "How did you happen to discover this new vocation?" he asked a bit sententiously, as if he were still talking to an eager undergraduate.

"I met a man who was already doing it."

Again Maitland smiled. "And lightning struck," he said with a hint of condescension. "That's what I call providential."

"You might say that."

"And your studies? What happened to them?"

"They took a different turn," Corman said, adding nothing else.

Maitland paused again, still watching Corman distantly. "Well, we missed you when you decided to leave graduate school." He squinted slightly, as if he were trying to figure out exactly where Corman had gone after that. "So, photography," he said idly.

"Photography," Corman repeated. He was reasonably sure that Maitland now thought of him as working in some sort of inferior world. It was as if the university were the one true penthouse of existence, the place with the really sweeping view. Everywhere else was somehow blocked in its perspective, hampered by trees, buildings, telephone poles, mounds of useless clutter. Maitland smiled. "Well, as long as you're happy," he said, forcing a certain lightness into his voice.

Corman glanced toward the bar and wondered what was holding up the drinks.

"And what about Lexie?" Maitland asked after a moment.

"We're not together anymore."

"Oh," Maitland said awkwardly. Then he shrugged. "Well, that's par for the course these days."

"What is?"

"Splitting up," Maitland said.

"I guess."

"In my opinion, it's all cyclical," Maitland added. "We've gone through a period during which the solution to a bad marriage was a quick divorce. Now we're coming into a different period."

Corman didn't feel like going into what this different period might be.

"We're going back," Maitland said authoritatively. "The solution to a bad marriage will be to live in it and keep your mouth shut. That's what people have done through most of human history." He smiled. "We're not talking about progress, David. We never are with human beings. We're only talking about a shift, the latest version of the Eternal Return."

It was the sort of statement Corman remembered from Maitland's classes. Only then they'd sounded truer, at times even faintly revealing, despite the superior edge. Now they sounded empty and pompous, something that could only fly in the rarefied air of the faculty lounge.

The beers came, and the two of them clinked their glasses together gently, then drank.

Maitland turned toward the front of the room, glancing at the other people in the bar, mostly young Columbia students.

"The elite," he said as he looked back at Corman. "What do you think of them?"

Corman shrugged but did not answer.

"You used to have opinions," Maitland said. There was a faintly knowing tone in his voice, as if he'd caught Corman doing something nasty in the woodshed, but was willing to keep it to himself. "Don't you have them anymore?"

"A few," Corman said.

"Like what?"

"More things seem ridiculous to me now."

Maitland's face soured somewhat. "You sound like Lexie."

"Really?"

"Absolutely," Maitland said.

Corman took a quick sip from his glass. "At this point, I don't think it matters."

Maitland leaned forward slightly, his eyes growing somewhat more intense. "Well, what is 'this point' exactly? I mean, with you? I take it you're not interested in coming back to graduate school."

Corman shook his head. "No, I'm not," he said. "Actually, I didn't come to talk about school at all."

"So I've gathered," Maitland said.

"It's about a woman."

Maitland laughed. "And you came to me?" he said. "I'm flattered."

"This woman, she ..."

"Of course, everybody knows that English departments are notoriously horny," Maitland interrupted. "It's all that romantic nonsense they read. 'How do I love thee? Let me count the ways.'" He laughed. "I mean, it's one thing to study that sort of thing all your life, it's quite another to take it seriously."

"She jumped out of a building last week," Corman said.

Maitland looked at him solemnly. "I'm sorry," he said. "I didn't know you were talking about something like that."

Corman pulled a photograph from his camera bag. "I took some pictures." He handed the picture to Maitland. "It turns out that this woman had been a student at Columbia."

"And that's what this meeting's about?" Maitland asked.

Corman nodded.

Maitland's eyes drifted down to the picture. "I don't recognize her," he said.

"She may have changed a lot since she was at Columbia."

Maitland's eyes continued to study the picture. He shook his head. "I don't remember her."

"Her name was Rosen," Corman said. "Sarah Rosen."

Suddenly Maitland's face turned very grave. "Sarah Rosen?" he said unbelievingly. He looked thunderstruck. "My God, I had no idea."

"Last Thursday night," Corman said quietly.

Maitland looked at the photograph again. "When I knew her, she didn't look like that at all."

Corman eased the picture from Maitland's hands. "She was starving," he said.

Maitland's eyes widened, and for an instant Corman could see something glimmering behind them. He had seen it before, even felt it in himself, a form of recognition that came up fast, like a man in your face, telling you that nothing could be taken lightly, that everything was real, and that this reality didn't care about your faith, your analysis, the precious little kingdom of your self-esteem, and that if you didn't back away from it, dodge it desperately somehow, you'd spend your days balled up in some clean white corner, rocking, wailing, facing the facts.

"Starving?" Maitland repeated.

"I'm trying to find out what happened to her," Corman said.

Maitland took his glass in both hands and rolled it slowly between them. "She was Samuel Rosen's daughter."

"A professor here," Corman said.

"Not just a professor," Maitland said. "Samuel Rosen. One of the world's great medievalists. A specialist on the Renaissance, too. Jesus, didn't you learn anything at Columbia?" He looked offended by Corman's ignorance. "Haven't you at least heard of him?"

"I think so," Corman said tentatively.

"His work is famous," Maitland insisted. "I know you didn't major in medieval studies, but for God's sake."

"How well do you know him?"

Maitland shook his head and looked embarrassed by his answer. "Not very well. I've read all his books."

"But you don't know him as a person?"

"No, not as a person."

"But you did know his daughter?"

"Yes."

"She took one of your courses her senior year."

"How did you know that?"

"Her husband."

"So you know about her examination then."

"Do you still have it?" Corman asked immediately.

Maitland nodded. "Absolutely." His face darkened. "It was written in a bizarre way."

"I'd like to see it."

"I'll look for it. It should be in my office."

"Could we look tonight?"

Maitland hesitated. "Is it that urgent?"

Corman nodded. "Yes."

"In a minute then," Maitland said. He smiled thinly. "I trust I can finish my drink." He took a quick sip, waited for Corman's next question, then took another sip when it didn't come.

Corman could feel his impatience growing. He needed facts, important facts. He could feel Trang and Lexie hovering over him, spectral presences hissing from above. He shifted restlessly and felt a clammy sweat gathering beneath his arms. "Can you tell me something about her?" he asked.

Maitland thought for a moment, his eyes rolling toward the ceiling as they did when he lectured, searching for his muse. "I always had the impression that she chose the words very carefully." He thought a moment longer, his eyes scanning the room until they finally came to rest on Corman. "Why are you investigating her?"

Corman thought of Lucy, Trang, Lazar, Julian, the pictures. It was all a maze. "Why does anybody do anything?" he asked, dodging the question.

One of Maitland's eyebrows curled upward. "That's a bit philosophical," he said. "I didn't know you were still interested in ideas."

Corman said nothing. From behind, he could hear a young woman laughing above the general hum of the crowd. He felt like turning and taking a picture of her, for no reason at all beyond its sweet relief.

"I thought of you the other day," Maitland said after a moment. "I was in the Columbia Bookstore, just browsing. And you know how, suddenly, from out of nowhere, something can remind you of someone? Well, this reminded me of you."

"What did?"

"It was a book of questions," Maitland told him. "Nothing but questions. You know the kind I mean: If a museum were burning, and you could save either the Mona Lisa or a cat, which would you save? That sort of thing. It reminded me of you." He smiled softly. "The way you used to be."

Corman could no longer get a handle on who that person had been. It was time to move on to other matters. "I'd like to see Sarah Rosen's exam," he said.

222

Chapter 29

"I THINK IT'S STILL IN HERE," MAITLAND SAID AS HE opened the door to his office.

Corman followed him inside then stood silently while Maitland felt about for the light switch, his fingers clawing at the wall until he finally located it.

"There," Maitland said as the fluorescent bulbs fluttered for a moment, then grew bright. He swept his arm out. "Looks the same, doesn't it?"

Corman nodded, took another step into the room and stared about, his hand unconsciously fingering the latch on his camera bag. The room looked almost exactly as it had that afternoon ten years ago when he'd sat in the plain wooden chair in front of Maitland's desk and told him he was leaving Columbia.

"Same bust of Poe," Maitland said. "Only a little yellower. Same diplomas hanging from the wall."

Corman glanced toward the diplomas, his mind instantly turning to the one they'd found in the burn-out, its cracked glass and shattered frame.

Maitland walked to the large metal filing cabinet at the other end of the room. "The paper should be in here somewhere," he said as he pulled open the third drawer and glanced down at a stack of undergraduate papers. "In twenty years of teaching, these are the only ones I've kept." He stepped back from the file cabinet. "Sorry I can't stay," he added. "Just close the office door when you leave."

Corman waited until he could no longer hear Maitland's footfall in the corridor before he began going through the papers. Sarah's was near the bottom of the stack.

It was very short, only a page and a half of tightly knotted sentences. As a paper, it hardly existed at all. Instead, it was a gathering of sentences, often disconnected, as if Sarah's mind had been incapable by then of stringing thoughts together in a coherent pattern. Fragmented, often broken off before completion, they suggested a mind that had simply shattered into thousands of tiny shards, like a large crystal vase that had fallen from a great height. It was still possible to catch individual, shining pieces, perhaps even to sense the overall beauty they must have once joined to create. But the whole had clearly flown apart. It was as if the law of gravity had ceased to operate in her mind, so that everything rose, sank and drifted according to weights and measures which were no longer assigned and limited by anything outside them. Because of that, as he read her paper again and again, Corman found himself ensnared in a similar randomness and indecipherability, so that the very act of thinking back over what he'd read drew him into Sarah's own swirling state, filled his mind with the wild, whirling sparkle of uprooted, weightless things.

And yet, she was there, clearly and powerfully, a voice so lost, and yet so entirely distinct, that her death suddenly came to him as something personal for the first time. He thought of her by the window, her mind shooting through the darkness that surrounded her, a vast sea of flickering lights, red, blue and yellow, burning in her head, burning in the darkness behind her and which, perhaps, she had finally tried to escape by easing herself to the ground on a cool white stream of rain.

He read the paper a final time before returning it to Maitland's file drawer, then headed toward the subway.

Outside, he could still feel her around him as he scuttled along the wet bricks of Columbia Walk, then took a train to the Village. It was as if she'd entered Maitland's office while he read and wrapped him in the texture of her anguish. Sentence by sentence, the web of her tiny black script had coiled around him, her words lined up like figures before a firing squad as she struggled madly for some bizarre frozen purity before letting it all fizzle away in long blank spaces and end finally in the coup de grace of an uncompleted sentence: "Given the note/

tone/mood of excresence here we may/can/will only/inadequately say/declare that it is/composed/authenticated/ with the heart of a ..."

He got off the train at 14th Street and headed east, still thinking of her, rooted in her, his eyes hardly taking in the legions of street-peddlers who spread their rain-soaked merchandise along the whole desolate strip that led to the river.

He could see Joanna already waiting for him as he stopped at the corner of First Avenue. She was sitting near the restaurant's front window, the table she always preferred, her eyes watching the flow of traffic as it moved southward toward the Bowery. As he watched her from across the street she looked hazy, incorporeal, an artist's sketch of a human being he'd decided not to paint. For a moment, Corman stood in the rain, watching her as she sipped her margarita casually, fingering the rim of the glass as she always did. He thought of taking a picture of her as she sat in the window, then decided it would seem posed, Joanna only a model who took direction well.

Her eyes drew over to him when he came through the door.

"Hi," Corman said quietly, as he stepped up to the table.

Joanna smiled. Her eyes misted. "Leo's going to be okay," she said, her voice breaking slightly.

Corman nodded, bent forward and kissed her, then started to move away.

She held on to him, her arms squeezing tightly around his body as he continued to stand over her. "Benign, that's what they said," she told him. "Completely benign. Like a wart, no worse than that, only inside."

Corman sat down opposite her and took her hands in his. For an instant, he saw Sarah's face float up from just beneath Joanna's, disappear, then return in a faint, wavering image that swam in and out of his vision.

"I knew you'd be happy about it," Joanna said. She daubed her eyes. "Sorry, sorry." She drew the handkerchief from her eyes. "You've never seen me cry before, have you?"

Corman gazed at her. "No, I don't think so."

"Yeah, that's part of it, I guess," Joanna said. She hesitated a moment. "You don't know all that's been going through my mind, Corman. What happens is, you lose control. You can think anything." She took out a cigarette and lit it shakily. "I asked myself all kinds of questions," she said. "Things about Leo. And about us, too." She squeezed his hand. "Especially, you know, in a situation like this. I thought maybe I'd been bad for Leo all these years. Bad for his life, I mean." Her eyes grew very serious. "You can take a lot of things, Corman, but you never want to think that anybody would have been better off if they'd never met you."

Her fingers were still in his, but he could feel himself releasing them one by one, small dry reeds he was feeding to the fire.

"I mean, nobody should give somebody else that much grief, right?" Joanna said.

He allowed the last finger to slip from his grasp.

"I even thought maybe I was bad for you," she added.

He drew back slightly and lowered his hands into his lap.

"You don't always know how things will end," she said.

"You never do," Corman said quietly.

Joanna put out the cigarette, lit another and laughed nervously. "I always wondered why you weren't involved with a younger woman," she said.

Corman shrugged.

"No, really."

Corman shook his head. "I don't see the point of talking about it."

Joanna glanced away from him, fingering the salted rim of her margarita. "I guess not," she said. "Anyway, I've been doing some thinking. I really have." Her face tensed. "David, I'm going to stay with Leo from now on. That's what I've decided." She paused a moment, drew in a second deep breath. "Just Leo."

In his mind Corman saw her curled in Leo's naked arms, snoozing beside him in their bed, living in the tightly sealed jar of predictability and taking comfort in knowing with absolute certainty how it would finally end.

"Did you hear me?" Joanna asked.

"Yes."

"It's what works," Joanna told him curtly. She waited for him to answer, then added, "Doesn't it?"

Corman didn't answer.

Joanna crushed out another cigarette. "But not for me, is that what you mean?" she asked with a sudden sharpness. "That look you just gave me."

"I don't know what works for you."

"No, I guess not," Joanna said brittlely, then waved her hand. "Forget it, Corman."

Suddenly, he realized she would be easy to forget since nothing of any real importance had ever happened between them. He felt closer to Sarah Rosen, had seen her more utterly revealed.

Joanna's eyes bore into him. "You have to make accommodations, don't you?" she asked. "You just can't live as if there's no tomorrow."

Corman stared at her silently.

"You were my hedge against being bored," Joanna told him matter-of-factly. "That's what it all comes down to." She reached for another cigarette, then stopped herself. "You can't have everything. Only a kid believes that." She waited for him to say something and continued when he didn't. "I wanted it all. That's always been my problem. I wanted Leo at home with the laundry. Good, steady Leo. But I also wanted someone waiting for me in a little restaurant or a hotel room. You, or someone like you." She looked at him as if she were making a final confession. "I've always had a lover. Long before you, Corman. Always." She drew in a deep, determined breath. "But I'm giving all that up now. Completely giving it up."

Corman leaned forward slightly and fought to keep his attention on her. But she already seemed very small and far away, made of gauze or flash paper.

"It's what I've decided, that's all," Joanna said firmly. "I just wanted to let you know." Then she reached toward him and touched his face gently. "My last lover," she whispered.

He hardly felt her hand, and let his eyes drift toward the street.

Joanna seemed to sense the distance that already divided them. She looked at him closely. "David? Are you all right?"

He turned back toward her, but saw Sarah's face again instead, all her agony building within him.

"David?" Joanna repeated.

His lips parted wordlessly.

Joanna's eyes hardened. "You don't care, do you? That I'm leaving. You're not even thinking about it."

Corman didn't answer.

"You're thinking about something else," Joanna said. "Your own thing." She glared at him fiercely, then began gathering her things, snapping up her cigarettes and lighter and dropping them angrily into her purse. "You turn everything into something else," she said hotly. "Some big fucking deal. In your head. A federal case."

She stopped for a moment and gave him an icy stare. "You know something? I never felt you were really with me. Even in bed— somewhere else." She jerked herself to her feet. "I'm getting out of here."

He didn't try to stop her, and in an instant she was gone, the sound of her high-heeled shoes clicking first along the tile floor, then beyond the door and out into the street.

For a long time after she'd left, Corman continued to sit in place, his eyes concentrating first on her empty glass, then his own hands, finally settling on the few dark figures who sat here and there in the shadowy light at the back of the restaurant. In photographs, each one would look dramatically alone, an isolated shape in a shroud of faded light. Inevitably, he knew, a grim futility would gather in every frame, and because of that, he tried to imagine a way to show each figure differently—to compose, once and for all, a picture that could say what is without declaring that it had to be.

Chapter 30

"IT'S AWFULLY LATE," THE WOMAN BEHIND THE RECEPTION desk told him.

"Well, he doesn't sleep much," Corman said.

"Yes, but, we have regular ..."

"I can't always make it during regular visiting hours."

The woman eyed him a moment longer, trying to determine what she should do.

"Look, nobody else comes to see him," Corman said softly. "Just me. Nobody else."

"Well, okay," the woman said reluctantly. "Go on down."

The room was at the end of the corridor and Lazar's face filled with quiet recognition as Corman came through the door.

"How you doing?" Corman asked.

The old man's light blue eyes rested silently on Corman's face. He sat up very slightly and pulled his head forward. A long strand of gleaming white hair fell at a slant over one eye.

Corman walked to the bed and sat down on the edge of it. "I'm sorry I missed you last weekend," he said. "I had some things I had to do."

The old man nodded. "D-d-d-d-d-d-d ... "

"I had to handle some things about Lucy," Corman continued. "Nothing big. Just some stuff with Lexie and her and ... you know."

One of Lazar's eyes narrowed. "D-d-d-d-d-d-d."

"Nothing bad," Corman assured him quickly. "She's not in any trouble or anything." He tried to smile. "This'll surprise you. I did a shoot with Harry Groton this week."

A small hesitant smile formed on Lazar's lips. "D-d-d-d-d-d-d-d-d."

"At the Waldorf," Corman said. "Some big wedding or something."

The old man grinned dismissively. A silvery string of drool descended slowly from the corner of his mouth and gathered in a glistening pool on his white bedshirt.

Corman took a cloth from the end of the bed and wiped the old man's mouth.

"Groton's leaving the paper," he said. "Pike offered me his job."

Lazar shook his head slowly. "D-d-d-d-d-d-d-d."

Corman smiled thinly. "You probably think I shouldn't take it."

Lazar nodded. A single hand came from under the sheet, crawled toward Corman's wrist, then encircled it.

"I haven't decided yet," Corman said. "But I have to have some money, Lazar."

Lazar's face softened almost imperceptibly.

"You know how it is," Corman added. "With money."

Lazar nodded. A second tangled strand of white hair fell across his forehead, dangling between his eyes.

Corman pushed it back. "Do you have a comb?"

Lazar shook his head.

"I'll bring you one next time."

The old man stared at him scoldingly for an instant, then smiled.

"I have to let Pike know in the next few days," Corman told him. "I don't know what to do."

Lazar's head drooped forward slightly.

"It's steady money. That's the one good thing about it."

Lazar raised his head slowly, the white eyebrows twitching slightly. "D-d-d-d-d-d-d."

"A woman jumped out a window down in Hell's Kitchen about a week ago," Corman said.

The old man's eyes widened somewhat.

"I took some pictures," Corman added. He drew the small stack from the camera bag and showed them to Lazar one by one.

He looked at them intently, eyes narrowing more forcefully with each one. Then he nodded slowly.

"I don't know much about her," Corman said. "She went to Columbia. She wrote an essay." He returned the photographs to his bag. "There's this guy I know in publishing. He says maybe a book, something like that." He heard his own words, how disjointed they were. He leaned forward and drew the old man gently into his arms. "Christ, Lazar," he whispered. "I'll never be the same because of you."

The old man began to cry softly, his shoulders shaking.

"I know, I know," Corman said, then waited until Lazar had regained himself and eased him back onto his pillow. "Lucy says hi," he told him.

Lazar smiled tremulously.

"I was going to bring her by on Sunday," Corman said. "But she's going to be with Lexie. You know, up in Westchester."

Lazar grasped Corman's hand again and squeezed.

Corman's eyes fled to the window, the dark city beyond it. He could feel small bones breaking in his soul.

"D-d-d-d-d-d-d-d-d."

Corman turned back to the old man. "I'll let you know what I find out about the woman," he said. Then he lifted himself to his feet. "I have to be going now, Lazar. Lucy's home, so I've got to head back."

Lazar's body suddenly tensed. His eyes searched the room frantically.

"You want something?" Corman asked.

"D-d-d-d-d-d-d."

"Water?"

"D-d-d-d-d-d-d."

Corman tried to follow the movement of Lazar's eyes. They were darting furiously in all directions, as if he were following the movements of an invisible bat.

"Food?" Corman asked. "You cold? Hot?"

The eyes continued to dart around. He seemed to be indicating everything in the room, the pictures on the wall, the television, the window. Then suddenly they stopped dead and fell toward the police band radio at Corman's side.

Corman smiled. "The city," he said. "You want the city."

Lazar nodded fiercely. "D-d-d-d-d-d-d-d," he said loudly.

"You want to hear what's going on." Corman took the radio from his belt. "SOD okay?" he asked as he wrapped the old man's fingers around it.

"D-d-d-d-d-d-d," Lazar said happily.

"Okay," Corman said softly. He switched the radio on, dialed the SOD code, then propped it firmly against the old man's ear. "That ought to keep you busy for a while."

Lazar nodded vigorously as the first click of the radio sounded in the silent room.

"See you soon," Corman said as he stepped away from the bed.

He walked to the door, then glanced back. The old man had eased himself into the pillow once again, the slender black receiver perched at his ear. His eyes grew intense, his brow slightly wrinkled in concentration as he listened to the first call. A fire was burning in a Brooklyn warehouse. No one knew if there were still any people trapped inside.

Trang was more or less poised at the entrance to Corman's building, squatting silently, his eyes following the traffic up and down the street. He rose quickly as Corman approached.

"How you doing," Corman said, as he tried to pass.

Trang stepped in front of him. "Good evening, Mr. Corman," he said. "As you know, we have a few matters to discuss."

"I haven't sold anything yet," Corman told him. "I'm still working on it."

Trang looked unhappy. "It is very serious now. You many months in arrears."

"I realize that," Corman said crisply.

Trang's body seemed to puff out slightly, make itself appear more formidable. "I'm afraid I have taken steps."

Corman stared at him expressionlessly.

"Filed papers." Trang looked exasperated. "I'm sure you know what I mean, Mr. Corman. Eviction. You left me no choice. I did it with regret."

In his mind, Corman saw two small white fangs slide down from Trang's mouth, then rise up again and slip behind the thick pink cloak of his upper lip. He felt his body tighten, make a quick, violent move toward him, then ease back, regain control.

"You'll get your rent," he said curtly, then turned quickly and headed for the elevator doors.

Lucy groaned sleepily as he kissed her. She looked up briefly from the pillow, her eyes fluttering softly before they closed tight again. "Oh, Papa," she groaned, a little irritably. "I was sleeping."

"Go back then," Corman said softly. "Good night."

He walked out of her room as the phone rang. It was Edgar.

"Glad to see you're home at night," he said. His voice seemed slightly strained. "Uh, I'm at home. I mean, in bed," he added quickly. "You know, with Frances."

"I understand."

"But, uh, I wanted to let you know that I've made all the arrangements with Lexie."

"Okay."

"Saturday night."

"Where?"

"She'll meet you at your apartment," Edgar said. "She's going to be in the city all day, she told me. Probably shopping for some art. They're building a new house, you know."

"No, I didn't."

Edgar didn't go into it. "Anyway, she says she can meet you at your apartment."

"Okay."

"I tried to talk her out of meeting you there," Edgar added.

"Why?"

"Come on, David," Edgar said. "The way it looks. Grist for her mill."

Corman glanced about the apartment, noting its disarray, and saw it as Lexie would, scattered, unkempt, collapsing at the center.

"She'll come by around eight," Edgar said.

"I'll be here."

"Make sure you are," Edgar warned. "If you weren't, she might take that in a very bad way."

"I'll be here," Corman repeated coolly and started to hang up.

"David?" Edgar said quickly, stopping him.

"Yeah?"

"You okay?"

"I'm fine."

"You don't sound it."

"I'm busy, Edgar."

"Developing?"

"Yeah, developing."

"Well, listen," Edgar said. "If anything happens. I mean, with money. It would be helpful if you could mention it to Lexie. Strictly in passing, of course."

"Okay."

"Technically, it's not her business," Edgar added. "But we're dealing with a mood here."

"I understand."

"Just a passing mention, that's all."

"If I sell anything," Corman assured him, "I'll let her know."

"All right," Edgar said. "Get some sleep, for God's sake."

"I will," Corman told him, then hung up and walked to the window. Outside, the city struck him with such broken beauty that after a while, he pulled his eyes away from it and let them drift downward until they caught on a little feather of dust which clung to the thigh of his trousers. He brushed at it softly, but the faint brownish mark only sank further into the cloth, so he slapped at it harder, then vehemently, with his fist, until suddenly he stopped and began to cry, gently at first, then in wrenching shudders until he finally stepped back from the window, raised his hand to cover his mouth, and waited for it to pass.

When it had, he returned very quietly to Lucy's room. She'd turned over on her back, sleeping deeply, her arms spread wide apart, head arched slightly back, throat exposed, as if waiting to be sacrificed.

Chapter 31

"I'M READY," LUCY SAID AFTER SHE'D FINISHED DRESSING the next morning.

Corman walked slowly to the door, opened it and ushered her into the corridor.

"Will you pick me up this afternoon?" Lucy asked.

Corman shook his head quickly, his mind concentrating on her with a sudden, biting pain, as if someone had slipped a needle into his brain. "Victor will," he said, then added impulsively, "I'll miss you tonight."

She looked at him oddly, then moved down the hall to the elevator.

They rode down silently, Corman clutching his camera bag while he thought of Trang, the eviction, the way it would send Lexie over the edge. He could see her sitting coolly across the table from him, her dark eyes as piercingly accurate as ever. She would know, no matter how much he lied. She would see it in the little feints, shifts, coughs. He was desperate, she would know that. Her true perception had never failed her in regard to his deficiencies.

"Did you and Joanna have a good time last night?" Lucy asked, prying gently, as she always did.

"Yeah."

"You don't look like it."

"We had an argument."

"Did you break up?"

"I think so."

She tucked her hand in his arm. "Sorry."

"It happens."

"Not to Mom and Jeffrey," Lucy said. "They don't ever fight."

Corman shrugged. "They're great people, that's why," he said facetiously, before he could stop himself.

Lucy jerked at him slightly. "That's not nice."

Suddenly the sound of her voice, the glancing touch of her hand went through him like a searing charge. He stopped and knelt down to her. "I love you," he said emphatically. "I will always love you."

She stared at him, alarmed.

"You must know that," Corman told her.

Her face tightened. "What's the matter?"

Corman caught the panic in her eyes. "Nothing," he said quickly, straightening himself, regaining control. "I just wanted you to know that I ..."

She watched him fearfully, her eyes glistening. "Stop talking," she said sternly. "Just stop talking."

"I didn't mean to ..."

"Just stop talking," Lucy repeated adamantly.

He reached for her hand, but she drew it away.

"I just wanted you to know that I love you," he said again, this time more calmly, trying to contain himself.

At the school, he gave her a brief hug. "See you," he said lightly, forcing a smile. In his arms, she was very stiff, a bundle of dry stalks. "I didn't mean to get something started," he explained. "Really, it's nothing. I just ..."

"Yeah, okay," Lucy told him. She turned away, then back to him in a quick, smoking whirl. "You're lying," she said sharply.

He started to lie again, then decided not to. Instead, he simply nodded and watched her eyes burn into him mercilessly before she spun around and disappeared into the moving crowd.

Corman found Lang on the second floor of Midtown North. He was sitting in the locker room munching a cheese Danish, a pair of handcuffs dangling from his one free hand. He looked brutish, and Corman realized that any photograph would only serve to make him look more so, moving the eye along the sloping belly, then up into the pudgy, featureless face, finally drawing it over to the chrome handcuffs, the way Lang's elongated head seemed plastered onto their shiny curving surface.

"What's up?" Lang asked as Corman walked up to him. "You working an EMS beat or something?"

Corman sat down beside him, his eyes moving up the long row of battered metal lockers. Several patrolmen were getting into uniform, struggling with their belts and citation pads, checking out the smudges on their brass buttons.

Lang offered a thin, reptilian smile. "I thought maybe you'd seen that guy I put in Saint Clare's this morning," he said. "Fucking skell. Tried to hoist an old lady off a roof on Forty-ninth Street." He shook his head. "I got there just in time. They may give me a medal." He laughed. "You should have been there. You could have taken my picture."

Corman reached into his camera bag and took out the notebook.

Lang eyed it suspiciously. "What's that?"

"For notes," Corman explained. "Just in case."

"Notes?" Lang said. His face tightened. "What kind of notes?"

"I'm still working on that woman,' Corman said. "And I was wondering if you'd come up with any background on her."

Lang shrugged. "I asked her father the routine stuff," he said. "Why'd she do it? Bullshit questions like that." He took a bite from his Danish and continued talking, his words slightly muffled. "They don't ever know, the parents. It's all a mystery to them. Shit, man, he didn't even know where she was."

"At the funeral, he was pretty upset," Corman told him.

"You went to the funeral?"

Corman nodded. "No one there but Rosen."

Lang washed the Danish down with a gulp of coffee. "Figures," he said. "With a broad like that."

"Like what?"

"A loner," Lang explained. "Nobody in the whole fucking neighborhood knew who she was. All they'd done is, they'd seen her. That was it. As far as shooting the shit with her, passing the time of day? Nothing."

Corman looked at him curiously. "So you did talk to a few people in the neighborhood?"

"That's right."

"Why? If it was a routine suicide."

Lang smiled. "Because of you, shithead."

"Me?"

"That fucking button," Lang told him. "We had to cover our asses." He shrugged. "So, we asked around a little."

"Did anything turn up?"

Lang shook his head. "Listen, Corman, I don't know why you got such a bug up your ass on this case, but take it from me, it's a complete zero. I'm talking, closed tight. You ask me, that girl dropped out of the whole human race. Put up that sign, you know, DO NOT DISTURB."

"But why?"

Lang smiled. "My guess is, some fucking guy screwed her up."

"But who?"

"Coulda been some drifter," Lang told him. "Maybe some asshole she bumped into while she was squeezing tomatoes at the A & P." He shrugged. "That's the way it is with women. Some scumbag comes along, they can't get over how great he is."

Corman glanced at his notebook, its cover still closed, the pencil in his other hand motionless beside it. "So you've got absolutely nothing?" he asked.

"Z-E-R-O, Corman," Lang said, his teeth already sinking again into the Danish.

Corman grabbed a hot dog outside the precinct house and strolled south, ending up across from the burn-out in which Sarah had lived the last days of her life. He sat down on the stoop, his eyes staring up at the fifth-floor landing. For a moment, she must have lingered at the edge, stared down into the blowing rain, tried to find the right sound, then settled on a final silence. He thought of how few facts he'd accumulated on what she'd done in the years before that moment, how little he had to give Julian. He knew the kind he needed, hard, brutal facts that sank deep then rose up to save the day, combined to make a story with a beginning, middle and an end. The end was directly in front of him, a slender line of vertical space from the window to the street. Everything else was considerably less defined, and he suspected that it always would be, not only in Sarah Rosen, but in everyone. A mystery of genes at the very start, and after that, only a slightly less consuming mystery. He thought of Lucy, saw her in a food store squeezing tomatoes while someone watched her from a few feet away, calculated the chances, made his move: *Nice tomatoes, huh?* Not to answer was to live in fear. To answer was to put your whole life at risk.

He was still considering it all when he heard voices down the street, and turned to see a group of children playing hopscotch on the sidewalk. There were two girls and a boy, all of them about the same size, with nut-brown skin and gleaming black hair. A break in the rain had released them, and they were taking full advantage of it, leaping happily in the moving slants of sunlight that periodically swept the street like enormous prison searchlights.

They laughed brightly as they played together, and after a moment Corman found himself inching toward them as unobtrusively as he could. He was almost upon them when a large woman came out of the building, sat on the stoop and watched quietly as the children played. She wore a flowered dress, and her hair was held tightly beneath a dark red scarf.

Corman smiled quietly and nodded toward his camera. "Photographer," he said.

The woman smiled back. "Nice now, the sun."

"Yes."

The woman nodded. "Very nice."

He pointed toward the abandoned building a few yards away. "A woman was living there."

The woman said nothing, and watched the children, a small smile playing fitfully on her lips.

"The woman," Corman said, "the one in the building. Do you remember her?"

The woman nodded and continued to watch the children. "Skinny woman," she said. "Didn't look too good. Jumped out the window." She turned to face him, twirled her finger at the side of her head. *"Era loca."* She returned her eyes to the children. "How come you talk about her? You her brother, somesing like that?"

"No."

"No blood?"

"No blood," Corman said. He let his eyes drift over to the children. One of the girls was skipping rope while two of the other children twirled it furiously. "Would you mind if I took some pictures of the kids?" he asked.

The woman smiled brightly. "No, that's good to take the pictures. They like that."

Corman moved a few feet away, then turned and began walking forward slowly, focusing on the children, taking a shot every few steps. Through the lens, he could see them caught forever in their play, held together and kept safe by the protective walls of the frame. Inside the camera they could be animated, yet suspended, full of life, yet shielded from it, forever clothed, fed, sheltered, with everything they needed ... but a life.

Chapter 32

CORMAN HAD BEEN WAITING FOR OVER AN HOUR BEFORE he saw Dr. Samuel Rosen come out of his apartment on East 68th Street, then head west, toward the rainy borders of Central Park. He looked as if he'd aged somewhat since the funeral, his white Vandyke just a bit whiter, his face slightly more lined. He was dressed in a long black coat and dark fur cap, his shoes carefully protected by glistening black galoshes as he moved forward determinedly, the wind whipping relentlessly at his umbrella.

Corman waited until he was a safe distance away, then reached for his camera and took a few shots of Rosen's tall, retreating figure. Then he returned the camera to his bag, walked into the vestibule of Rosen's building and pressed the buzzer.

"Yes?" It was a woman's voice, black, with a faintly Southern accent.

Corman leaned forward and spoke into the wall speaker. "My name is David Corman. I have an appointment with Dr. Rosen."

"Dr. Rosen's not here."

"I know," Corman told her. "I saw him on the street. He asked me to wait for him."

"And you're who, now?"

"David Corman. I'm an old student of his."

"Well, okay," the woman said reluctantly. "I guess so."

The buzzer sounded. Corman stepped into the building and headed up the stairs to Rosen's apartment.

The woman was standing in the door, eyeing him from a distance.

"Hi," Corman said as brightly as he could. He slapped a few droplets of rain from his jacket. "Looks like it's going to go on forever."

The woman nodded. "Worst it's been in a long time," she said.

"Yeah."

"Well, step inside," the woman said. "It's dry in here."

Corman walked into the foyer, then followed the woman into the living room. It was elegantly arranged, but with a dark modesty that resisted showiness of any kind. There was a baby grand piano with a marble bust of Socrates on it. Other busts were scattered around on slender wooden pedestals. Corman recognized some of them: Johnson, Wordsworth, Shakespeare. Others were more obscure figures, medieval thinkers, poets, gathered together as if in silent enclave, mutely watching the rain trail down the large French windows at the back of the room.

"I dust them every day," the woman said. "Dr. Rosen likes them polished up." She stepped over to a bust of Erasmus and began wiping its surface with a white cloth.

Corman hesitated a moment, then launched in, because he had no choice but to move quickly. "Well, I guess they're his life," he said, "especially since Sarah."

The woman's eyes swept over to him. "Terrible, what happened to that child," she said darkly.

"Yes. Did you know her?"

The woman shook her head. "Seen her a few times, that's all."

"What was she like?"

"She was shy. Always. You know, like lots of people are. Off in the corner, that sort of thing."

"And she stayed that way?" Corman asked casually, trying to suggest no more than ordinary interest.

She thought about it for a moment. Her hand stopped dead in its rhythmic sweeps across the marble surface of the bust. "She wasn't fit for nothing."

"Fit?"

"For living," the woman added. She started polishing the marble again. "Dr. Rosen done his best for her. But Sarah, she just wasn't fit for nothing."

"How long had she been gone?"

"You mean from here?"

242

"Yes."

"Since she got married," the woman said. "Then something happened, and that was the end of her."

"She just disappeared?"

The woman nodded. "Hadn't nobody seen her, far as I know."

"That must have been hard on him," Corman said.

The woman finished polishing the bust and moved on to the next one. "I got to do his office now," she said when she'd finished it. "You want to come in?"

Corman got up immediately. "Sure."

The woman headed down a short corridor, past the closed doors of the bedroom and into Dr. Rosen's office at the back of the apartment. "He stays here most all the time now," she said as she led Corman into the room.

Corman glanced about. "It's a nice room."

"He likes it dusted every day." She stepped over to the large wooden desk and began straightening the few papers that were spread out across his work. "He does all his work in here."

"He's a great scholar," Corman said.

"Don't keep things messy, that's for sure," the woman told him. "Always pretty much keeps things nice."

"I guess he likes things to be in order," Corman said.

"Neat and clean. That's the way he likes it." She leaned over and began dusting a tall stack of reference books which rested at one corner of the desk. "I dust and polish everything in here once a week."

While she worked, Corman let his eyes roam about the room. A large bookshelf rose all the way to the ceiling along the right wall. It was filled with books, papers and a scattering of professional journals.

"You a teacher, too?" the woman asked, as she finished the last of the books and started wiping the top of the desk.

"Not anymore," Corman said.

The woman pulled a bottle of lemon oil from her apron, poured some of it onto her cloth, took one of the paintings from the wall to her left and began polishing the frame. The odor of the lemon oil filled the room immediately.

"Got out of it, huh?" the woman asked.

Corman nodded. "Yeah," he said, as he glanced at the wall behind her. It was covered with various framed documents, honors, diplomas, most for Dr. Rosen, but several for Sarah, certificates of mastery from her many tutors. And just beneath them a single empty square.

It was only a short subway ride to Midtown North, and Corman made it in only a few minutes, then headed into the building and down the stairs to the basement. He lifted the frame from the box, sniffed it quickly and drew back slightly from the heavy lemon odor.

"Still chasing ghosts?"

He turned toward the door.

Lang was standing massively within it, tiny streams of rain still pouring off the hem of his coat and gathering in small translucent pools on the basement floor. Something in the way he slumped against the doorjamb made Corman want to snap up his camera and take a picture of the sinister hunter in the darkness of his lair.

"You in love with a corpse?" Lang asked. His eyes settled on the diploma. "What's on your mind, Corman?"

Corman tried to look casual, tucked the frame back inside the box, then closed it silently.

"You solve the mystery, Corman?" Lang asked with a sudden, hard-edged tone. "Because if you did, I'd like to hear it."

Corman picked up the box and returned it to its place on the shelf. "I'm just a shooter," he said.

"With an eye, so they say."

"No better than most."

Lang watched him closely, inching himself up slightly, his shoulder crawling up the side of the door and leaving a wet streak behind it. "What do you see, Corman?" he demanded. "With your eyes?"

Corman drew the camera bag over his shoulder and headed for the door.

Lang blocked his way. "Don't fuck with me," he warned. "If you got something, you give it to me first."

Corman looked at him evenly, and decided he would bring it first to whomever he damn well chose. "No."

Lang's lips parted wordlessly in surprise as he stepped out of Corman's way.

Corman could still smell the lemon oil on his fingers as he walked slowly across town toward Groton's apartment. In his mind, he could see Julian leaning toward him from the other side of the desk, his wolfish eyes staring intently as it was laid out for him, the freshness of the oil, the fact that Sarah had not been in Dr. Rosen's apartment for months before her death. Julian would know exactly what he had, a blood offering, Dr. Rosen's body greased and ready for the fire.

The doorman at Groton's building nodded politely as Corman came into the lobby.

"I'm here to see Mr. Groton," Corman said.

"I remember you," the doorman said. "You can go on up."

Corman walked to the elevator and rode up smoothly, his mind still trying to go through all the possible scenarios for how the diploma might have ended up on the fifth-floor landing, its frame shattered and glass cracked, all of it as broken as Sarah's body must have been a hundred feet below.

At Groton's door, Corman knocked, waited and knocked again. There was still no answer. He waited a moment longer, knocked a third time, then a fourth. Inside, a radio was playing softly, but otherwise there was no sound, and after a moment, Corman pressed his ear up against the door. "Harry?" he said. He rapped at the door a final time. "Harry?"

The door opened slowly, and Corman could see Groton staring at him, his large swollen face slightly pink in the dim light of the room.

"Didn't know it was you," he said grimly.

"We have a shoot," Corman reminded him.

Groton stepped back and swung the door open. A severe smile spread across his lips. "You probably thought I was dead. Either that, or drunk."

Corman walked inside and said nothing.

"The job's yours," Groton said as he closed the door. He nodded toward a single swollen suitcase which rested heavily at the end of the bed. "I got a flight. That's what I decided a few hours ago. That I was going home."

Corman turned toward him. "Home?"

"Back west. South Dakota."

"I didn't know you were from South Dakota."

"I'm not," Groton said. "But my brother is. At least, that's where he lives now." He shrugged. "We never were that close. But here. Well. There's just . . . the way you feel . . . like nothing stuck. Through the whole thing, nothing."

Corman nodded.

Groton stepped over to the bed and began tightening the last strap on the suitcase. "Anyway, that's what I decided. I called Pike. I guess he couldn't get in touch with you."

"I guess not."

"The shoot's at Tavern on the Green," Groton said matter-of-factly. "Be there by six. You'll like it. They got all those little lights wrapped around the trees, little ones." He drew the strap up very tightly, pulled the suitcase from the bed, and lowered it onto the floor. "That's all I'm taking. The rest can go get fucked."

Corman's eyes swept the room, taking in all Groton had decided to leave behind: the bed, a rickety chair or two, a gray metal desk, a calendar from a Brooklyn bank. The walls which surrounded them were dirty, but completely unadorned, as if in all the years he'd lived in the room, Groton had never bothered to lighten the atmosphere with even so much as a single dime store painting of a fuzzy kitten in balled-up blue twine.

Groton smiled. "You need any of this stuff? You see something, take it. The landlord'll just toss it."

Corman shook his head. "My place is already a little cluttered," he said.

Groton nodded quickly, walked to the front door, drew his raincoat from a small brass peg and pulled it on. "Well, good luck, Corman," he said as he thrust out his hand.

Corman didn't take it. "I'll go down with you."

They rode silently down the elevator and walked out onto the bustling sidewalk. For a moment, Groton stood very still, his hunched frame poised like a rumpled statue. "It's not easy, leaving," he said finally.

"You'll miss the city," Corman said absently, without conviction.

Groton looked at him irritably. "That's not what I meant," he snapped, then whirled around quickly, hailed a cab and disappeared into it as fully as if it were a faded yellow cloud.

Chapter 33

THE LITTLE WHITE LIGHTS WERE TWINKLING BRIGHTLY at Tavern on the Green by the time Corman arrived. Clayton was already staring about anxiously, waiting for him.

"Groton out again?" he asked as Corman came up to him.

"He's gone to South Dakota," Corman told him. "Pike knows."

"And you're the official replacement?" Clayton asked.

Corman nodded.

"So you took the job?"

Corman shook his head. "Not yet," he said. "But I'm here for the night."

Clayton smiled pleasantly. "Good," he said. "Then let's get to work."

Corman started immediately, moving through the crowd as invisibly as he could. He shot little knots of tuxedos and evening dresses, tables of densely packed hors d'oeuvres, flower arrangements, the slightly overweight members of the classical quintet that played in a distant corner.

As the minutes passed, the room grew increasingly more crowded until, toward eight, it was entirely filled. Corman had taken five rolls of film by then, and he was busily putting a sixth into his camera when he glanced up and saw Lexie standing only a few yards from him, her face smiling quietly through a clutter of shoulders, champagne glasses and gliding silver trays. He felt his legs go rubbery beneath him, his stomach empty, and began to shrink away, just as she glimpsed him suddenly, excused herself and made her way toward him through the crowd.

"David," she said quietly when she reached him. "To say the least, I didn't expect ..."

"No, of course not," Corman said.

"What are you doing here?"

Corman lifted his camera and smiled lamely. "Filling in," he said. "For the regular guy."

Lexie looked at him doubtfully. "I see."

Corman shrugged. "Just for the night."

She was dressed in a shimmering green dress, cut low, so that the rounded tops of her breasts shone toward him whitely, like two muted lights. She was incontestably beautiful, but there were distractions now—a diamond choker, a gold pendant—things so radiant she seemed lost within their glare.

"You look very nice," he said.

"Thank you," Lexie replied. "You look ..."

"The same," Corman said quickly, helping her out.

"Yes."

For a moment, Lexie's eyes studied him with that quietly burning stare that peeled back his soul the way heat peeled back curls of liquefying paint.

"As a matter of fact, I was just about to leave," he told her. He smiled again, tried to look at ease, and shifted the subject away from himself. "Is Jeffrey here?"

Lexie glanced about idly. "Somewhere in the room."

"I guess you know these people."

"People?"

"Whoever this party's for."

Lexie smiled indulgently. "It's for the seals."

"Oh ... the Seals. They live around here?"

Lexie laughed. "Christ, Corman."

"What?"

"In the ocean," Lexie explained. "Those seals."

A quick frantic little burst of embarrassed laughter broke from him. "Oh, those seals." He shook his head. "Sorry."

Her face softened. "Are you all right, David?"

His face stiffened. "I'm fine."

The look came back. He could feel the heat from it sinking into his bones.

"We have to talk, you know," she said.

Corman nodded.

"Edgar said that he'd spoken to you," Lexie added significantly.

"Yes, he has," Corman told her. "And you and I are supposed to talk tomorrow night, right?"

"That's right," Lexie said. She smiled sweetly. "I'll meet you at your apartment, if that's all right."

Corman didn't want her to see the apartment any more than Edgar had, but didn't know how to prevent it without looking like a felon hiding evidence of his crime. "Okay," he said.

"Eight o'clock, I believe."

"Yeah, fine."

For a moment she watched him silently, her eyes turning oddly inward, as if they were watching something other than him, a movie playing in her mind.

"Well, I'll see you tomorrow night," she said finally. A tiny smile fluttered onto her lips, clung there like a little girl holding to a liferope, then fell away. "Good night, then, David," she said, turned and made her way back through the jungle of silk and satin until she seemed far, far away from him, beyond the rolling surf of even the most distant sea.

He left Tavern on the Green an hour later, and by that time, he'd run into Jeffrey, too, exchanged empty pleasantries, and slunk away. It was a relief when Clayton had finally come by and dismissed him with a quick nod.

The lights were still twinkling behind him as he headed downtown along Central Park West. For a moment he stood silently under the sheltering trees, stared back at them, then turned south again, making his way slowly down the cobblestone walkway that bordered the park. The rain had stopped, but large, isolated droplets still fell from the overhanging branches, splashing against his jacket or streaking past his face as he moved slowly under them. The traffic was very heavy, but there were only a few people along the edges of the park. Across the avenue, a tall slender man hurriedly walked an even more emaciated Airedale. A few yards away, a doorman slumped listlessly in a lighted vestibule, then pulled himself quickly to attention as an elevator door opened in the lobby behind him.

At 65th Street, Corman crossed the avenue, then continued south. He walked on a few blocks, glanced back toward the park, then slowed immediately, finally coming to a full stop. He could see an old man sitting silently on one of the wet wooden benches. The white beard glimmered slightly in the street light, and as Corman inched closer to the curb, he saw the face emerge slowly from the darkness, assuming the features he thought he recognized from his encounter in the chapel. There were the same bushy eyebrows and carefully manicured silver beard, the same dark, deep-set eyes with their long black lashes, but it was not Dr. Rosen, only some other lone figure, hunched in the rain. The resemblance held him nonetheless, and for a long time, Corman stood a few yards away, his eyes focused on the old man while he let the impulse build slowly, steadily, until he had no choice but to follow it.

For an instant he couldn't move but simply stood in the door, facing him. Then he drew in a deep breath, like a swimmer before a long dive, and plunged forward. "I was at Sarah's . . . the photographer."

Dr. Rosen stood rigidly at his door, staring at him expressionlessly. The pen in his hand twitched gently, but everything else remained utterly still. The earlier rage was entirely gone, replaced by a strange resignation, the eyes settled, firm and untrembling. It was as if the explosion in the chapel had sounded the final note of his resistance. "You came earlier," he said finally.

"Yes."

"Posing as a graduate student."

Corman nodded.

"Did you use your real name?" Dr. Rosen asked. "Corman, isn't it?"

"My real name, yes," Corman said.

Dr. Rosen's face grew stoney, as if his body had suddenly turned into a slab of granite, solid, immobile, unimaginably old. "What do you want, Mr. Corman?" he asked.

Corman realized that he had no precise answer to that question. For a moment he felt stymied. "The diploma," he said finally, nodding toward the office. "The one they found with Sarah's things. It came from your office."

Dr. Rosen's gray face studied him with a concentration Corman remembered only in pictures of doomed romantic poets, driven, tormented, people caught within the throes of tragic fermentations.

"What do you want?" Dr. Rosen asked again.

"To talk about her."

"Why?"

"I'd like to understand what happened."

Rosen shook his head. "You will never know what happened to Sarah." He began to close the door slowly, with a strange courtliness, as if he were doing it with regret.

Corman raised his hand to stop it. "The diploma," he repeated. "It came from here."

Rosen eased the door forward again. "Yes, it did," he whispered, lowering his head somewhat, his voice growing less robust and taking on the muffled quality of a whisper.

"It still smelled of lemon oil," Corman added. "So you must have brought it down with you that night."

Rosen looked at him plaintively, and with an expression of such overwhelming grief that Corman realized immediately that all his darkest ruminations about Rosen were entirely wrong. "To save her," he said.

The door stopped its forward progress as Dr. Rosen stepped back slightly, watching Corman intently, but with eyes that seemed battered into softness. "To save her," he said quietly. "But she's dead now, and nothing can be done about it."

The last words came in a gentle coda, and instantly Corman understood how much the sounds of things mattered to Dr. Rosen, how much he shaped each word with the intonations of his voice, giving each one the music called for by its meaning in the context of the sentence, pure as his daughter's indecipherable imitations, her titanic striving to be like him.

"She's gone," Dr. Rosen said. "Gone. So what's the use of going into Sarah's death?"

"I want to know what happened," Corman said. "Over the last week or so, I feel that I've sort of ..."

"Come to know her?" Rosen asked.

"Not exactly."

"What then?"

"Come to know you," Corman blurted before he could stop himself.

Rosen looked at him, amazed. "Me?"

"As a father," Corman added. "How you tried to save her."

Dr. Rosen's eyes studied him thoughtfully for a few seconds before he spoke again. "After the accident, the way her mother died ..." He shook his head. "It's how arbitrary things are. Random. You have to work within that frame, don't you?"

Corman said nothing.

"That there is absolutely no pattern to anything," Rosen said. "None at all."

Corman watched silently as Dr. Rosen drew in a long slow breath, then continued.

"And so, you try to intervene," Rosen said. "Rewrite the world, you might say. You have a daughter, and you try to save her. You try to teach her everything she needs to know. You try to control her experience. That's all I ever wanted to do for Sarah."

She rose in Corman's mind as he listened, the air surrounding her dense and lightless, the rain falling in long gray sheets as she stood at the window, the doll clutched to her breast.

"She lived on my terms," Dr. Rosen went on. His eyes took on a fierce wonderment. "She was a perfect daughter." The wonderment deepened into amazement, intense, magical, a prophet in the midst of his promised transformation. "She heard every word I said, did everything I asked."

"Even with the baby," Corman said.

Rosen's face darkened. "Yes, even that."

"You wanted to eliminate the risk."

"All risk," Rosen said. He looked at Corman pleadingly. "Isn't that what every father wants to do?"

Corman saw the rain sheeting in windy blasts across the dark windows of the fifth-floor landing. She was leaning against the wall, the doll held loosely, dangling from her hand, the rain slapping mercilessly at its bare plastic legs. "Is that what broke her?" he asked. "The baby?"

Rosen shook his head. "Only the last thing. She was already slipping away."

"Why?"

"She was never well, Mr. Corman," Rosen said. "There were tendencies. In her mother's family."

"Toward what?"

"The general term?" Dr. Rosen asked. "Schizophrenia." He smiled mockingly. "It's just a word for something no one understands. It means 'broken soul.'"

Corman recalled her short paper, knew now that her scattered sentences had been an effort to draw her soul back together through a rope of words.

Rosen looked at Corman as if he were explaining himself to a tribunal of ancient gods. "And so, given all of this, I felt that I had to control her environment as much as possible." He took a pair of glasses from his pocket and wearily drew them on. "I thought about some kind of institution for her," he said. "Especially after the baby." His face took on a terrible conviction. "We have to have what our souls require, don't we?" he asked passionately. "No matter how strange it may seem to some other person, we have to have it."

Corman looked at him evenly. "What did your soul require?" he asked.

"That she be safe," Dr. Rosen said desperately. "Isn't that what we all want for our children, just to keep them safe?"

Corman studied Dr. Rosen's face and understood the terror that drove him. In him, the passion of fatherhood had taken on a mystery beyond what could ever be described to someone else. It had become heroic in its refusal to accept what all fathers had heretofore accepted, that they could not rid the world of its dark snares, nor provide safe passage through them for their children. It was an effort that had lasted all the years of Sarah's childhood and adolescence, and which she had resisted only once, perhaps in dreams during one long night, her small white teeth tearing fiercely at her bottom lip.

"You were there the night she died," Corman said matter-of-factly, with no sense of accusation.

"Yes, of course," Dr. Rosen answered without hesitation.

"How did you find her?"

Rosen's eyes fell toward his hands. "By chance. I was down at the library annex, the one on Forty-third Street. I'd been working there all day. It was late in the afternoon. I started home, and there she was. Across the street."

"You followed her?"

Rosen nodded slowly. "To that ... place ... that ..."

"Did you talk to her?"

Rosen shook his head. "No. I didn't know how. I didn't know where to begin. I just went home." His eyes darkened. "After the baby, I realized what I'd done, so, when she disappeared, I didn't try to find her. I had learned by then that she had to get away from me, make a life of her own, regain, if she could, the sanity she'd lost. But when I saw her that day, the way she was, I knew I had to intervene, so I went back that same night." He seemed to tremble at the thought of it. "The rain was terrible," he said. "There was no one on the streets."

Corman nodded. He didn't have to imagine the rain, the streets, only Dr. Rosen moving through them, glancing fearfully at the wet, unpeopled stoops, then up toward the dripping metal fire escapes, down again to where the gutterwash swirled toward the steadily clogging drains.

"It seemed unreal," Rosen said. "That she was in a place like that."

Corman's mind moved through it again, saw the littered alleyway, the naked ceilings, the empty cans of Similac, the pictures he'd taken as she lay on the street, her arm reaching desperately for the doll. "What happened the night she died?" he asked.

Dr. Rosen drew in a deep breath and began to speak very rapidly, as if trying to get it all out before drawing in another one. "I brought the diploma, something to show her, something to remind her of her life. But when I saw her again, in that place, the way her hair was so wet with the rain, I couldn't imagine that it was Sarah at all. She was a ghost, a spirit waiting to die. She hardly spoke while I was there. She just looked at me while I tried to get her to come with me. I handed her the diploma, but she tossed it away. She kept holding to that doll instead. She even tried to feed it. That's when I grabbed it from her. She got it back and ran upstairs. I went up after her." He stopped for a moment, lowering his voice when he began again. "She kept clutching to that doll while I kept trying to get her to hear me. Finally I pulled it away from her. She tried to get it back. That's when I threw it out the window." His eyes opened wide as he stared piercingly into Corman's face. "She looked at me at that moment in a way no one ever had. Then she turned toward the window. I grabbed at her dress, but she pulled away. And then she was gone." He bent over slightly as if a hand had pressed his head forward, readying it for the axe. "I knew she was dead," he added quickly, his eyes focusing intently on Corman. "Are you a father?"

"Yes."

"Then you know what I mean," Dr. Rosen said. "That I didn't have to look, that no one had to tell me. I absolutely knew what had happened to my daughter."

At that instant, Corman realized that there would be no book on Sarah Rosen, no exposure on film or otherwise. At the same moment, he saw Lucy in Sarah's place, standing at the window, staring down as Sarah had, as all daughters did, poised on the excruciating ledge while their fathers watched them helplessly, watched as they retreated further and further from their care until finally they could grasp no more of them than the small white button of a dress.

Corman walked home to his apartment very slowly, often stopping to peer into a shop window or, more often, into the yellowish interior of a bar. The old city was no more. Like all things held too dear, it had become a phantom. Now there was only Lucy. He felt her like a wreath of smoke around his head, dense, powerful, and yet beyond his grasp, a presence he could neither hold on to nor bat away, and as he continued toward home, he wondered if he would always have to live with her in this new way, love her at a distance, visit only on recommended days.

She was standing at the window when he came in and turned toward him slowly, her face very solemn. He felt himself quake and shiver, swallowed hard, and gained control.

"You got a call, Papa," she said.

Corman pulled the camera bag from his shoulder and let it fall into the chair beside the door. "Who from?" he asked in a whisper.

"That home where Mr. Lazar is."

Corman looked at her and waited.

Lucy hesitated a moment, then spoke. "He died, Papa," she said tenderly. "They want to know what to do with him."

Corman's thought came immediately. "Do with him?" he asked himself silently. "What could anyone ever do with such a man?"

Chapter 34

THEY NEEDED A SUIT TO BURY HIM IN, AS CORMAN found out early the next morning. As he dressed himself he tried to decide what would look best on Lazar. It was the kind of highly limited detail his mind could concentrate on, and he felt grateful for the way it kept everything else at bay.

"I guess there'll be a funeral," Lucy said quietly as she strolled into the living room.

"Yes," Corman said, "but not today. You can just hang around here. I have to get some things before they bury him."

She rubbed her eyes wearily. "He was a nice man."

"Yes, he was."

"Remember when he gave me that toy typewriter?"

Corman nodded, pulled on his jacket and headed for the door.

"I still have it," Lucy said as she followed behind him. "I don't play with it anymore." She considered it for a moment. "But maybe I'll keep it anyway," she said at last. "Because he was a nice man."

Corman bent forward and kissed her lightly on the forehead, carefully resisting his need to pull her fiercely into his arms and rush away with her, as animals sometimes did when their young were at risk, holding them like tender morsels within their open mouths.

"See you this afternoon," Lucy said as she opened the door for him.

He nodded crisply, then stepped into the hallway.

She drew him down to her again and kissed him very softly on his cheek. " 'Bye," she said as she slowly began to close the door.

He watched her disappear behind it as he usually did, but differently too, in the way he thought must inevitably accompany the dwindling of life, when everything counts more in number than degree, and each sensation asks how many times are left to see, hear, feel or taste it.

It was only a short walk from the Broadway to Lazar's apartment on West 44th Street. It was in a rundown five-story building where some of the older tenants, unable to live on Social Security, rented out their rooms for thirty minutes at a time to the small army of Eighth Avenue prostitutes who swarmed over the neighborhood. They were mostly old Broadway types, bit players in the long spectacle, who chatted casually on the stoop while their rooms were being used upstairs.

Corman rang Chico's buzzer and waited the few seconds it took for him to come up from his own basement apartment.

"I need to get into Mr. Lazar's apartment," Corman told him.

"Sure, no problem," Chico said. "How's he doing? He doing okay, or what?"

"He died."

Chico's face remained oddly cheerful, despite the news. "My mother, the same. Sometimes, you know, it's the best thing." He smiled quietly. "You his son, right?"

"Just a friend."

"You the only one I ever see him with," Chico said. "So I figure you was his son."

"No. We worked together."

Chico nodded quickly. "So, what you want? The key?"

"I need to get a suit to bury him in," Corman explained.

"Yeah, sure, no problem," Chico said hastily. He pulled a huge ring of keys from his pocket, pulled one off and handed it to Corman. "What's going to be with the apartment? You going to clean it out, or what?"

"I don't know."

"It's decontrolled now, you know," Chico said. "So, the landlord, he's going to want to take it back, okay? I mean, right away."

"He can have it tomorrow," Corman said.

Chico looked unsure. "You sure that's okay? The old man, he didn't have nobody?"

"Nobody."

"So, okay if we clean it out?" Chico asked. "You give me the okay to do it?"

"Yes."

"That's good, then," Chico said happily. He slapped Corman gently on the shoulder. "You take whatever you want. The rest, we'll dump it."

Corman nodded quickly and made his way upstairs, then into the apartment.

It was a one-room apartment which overlooked the street. Long, dark blue curtains hung over a tangle of battered Venetian blinds. The sink was stained and rusty, the toilet ran incessantly, filling the air with a soft gurgling rattle. The bed sat in one corner, its covers rumpled, the torn sheets piled up along the floor beside it like a drift of faintly yellow snow. In a photograph, Corman realized as he walked to the window and raised the blinds, it would look like a stage designer's idea of a loser's apartment, a dusty little room in a pathetic has-been of a building full of people who had nothing left to turn a trick with but their beds.

He walked to the single, nearly empty closet at the back of the room. The door was already ajar, the upper hinge pulled nearly free from the wall so that it slumped to the right. There were two suits, five shirts and four pairs of trousers. A cracked leather belt hung from a wire hanger, along with a scattering of ties. Corman picked the dark blue one, then added a white shirt and a black suit. The world could hardly contain the vast irrelevancy of his shoes.

A large suitcase rested on the upper shelf of the closet, and as Corman pulled it forward, he felt its unexpected heaviness suddenly shift toward him, then stood by helplessly as it tumbled over the edge and slammed into the floor below, the top springing open as it fell, spilling hundreds of photographs in a wide, black-and-white wave across the bare, wooden floor.

Reflexively, he dropped to his knees and began sweeping the scattered pictures back into the gutted suitcase. At first he returned them in large handfuls, then slowly, one by one, taking a long, lingering moment to stare appreciatively at each of them. These were what the old man's soul had needed, and as Corman continued to look at them, staring longer and longer at each one, he knew that this was his way of paying homage to a life he'd only come to know in its final years. All through the morning and then into the afternoon, he sat on the floor and looked at the photographs Lazar had saved through his long career. While the air grew steadily darker, he peered at pictures of children playing in the park, women leaning from their windows, men slumping against parking meters, cars and brick walls, and over and over, in one picture after another, in a theme that seemed to have developed slowly throughout the old man's life, pictures of people huddled beneath awnings, in doorways, under the fluttering batlike wings of a thousand black umbrellas, but all of them staring out toward unseen open spaces, as if still searching for some break in the unrelenting rain. And as Corman returned the last picture to the suitcase, it struck him that this was what had been missing from Groton's apartment, that there'd been no photographs hanging from the walls or stuffed into his bag, not one picture after all those years to stand forever as something he did right.

He was still in Lazar's apartment when he called Pike. "I'm going to pass on Groton's job," he told him quietly.

"Suit yourself," Pike said casually. "It's not a job I'll have any trouble filling."

"No, you won't."

"Too bad, though," Pike added nonchalantly. "The fag liked you, said you were a pretty good shooter."

"I'm glad to hear it."

"Said you had an eye for things."

"An eye," Corman repeated unemphatically, then with more significance. "Lazar died yesterday." He tapped the side of his camera bag. "I'm taking some of his clothes up. For the body."

"He was good," Pike said, "a good shooter. But he was weak, Corman. What the Irish call a harp."

"He seemed tough enough to me."

"How tough's that?"

"He drank it down to the worm," Corman said. "He didn't fake anything." If he'd been a sculptor, he thought as he hung up the phone, he would have etched the same proud words upon the old man's stone.

* * *

Corman laid the bag on the desk beside a tray of hospital plates. "This is for Mr. Lazar," he said.

The attendant recognized him immediately and gave him a quizzical look. "Did anyone call you?" she asked delicately.

Corman nodded. "I know he died," he told her. "I brought some clothes for him."

"Oh, I see," the woman said. "Well, Mr. Lazar is ... we have ... I mean he's downstairs."

"Yes."

"Would you like to see him?"

Corman shook his head. "No, I don't think so."

The woman smiled softly. "He died in his sleep," she said. "Very quiet. We didn't know anything had happened until we made our regular rounds." She glanced at the bag for no reason, then returned her eyes to Corman. "He was sitting up. I mean, when it happened. I guess he was listening to the radio. He had it propped up against his ear."

"Yes, he was probably doing that," Corman said. He could feel a strange restlessness somewhere deep within him and worked to keep it down. "As far as a funeral, I'll make the arrangements. He owned a plot in a cemetery in Brooklyn. The one you see from the train on the way to Coney Island. It's very crowded. He liked that, crowds."

"I know the one," the woman said with a sudden cheeriness. "I live near it."

"They would know about the plot," Corman added. "Where it is. That kind of thing. I'll call them, make the arrangements." He slid the bag over toward her. "I guess you can take these now?"

She pulled them toward her, peeked in. "Looks fine," she said.

Corman placed his hand on the suitcase. He could feel the many miles it had traveled, smell the hotel beds where Lazar had flung it, see the roads, tracks, rails it had been hustled down. "Yes," he said as he spread his hand across it, left it there a moment, then drew it achingly away.

Lucy had left a note on the door telling him she'd gone to Mrs. Donaldson's, so he trudged back down the hallway to get her. She answered the door immediately.

"Why are you here?" she asked, surprised.

He smiled quietly. "Just to pick you up."

"I thought you were going out with Mom."

"I am, a little later."

"And I'm going home with her tonight, right?"

Corman nodded. Tonight and forever, he thought, and ever and ever and ever. And he would be away as she grew tall and her voice changed by imperceptible degrees. He would be away when she failed at this, triumphed at that, away when she woke up with a start, when the cat died, the bird escaped, away when she fell, away when she got up again. And in the end he would no longer feel familiar with the shape of her leg, the length of her hair, because, by some formula the world took powerfully to heart, he had failed to be what he should have been.

"So when are you meeting Mom?" Lucy asked.

"Around eight," Corman told her. "Mrs. Donaldson will stay with you until we get back."

Lucy turned excitedly and called to Mrs. Donaldson that her father had arrived, and that she was going home. "Is it okay if I eat with her tonight?" she asked as they headed toward their apartment. "She cooks better."

"Yeah, it's okay."

Lucy slapped her hands together. "Great," she said happily, then rushed away, bounding down the corridor ahead of him for a few yards before she stopped abruptly, as if caught by a sudden thought. Then, for no reason he could understand, she returned to him slowly, her eyes oddly tender, tucked her hand in his arm and walked beside him silently to their door.

Chapter 35

LEXIE ARRIVED ALMOST EXACTLY AT EIGHT. SHE SMILED tentatively when Corman opened the door, then came slowly into the small foyer as he stepped back to let her pass.

Lucy rushed from her room to greet her. "Hi, Mom."

Lexie pulled her into her arms, smiled warmly. "Hi. How are you?"

"Fine," Lucy said. "I'm staying with you tonight."

"Absolutely," Lexie said. She looked at Corman, then spoke to him finally, her voice already a bit strained. "Hello, David."

Corman nodded.

"You left the party quite early."

"The shoot was over."

Lucy tugged Lexie's hand. "Did Papa tell you?"

"Tell me what, honey?"

"Mr. Lazar died."

Lexie's eyes shot over to Corman. "I'm sorry, David."

"He'd had a stroke," Corman said, almost dismissingly, carefully controlling himself. "He wasn't in very good shape."

"Still, it's . . ."

"Yes, it is," Corman said, cutting her off. He reached for another subject. "Well, this restaurant we're going to, do I need a tie, jacket?"

"Well, yes, I think so," Lexie said. "I hope you don't mind."

Corman shrugged. "No, I don't mind. Where are we going?"

"I thought we'd make things a little classy tonight," Lexie told him. She smiled. "If that wouldn't bother you."

"Not at all."

"He'd like it," Lucy said enthusiastically. "He eats pizza most of the time."

Lexie's eyes remained on Corman's face, as if she were trying to determine exactly what was left between them, affection, amusement, just the pull of years.

"I'll be ready in a minute," Corman told her. He turned, walked into the living room and pulled his jacket from the table. He could hear her moving toward him, stepping cautiously into the room, as if odd things might be lurking in its shadowy depths.

"Okay," he said when he turned back toward her. "I'm ready."

For a moment, she didn't move. Her eyes scanned the room, surveying its stained walls and battered furnishings, the way everything seemed crippled by age and wear, the downward tug of squandered chances. She looked like a lawyer taking notes, building a case for impermissible disarray.

"I said, I'm ready," Corman repeated.

"Oh, good," Lexie said, coming back to him. She looked toward the door, smiled at Lucy as she headed toward it then hugged her once again when she got there. "See you later," she said lightly.

Corman stepped around her and opened the door. " 'Bye, kid," he said to Lucy. "I'll tell Mrs. Donaldson to come right over."

"She's bringing dinner," Lucy said to Lexie. "Pot roast. It's great."

Lexie smiled thinly. "Sounds wonderful," she said, her voice faintly distant, as if it were coming from a better part of town.

Corman headed down the corridor, stopped at Mrs. Donaldson's door and knocked lightly.

The door opened immediately.

"Lucy ready for dinner?" Mrs. Donaldson asked.

Corman nodded toward Lexie. "This is Lucy's mother," he said. Then to Lexie, "Mrs. Donaldson."

They shook hands quickly.

"You have a wonderful little girl," Mrs. Donaldson said. "Such a sweetie." She smiled sympathetically at Lexie, as if in commiseration for all the times she'd had to put up with a rootless man.

"Well, we'd better be going," Corman said to her. "We should be back fairly early."

Mrs. Donaldson waved her hand. "Take your own sweet time," she said expansively. "Me and Lucy always have a grand old time."

Lexie led the way to the restaurant, walking briskly, as she always did, until they'd made their way silently across town to a place called Pierre-Louis on East 56th Street. Pierre himself was standing at the door as Corman followed Lexie in. For a few minutes, the two of them stood together, talking of mutual acquaintances and the state of things in the Hamptons while Corman shifted awkwardly just to Lexie's right, silent, patient, one of her retainers.

"Well, it's very good to see you again, Mrs. Mills," Pierre said in conclusion. "Mathieu will show you to your table."

Mathieu did precisely that, then directed a few other people around until the table had been served with drink, bread and butter. The bread was good, like the butter. Corman recognized the scotch as the same Jeffrey had ordered for him at the Bull and Bear.

"So, it's . . . the restaurant . . . it's nice," he began haltingly after the first sip.

Lexie smiled. "It's funny how little we have to talk about."

"Divorce puts a clamp on things."

"Yes."

"That's just the way it is."

"I'm afraid so," Lexie said. She took another sip from her drink. "I'm really sorry to hear about Mr. Lazar."

"I was, too."

"Was it painless?"

Corman shrugged. "I don't know."

Lexie bowed her head slightly. "Anyway, I was sorry to hear it."

Corman nodded and finished his drink.

Lexie immediately ordered another and waited for it to come before continuing.

"I hear you have something going," she said. "Some sort of project."

"Who told you that? Frances? Edgar?"

266

Lexie didn't answer. "A book, isn't it?" she asked instead.

Corman shook his head. "There's no book," he said.

Lexie looked surprised, but Corman couldn't tell whether it was because he'd dropped the book idea or simply been willing to admit it instantly.

"But why?" she asked. "Julian says . . ."

"Julian?" Corman blurted. "I didn't know you were still in touch with Julian."

Lexie's face tightened almost imperceptibly. "Sometimes."

Corman looked at her pointedly. "Lexie, you think I care if you're seeing Julian?"

"It's not like that."

"I don't care what it's like," Corman said. "It's not my business." He looked at her very seriously, trying to find a route into her that would broaden both of them and let them live in some sort of collusion against whatever it was that had spoiled things for them. "Anyway, there won't be a book," he told her.

"Why not?"

"Because it didn't add up to anything Julian would be interested in."

"He said something about a woman."

Corman shook his head. "They weren't really interested in her, I don't think. They had their own ideas. I'm not sure what. Maybe to get the father somehow. For a villain."

"And the father wasn't one?"

"No, I don't think he was," Corman said. "At least not intentionally. I mean, who's to blame when it all goes wrong?"

Lexie's eyes rested on him. They seemed oddly lifeless. He half-expected them to tumble from their sockets, roll across the table and drop into his lap.

"So, what it comes down to," he said, "there's not going to be a book."

"I see," Lexie said. She hesitated a moment, as if trying to get her bearings, then began, "I know Edgar talked to you."

"Yes," Corman said. He could feel it coming, like an executioner moving slowly down the corridor toward his cell, grim, unstoppable, prepared to carry out the court's inflexible decree.

"The worst thing for a child is bitterness," Lexie said, as if quoting the latest manual on the subject. "Friction. Hostility. Even ambiguity. Things like that have to be avoided."

Corman said nothing. He felt that any words from him would fall upon her like tiny drops of water, explode on impact then turn to little dribbling streams.

"It's always been very smooth between us, David," she went on. "Especially these last few years." Her eyes narrowed significantly. "I don't want that to change."

Corman cleared his throat weakly, offered a quick, inconsequential remark. "I don't want anything to change."

"Which brings us back to Edgar," Lexie said. "Or should I say, to Lucy." She stared at him solemnly. "You have to understand, David, that whatever I want, I want it for Lucy. Not for me at all. And I mean that." She gave him a quick smile. "To tell you the truth, I don't get the feeling Jeffrey's terribly excited about having a little girl around. But I can't think of him, of his interests, anymore than I can think of yours. It's Lucy's welfare. That's what I'm interested in. Only that. Nothing else."

He was feeling the sweat again. It was gathering beneath his arms and along the creases of his palms, dank, clammy, softening his skin, making it more pliant, as if preparing it to receive the blow.

"I have quite a few concerns," Lexie added without a pause. Then she ticked them off. "Lucy's school, her neighborhood." She stopped, as if deciding whether to release another volley, then went ahead and released it. "And there's the apartment, too, your work. Especially at night. Really, it's more or less everything, David. The whole situation she finds herself in."

It was the last three words that caught him, snagged his mind like a hook, jerked him from the rising waters. "Finds herself in?" he asked.

"Yes."

"What do you mean, 'finds herself in'?"

"The way she has to live."

"You make it sound like a swamp," Corman said. "Or a hole. Like I've thrown her in a hole."

"Not a hole, David," Lexie said. "Just your life, the way she lives it with you."

"My life?" Corman asked. "What about my life, Lexie?"

She looked faintly surprised by the question, but wary of it, too, as if she'd heard the hard, alarming sound of a pistol being cocked behind the seamless curtain of his face.

"Well, I mean the situation," Lexie said. "It's not her fault that she doesn't have certain advantages, things that would make her more comfortable, things that I could give her."

Corman could feel something growing steadily more luminous in his mind, shoring up walls he thought had crumbled, restoring the shattered battlements of a city under siege, yet still unready to surrender. "There are other things," he said. "Besides the things you can give her. Things that matter." As he spoke, he could see Lazar alone in his room, pressing yet another picture down into his old suitcase. "Things that matter, Lexie."

Lexie shifted uncomfortably. "David, I think you've . . ."

He raised his hand to stop her. "We're all sailing, Lexie," he began, still struggling for the words. "Sailing through this . . . life."

Lexie stared at him. "Sailing?"

"And so, you have to . . ." He stopped, wrestled mightily to gather it all in. He could feel his mind focus slowly, like a great camera, bringing everything into view, and after a moment he understood, very clearly and with the full force of his conviction, precisely why Lucy should stay with him.

"She doesn't need to be protected," he said explosively. "It would take something from her, Lexie, something that matters."

Lexie sat back slightly, but said nothing.

"Her neighborhood, her school," Corman said. "The way she walks the streets. Lexie, if you could see it. The way she moves toward any little craziness around her, the way she's drawn toward things that aren't safe."

Lexie watched him silently, her eyes immobile, as if fixed on something she could not quite bring into view. "I can provide a nice life for her," she said finally. "A very nice life."

Corman looked at her stonily. "She has the life that's best for her."

Lexie drew her napkin from her lap and began fiddling nervously with its lacy edges. "I'm talking about a good life, David. Opportunities."

Corman shook his head. "No."

Lexie's eyes deepened slightly, but she said nothing.

Corman leaned toward her and felt the high rapture of a well-delivered blow. "Do you know why she should stay with me, Lexie? Because I trust her, and you don't."

Lexie glanced down, then up again, her eyes glistening suddenly.

"You never trusted yourself," Corman added determinedly. "And now you don't trust her."

Lexie labored to recover then sat up stiffly. "That's all very well, David, but there are also some practical matters, you know, such as . . ."

Corman knew what was coming, but also that he could face, even surmount it, because suddenly he realized that fatherhood created a life whose downward pull was always toward the deeper regions, a place where heroism took the form of washing dishes, doing clothes, holding down a job, where compromise miraculously reversed its course, and shot you to the stars.

"I've been offered a job at the paper," he said, interrupting her. "A steady job. Good pay. I'm going to take it."

Lexie stared at him, amazed. "But, David, I thought you . . ."

He lifted his hand to silence her. "But I won't give up the night," he added determinedly. "I won't give that up, ever. But as often as I can, as often as it's right, I'll take Lucy with me, show her what I think she needs to see."

Lexie continued to stare at him but said nothing.

"My eyes," Corman said. "I have a right to them. And so does she."

Lexie studied him intently for a moment, then started to speak.

Corman put up his hand again. "That's the bottom line," Corman told her. "What happens now is up to you." He added nothing else, but merely rested in the silence that drifted down upon them, felt the air around him, the whole dark envelope of the city, and waited for a blow that never came.

Lucy had already packed for the weekend by the time they got back to the apartment, and within a few minutes the three of them were standing beneath the Broadway's battered awning, waiting for a cab. Lucy stood under Corman's arm, nuzzling him gently while she talked to Lexie about the time she'd spent with Mrs. Donaldson. Lexie smiled, nodded, gave her every encouragement, but something in her looked ravaged.

"I'll bring Lucy back tomorrow night," she said to Corman after Lucy had finished her story.

"Fine."

"Any particular time?"

"I'll make sure I'm home before seven."

Lucy stepped from under Corman's arm, walked over to Lexie, and took up the same position, as if trying to balance things with absolute precision.

The cab arrived. Corman opened the door, watched as the two of them slid inside, then handed Lucy her small blue traveling case, closed the door and bent down beside the window.

It was streaked with rain, and a small layer of water formed a watery edge as Lucy rolled down the glass.

" 'Bye, Papa," she said.

Corman pressed nearer and kissed her lightly. "Have fun," he said.

The cab pulled away a few seconds later. Corman returned to his apartment and dialed Pike immediately, afraid that Groton's job had already been given to someone else.

"I've changed my mind, Hugo," he said when Pike answered. "Groton's beat. Is it still open?"

"Yeah," Pike said. "By the skin of its teeth."

"I've decided to take it."

"Oh yeah?" Pike asked. "What brought on the change?"

"Just things."

"Wolf at the door, am I right?"

"Close enough," Corman said. "I'll be there Monday morning."

"Nine sharp," Pike told him.

"Nine sharp," Corman repeated, then hung up.

For a time he curled up on the sofa and tried to take a short nap. But the intensity of the last hours still lingered like a faint electrical charge in the air around him, and so, after only a few minutes, he returned to the streets, heading south, crossing the avenues at random, simply moving forward with no direction in mind. He passed down Broadway, through the swarming neon of Times Square, then down Seventh Avenue. It was nearly deserted until he reached the plant and flower district in Chelsea. The trucks were unloading everything from common ferns to the most exotic tropical flowers, and for a long time, Corman watched the whole striking process from the front booth of a small diner on 26th Street.

Before he left, an idea struck him, a series of photographs that would show how the city reprovisioned itself during the night. He would record the flower district, the meat, fish and vegetable markets, the unloading of trucks, freight cars, planes, boats, barges, how the city was fed by tubes of streets, bridges, waterways, airlanes. He would take Lucy with him, teach her the mystery of replenishment.

By dawn he'd reached the great stone ramparts of the Brooklyn Bridge, faintly blue in the chill morning air. The rain had stopped, and a heavy mist rose from the gray waters. As he looked at it, he thought of Lazar, all the photographs he'd taken of people huddled together, shrouded in the mist, waylaid by the storm, but searching through it anyway, enduring and eternal, relentless as the unrelenting rain.

A chill breeze swept up from the river. He lifted his collar against it, briefly headed back uptown, then thought better of it and turned southward again, moving out onto the bridge, walking steadily until he'd reached its towering center. The wind was cold as it blew unhindered over the river. It chilled his lungs and tore madly at his hair, but he continued to stand silently between the great gray arches, with emptiness below, he knew, and above, more emptiness.

And yet?

Standing.